ANN APTAKER

HUNTING
GOLD

Bywater
BOOKS

Ann Arbor
2022

Print ISBN: 978-1-61294-237-7

Bywater Books First Edition: July 2022

Printed in the United States of America on acid-free paper.

Cover design: TreeHouse Studio

Bywater Books
PO Box 3671
Ann Arbor MI 48106-3671

www.bywaterbooks.com

This novel is a work of fiction.

ANN APTAKER

HUNTING GOLD

*This book is dedicated to everyone who insists
on having a place in the world.*

Chapter One

April 1955
The Green Door Club, a Lesbian nightspot in New York City
Around 11 p.m. on a Tuesday night

The goons in blue burst in, rush the dance floor, flash their badges, and laugh in our faces as they shove their billy clubs between dancing couples, forcing us apart. Women scream in fear and fury.

The smack of the sticks against female flesh along low-cut backs of dresses lets loose more screams. Billy clubs crack the heads of swells decked out in tailored suits. Blood drips onto lapels and the collars of white shirts. The sticks slap against legs in sheer stockings and high-heeled shoes as the goons herd us out the door of The Green Door Club and into a paddy wagon at the end of the alley. One of the badge boys even shouts that what we all need is a good fuck by a real man to straighten us out.

Someday I'll knock his teeth down his throat.

That was an hour ago. Now, instead of romantic conversations in the glow of amber-shaded lamps at little tables or in the shadows

1

on the dance floor, all I hear are terrified sobs, bursts of seething anger, frustrated slaps against the bars of our cell, and the galling laughter of the police matron at her desk. It's the noise of hell.

The sweet blonde I was dancing with when the club was raided—a purring little kitten who enjoyed running her fingers through my always unruly short brown hair—is crouched in a corner, too numb to cry. The Green Door's barkeep, Peg Monroe, sturdy in black trousers and pale blue shirt, and whose mahogany skin harbors a soft heart and tough spine, is doing her best to comfort a group of terrified young women who'd come to New York for a few days of freedom from the small minds of their small towns.

Some of us in the lockup realize we're actually lucky tonight. This one's been an easy raid, the blood and beatings stopping at the jailhouse door. It's a less brutal ordeal than a raid a few years back when the badge boys weren't satisfied with just slapping us around but cheered when a couple of them unzipped their pants, let their peckers out, and forced themselves on some of their jailhouse captives.

Sometimes I still hear the women's screams in my sleep.

My souvenirs for tonight's police frolics are blood splotches on the collar of my black shirt and the lapel of my light gray silk suit. The stains aren't too visible on my shirt collar but the splotch on my lapel is red as a girlie show marquee. The blood's from a gash on my forehead where the tip of a billy club caught me. If it scars, it'll join the company of the other souvenirs given to me by cops or various other thugs. There's a curved scar over my right eye, a jagged one on my left cheek, a straight line cut into my chin, a knife-shaped bit above my lip, and a small, angled slice at the corner of my mouth.

The scars aren't exclusively the result of my illegal romantic preference for women. My life's dangerous all the way around. I'm a thief and a smuggler, an outlaw, because as far as I'm concerned if the Law's gonna label me a criminal just for who I kiss, I figure I don't owe the Law any allegiance at all. So I make my dough on the dark side of the art game, smuggle art and other treasures into the Port of New York, having lifted the stuff in the first place from people or places that had no plans to get rid of them. The goods eventually end up in display cases of major museums, where at least the average Joe and Jane can see them, or in private collections, where they can't. I prefer the first outcome, but I don't turn my nose up at the second, for which my bank account, my landlord, my tailor, and my lawyer are all deeply grateful.

A pudgy cop, a rookie by the peach fuzz look of him, walks into the lockup area, shouts, "Gold! Cantor Gold!"

"Yeah?" I say.

"Your shyster's here. Posted your bail. You're out."

A slug of Chivas scotch followed by a hot shower eases my bruised muscles. The shower's needles of heat drill down to break up knots of tensed nerves and sinew. My body feels better but my mood's still raw. Smug cops and the Law that unleashes them always put me in a raw mood.

My face cleaned of blood and my body wrapped in a favorite silk robe, I take a bottle of Chivas with me to the living room where my mind's eased a little by a phone call from my lawyer letting me know he was able to bail all the other women out of lockup. Before I left the jail, I'd told him to put the women's bail money on my tab. I can afford it. My racket pays me plenty of dough, enough to have my silk suits custom tailored, buy a new car whenever I want, and pay whatever it takes to keep my freedom and the freedom of my kind.

I pour myself another slug of Chivas, shake out a smoke from my pack of Chesterfields, turn off the living room light, and sit down in my favorite big red club chair. A slug of whiskey and a drag on my smoke takes the edge off my raw mood. I even find a little peace in the view out my window to my theater district neighborhood. Its nighttime neon glow filters into my darkened living room, tinting the air with pretty colors that brush the furniture and wash over me. This view of the city reminds me that despite the brutal Law that hates me and people like me, despite the crooked judges and rotten cops who either want to jail me or kill me, there's plenty to love about New York. There's enough energy and creativity in this town to enrich the soul of the whole world.

But there's a darker side to New York, too, a side I know well, a side I thrive in because it lets me. Its only judgment of me is how well I survive among its gangsters and killers, its thieves, hustlers, con artists, and thugs. The citizens of my shadowy slice of the city don't give a fig for the Law. Some of them because, like me, the Law doesn't give a fig for them. The Law would be just as happy to see certain segments of the population disappear, or even die, or just shut up: people whose names have too many vowels or consonants, or whose accents are too musical or their skin color too dark, people whose idea of romance doesn't fit the Mommy-and-Daddy-and-two-kids mold. People like us owe the Law no loyalty at all.

So until the world changes, until the day I can walk down the street holding hands with a woman, even kiss her and not worry about having some passing schmo or a gang of schmoes take a swing at us with fists or baseball bats, or until the night I can dance with a woman and not get arrested for it, my loyalty's reserved for my own survival and for the people who help me maintain it: Judson Zane, my Guy Friday who takes care of the desk-work side of my business, a young genius whose talent for digging out information from even the deepest holes would make the CIA boys feel inadequate; Rosie Bliss, a cabbie with the slickest driving skills in town; Red Drogan, a tug boater who knows how to slide me through the city's waterways and past the harbor cops; and my lawyer, whose manicured fingers play the levers of power as elegantly as a concert pianist. Any remaining loyalty goes to the clients who pay me big money to risk my life to satisfy their lust for art and treasure.

Tonight, though, my loyalty is to the bottle of Chivas on my lap. Good scotch has seen me through even tougher nights than this, nights of violence, nights of betrayal, and the worst night of all, a night of heartbreak, when the woman I loved more than life itself disappeared into the worst kind of hell. It's a wound in my soul that will never heal. Best I can do is numb it with hefty dollops of booze. So I pour myself another slug, toast my loyalty to our ongoing relationship. I take a swallow, let the whiskey warm my insides, calm my anger about the Law and what its goons did tonight.

The phone rings. I let it ring, wait for the caller to give up, let 'em figure I'm not home. It's after midnight, too late for clients to call, and I'm not in the mood to chatter with anyone anyway.

The ringing doesn't stop. I'm tempted to throw the phone across the room or out the window and just get back to drinking in peace, get back to letting the scotch and the soothing balm of nicotine blot out this crummy night of vicious cops and crying women.

The phone keeps ringing. I finally tear out of my chair and answer the phone just to shut it up. My "Yeah?" is about as friendly as a jungle cat about to pounce on prey.

"Cantor?" I know the voice. It's usually rich and silky but now sounds ragged, the voice of a woman whose night's been as lousy as mine. "It's Vivienne," she says. "Can you come over? I'm terrified. And you should be too."

Chapter Two

Vivienne Parkhurst Trent is the kind of woman you dream about, if your dreams run to women who are gorgeous, brilliant, sophisticated, and savage in the same package. That dream came true for me one night five years ago when Vivienne showed up at my door and decided to try me on for size. But it was only for that one night. She never indulged again. Maybe she figured the size didn't fit, or maybe she decided the style didn't suit her, or that it was too much of a threat to her position in society. Whatever the reason, she's since restricted her socializing to the escorting arms of men. My loss, their undeserving gain. Still, I sometimes get the feeling Vivienne didn't let go of that night completely, that there's a thread still tickling the palm of her hand. That's why I'm on my way to her place at nearly one o'clock in the morning, spiffed up in a black silk suit, pale apricot shirt, black tie, the outfit finished off with an apricot pocket square.

There's serious business under the dressy duds, business in the form of the hard blue steel of my Smith and Wesson .38 nestled in its shoulder rig. It might prove helpful in convincing whoever's frightening Vivienne to change their plans.

The sophisticated part of Vivienne comes from her patrician Parkhurst lineage. The savage part from her up-from-the-gutter Trent bloodline. The brilliant part was bred in her bones but sharpened by her hard work to become a respected curator of

European Renaissance art at the city's premier museum. As for the gorgeous part, well, that's just icing on an already impressive cake.

She lives in the house where she grew up, the Parkhurst Trent mansion on the city's tony East Side. It's the sort of neighborhood where kids don't wear dungarees and don't play stickball or potsie in the street, but walk politely in pressed pants or pastel pinafores while they hold their governess's hand.

The Parkhurst Trent pile is bigger than the other fancy townhouses on the block but smaller than Buckingham Palace. I guess only the Queen of England could consider the place cramped.

Vivienne's butler, George, who's been old as long as I've known him, greets me at the door. At this hour he's in his pajamas and a wool robe instead of his butler's getup. He's usually not happy to see me, considers me a lowlife influence on the lady whose family he's served since Vivienne was a tot. Tonight, though, his attitude's a bit more welcoming. If something bad happened here tonight, I guess he figures it might take a bad character to handle it.

He takes my cap and coat, notices the newest wound to my face, but his butler's upright restraint stops him from mentioning it. He just says, "Miss Vivienne's waiting for you in the living room."

"What happened here, George? Is Vivienne all right? What frightened her enough for her to call me in the middle of the night?"

"Miss Vivienne is unharmed, but the house has been broken into." He says it with more than a touch of shock that anyone would have the nerve to invade such a blue-blooded household. I'm tempted to remind him of what I do for a living.

"I assume something's been stolen?" I say.

"Perhaps I should let Miss Vivienne give you the details."

I don't have to wait long for those details. I get the story as soon as I walk through the mahogany-paneled hallway on my way to the living room. The hallway's walls are usually covered with priceless artworks by Leonardo da Vinci, Jan Van Eyck, Caravaggio, Vermeer, Fra Filippo Lippi, among others. Tonight, there's only naked picture hooks where two of the smaller pieces should be: a Caravaggio portrait of a young boy, and a honey-toned Madonna by Fra Filippo Lippi.

I understand why Vivienne is terrified. Being robbed is like being violated. I know because I often do the violating. And no, I won't apologize for it. I risk my life to earn my daily bread my way. You can go right ahead and earn your living your way. I won't judge.

But I understand why Vivienne thinks I should be terrified too; both of the stolen artworks were supplied by me.

Could be coincidence. Of all the artwork on the hallway walls, the Caravaggio and the Lippi are the smallest, the easiest to grab and get out with. And anyway, how would the thief know I supplied the goods? Vivienne's always tight-lipped about how she gets artwork for her personal collection as well as for her museum. Every curator and collector in town knows to keep their mouths shut. Still, I have a queasy feeling about the thief walking off with only those two paintings from Vivienne's hallway.

In the living room, an elegant but cozy room of rich greens, browns and golds, Vivienne's seated on the sofa, its slate green silk velvet upholstery shimmering in the light of the room's shaded lamps. Vivienne, sipping a brandy, shimmers too, dressed for an evening out in a pale blue chiffon gown that floats like breath along her body. The strapless number goes well with her green eyes, allows the waves of her brunette hair to brush her bare shoulders. The whole picture holds my attention, nudges me to straighten my tie in response to my envy of whoever was her escort this evening.

She starts, "Thanks for—" but doesn't finish the greeting. She sits up instead, her eyes wide then narrowing with concern. "Cantor, you're hurt," she says. "That wound on your forehead looks ghastly."

"I'm fine," I say. "Don't worry about it. I'm more concerned about the stuff missing from the hall."

Vivienne lifts her eyes to a living room wall, directing me to empty spots where a couple of small seventeenth-century Dutch landscape paintings usually hang: an Aelbert Cuyp woodland scene, and an Aert van der Neer nightscape. There's nothing in their place but empty picture hooks.

That queasy feeling I felt in the hall just got queasier. Both paintings were supplied by me, lifted three years ago from a Dutch swindler who had a taste for art.

Vivienne says, "You look like you need a drink. You know where the bar is. Help yourself." Her voice has that rich-as-wine quality again, but there's confusion under it, and that trace of fear I heard on the phone. Confusion and fear are not typical of Vivienne Parkhurst Trent. Her aristocratic Parkhurst lineage endowed her with a haughty confidence of the sort only the highborn enjoy, while the Trent bloodline of her great-grandfather Malachi Trent, a brute who made his shipping fortune along New York's tough-as-nails waterfront during the city's gaslight days, gives Vivienne her taste for what the elite politely call country sports, meaning hunting four-legged creatures across forests and fields. She's got the skill with a firearm to bag game from yards away, and the steady nerves to gut it when it's down. Both traits, the sophisticated and the savage, are visible in those seductive green eyes of hers, the eyes of a pampered palace cat who'll purr for you or eat you alive.

I pour myself a Chivas from the small bar behind the sofa, then sit in a club chair opposite Vivienne. Her eyes are on the cut on my forehead. "How did you get hurt this time, Cantor?" There's worry in her voice, not for the first time.

"I'll survive," I say.

"You always do."

"Then you don't have to worry about me. So let's talk about what the hell is going on here."

"What do you think is going on? Someone was very particular about what they stole."

I take another swallow of scotch while I look around the

room. In a house full of priceless artworks, the only things missing are paintings Vivienne obtained through me. Makes me wonder who's got me in their crosshairs. And why target Vivienne's place? I've got other clients around town.

I think about the stuff on their walls, wonder if some of it will be missing tomorrow or the next day or the day after that or until the thief is done with whatever this is all about. Or until my operation's destroyed, or I'm in jail, or dead.

I know the other light-fingers in town and they know me. We don't give up the names of our clients, and we don't rat on each other to cops or other busybodies asking questions. But someone knew about the stuff in this house, and they knew which stuff was mine. There's a crack in what's supposed to be the wall of silence. I'll have to slip through that crack to find whoever made it. And when I find them, I'll have to decide what I'll do about it. And like I said, I don't rat out anyone to the cops.

Vivienne finishes her brandy, takes a cigarette from the brass box on a side table, lights the smoke with the matching lighter, and closes her eyes as she leans back into the sofa's cushions. She lifts her hand to brush a stray wave of hair from her cheek. The movement sends curling trails of smoke along her face. Her delicate chiffon gown ripples along the length of her.

I could easily be mesmerized by all that, but I don't dare. I have to put that off for another time. Right now I need to stick to business to save my business, maybe save my life. Maybe save Vivienne's life.

I say, "What time did you get home and discover the paintings were stolen?"

Vivienne says, "A few minutes before I called you."

"So around midnight. Was the door open when you arrived? The lock broken? Maybe a window broken or open?"

Vivienne opens her eyes, shakes her head. "No, none of those things. The front door was locked. I had to use my key. The windows were all closed and locked too. George and I checked while we waited for you."

"What about George? Did he see or hear anything that

might be helpful?"

"Not a thing. When I came home and saw the house had been robbed, I went upstairs to George's room to make sure he's all right. He was asleep. I had to wake him."

Whoever walked off with Vivienne's artwork knew what they were doing. They knew how to pick a lock, how to slip into the house without a sound, work without a sound, slip out without a sound. Whoever did this has good hands, skilled and quick. It's as elegant a job as I've seen.

"I assume you didn't call the police," I say.

Vivienne gives that a shrug and a you-should-know-better *tsk.* "Of course not," she says. "How could I?"

She couldn't. You can't report the theft of something that was stolen in the first place, not unless you're willing to serve time for receiving stolen goods.

"Cantor? What are you going to do?"

I get up from my chair, go to the bar behind the sofa, and pour myself another scotch. "I'm going to get your paintings back," I say.

"Are you saying that you know who might've taken them? And why?" There's hopefulness in her voice, in her eyes.

Disappointing Vivienne can't be on my menu, but disappointing Vivienne never is.

But I can't lead her on either. "Look, the only stuff they stole was stuff that came through me," I say. "And they didn't take just one or two; they took four, so someone really wants to make a point."

"A threat?"

"Maybe. Or maybe just a challenge. Maybe some new player nipping at my heels."

Vivienne gives that a knowing nod. She's no stranger to challenges. As one of the few women curators in a profession dominated by snobby men, Vivienne's had to fend off threats to her success almost from the day she started at the museum. "Just be careful, Cantor. You don't know what the threat is."

"I can't worry about that."

"But I do worry about it. My home has been invaded, you've already been hurt tonight, and I don't need the violence of your world in my life."

"There won't be. Well, not unless I take you dancing."

Scotch whiskey and dancing with pretty women at the Green Door Club are two of the medicines I use to try to kill the pain of that wound that won't heal. A third medicine is sex. Rare is the night I sleep alone.

But tonight is going to be one of those nights. After the billy-clubbing cops, the crying women in the jail cell, and now the break-in at Vivienne's place, I've had all the excitement I can stomach for one night. All I want is a nightcap stiff enough to help me collapse into sleep so I'll have the wherewithal to deal with all this in the morning. What I don't want is the note I find slipped under my door.

Chapter Three

The cobblestone streets in the Meatpacking District used to be slick with the blood and discarded innards of cows, pigs, lambs, and horses. The offal has since been washed away by the requirements of modern city ordinances, but the butchery smell of the meatpacking plants lingers, even after hours. I'll try to forget it the next time I order lamb chops or a steak.

The address I'm going to is a warehouse on Washington Street off Gansevoort in the shadow of the overhead High Line tracks, a train line that moves goods to and from the area's meatpacking plants, various West Side warehouses, and the Hudson River's freight docks. I'm here at nearly two-thirty in the morning because of what was in the note under my door:

> YOU THINK YOU'RE THE SMART
> ONE, CANTOR GOLD. I SLIPPED
> THOSE PAINTINGS OUT FROM UNDER
> YOUR NOSE. I CAN COME AFTER
> EVERYTHING IN YOUR LIFE ANY
> TIME I WANT. I CAN RUIN YOU ANY
> TIME I WANT. IF YOU WANT MISS
> PARKHURST TRENT'S PAINTINGS BACK,
> COME TO HARTMANN'S WAREHOUSE
> ON WASHINGTON STREET. NOW.

There's so much wrong with the note my skin hasn't stopped prickling from the minute I read it. The first thing that's wrong is there's no demand for cash. What do they want in return for the paintings? A kiss? And what the hell does *Now* mean? What if I'd been out all night, didn't see the note until dawn?

The handwriting's no help either. Just crude, blocky capital letters scrawled to hide a personality. It could've been written by a man or a woman, could've been written by someone old or young. The note's all riddles, and about as kosher as a dish of pig's guts, but it's my only lead to the stolen paintings and to whoever's nipping at Vivienne and coming after me.

The note's folded up and snug in my coat pocket when I arrive at Hartmann's Warehouse, a big brick nineteenth-century building with tall grimy windows along a shadowy stretch of Washington Street. There's nobody around at this hour, and except for a dark prewar Dodge parked at the curb and a beat-up two-tone three-year-old Chevy parked across the street, the area's deserted and quiet. The only action comes from random pages of discarded newspapers skittering along the cobblestones or flying around in the wind off the river. The only sound is the middle-of-the-night-music of empty whiskey bottles and beer cans rolling in the gutter.

The light of streetlamps is cut through by the High Line tracks throwing a hard pattern of dark and light slashes on the pavement and across the brick face of the warehouse. The light shines in glittering blades across the warehouse windows and cuts through the faded Hartmann's sign. Mists of steam rising through manhole covers and curling into the harsh light gives the warehouse the sort of charm Dracula might find cozy.

There are two ways in: a wide loading dock door and a regular door to the street. I try the street door.

The old-fashioned brass doorknob turns. The door's unlocked. No surprise. Whoever wrote that note wants me inside.

I walk into a dark, cavernous room. The place smells of dust and dead animals. The damp, meaty air's clammy on my skin. I nearly lose my footing on the floor's greasy remnants of the warehouse's meatpacking days. Slivers of streetlight through the High Line's tracks slice through the windows and hit the floor like luminous knives.

The light cuts across a couple of shapes a few feet in front of me on the floor. One of the shapes appears to be a large canvas sack. I recognize the edge of a picture frame sticking out, the scrollwork corner of Fra Fillipo Lippi's Madonna.

I figure the sack contains Vivienne's stolen paintings. I should be happy about it, but getting the stuff back this easy is all wrong. As wrong as the note that sent me here.

The other shape sends another twist through my gut. The shape is the unmistakable lump of a dead body. The guy's bloody face is toward me. His fedora's rolled off his head. His gray hair is streaked with blood.

When I get close, I don't recognize the old guy, don't think I've ever seen him before. I only know that his coat, his shirt, and his tie are stained with blood. And he's dead.

What the hell has this guy got to do with me or Vivienne's paintings?

I take the note from my coat pocket, read it again in a streak of light from the window. I look for any clue in the heavy-handed lettering, pick through each sentence for any meaning maybe I didn't catch the first time.

It doesn't matter. I could read the note a thousand times and still find nothing about why I'm here with a corpse.

The mystery is suddenly answered by the approaching wails of sirens and smears of red light sliding through the windows.

I've been set up.

I've got to get out of here. If the cops find me with a sack of paintings and a dead body, I'm a jailbird. My earlier visit to the lockup was enough for one night. I don't want a second, especially one tied up with a murder the cops will only be too happy to fry me for.

The cops will find the body but they won't find me. I grab

the sack of paintings, run toward a window but slip on the greasy floor and fall to my knees. Pain shoots through my kneecaps sharp as bullets but there's no time to nurse the misery. The wail of police sirens is getting louder, the smears of twirling red lights brighter. I pull myself and the sack of paintings up from the floor, run to the window and crash through it. I'm gone.

It's a little after three in the morning when I ring Vivienne's doorbell, my bruised knees aching, though a hefty slug of scotch could smooth that out. A minute later, George opens the door. His robe is barely tied over his pajamas, his white hair disheveled.

"Sorry to disturb your sleep again, George," I say. "Won't blame you if you're annoyed."

"It's not my place to be annoyed," he says. "I'll tell Miss Vivienne you're here." He eyes the canvas sack, no doubt guesses what it contains, but the expression on his face stays neutral, all stoic propriety. I guess he figures it's not his place to show relief or happiness. He notices the grease stains on the knees of my trousers, but says nothing about that either.

Of all the high society types I deal with in my racket, I've always found Vivienne to be the least snobby when it comes to dealing with the common classes, but evidently the old hierarchies still hang on: servants, no matter how beloved, know their place. Makes me wonder if Vivienne was just slumming the night she shared my bed.

I tell George I'll wait for Vivienne in the living room.

I'm tempted to take the paintings from the sack, rehang the Caravaggio portrait and the Lippi Madonna in the hall, and hang the Dutch landscapes in the living room, but decide to let Vivienne have the triumphant pleasure.

I turn on a lamp on one of the side tables when I walk into the living room, then pour myself a stiff scotch from the bar behind the sofa while I wait for Vivienne. I down the whiskey in one gulp. It warms me, takes the edge off the pain in my knees. I pour another one, drink it down, too, let it do its work to further dull the pain. I pour another.

The soft light and mellow shadows around the room, and another deep swallow of booze, help soothe some of the rawness the night's scraped all over me: the raid on the Green Door Club followed by the ugly time in the clink, and finally a dead stranger at my feet in a frame for murder. I have no idea if there's a God but if there is, after a night like tonight I'd say the sonovabitch hates me.

Well, maybe I can have the last laugh. Whoever set me up didn't get their way. The cops didn't find me standing over a dead guy, and at least I got Vivienne's paintings back. But I can't enjoy that laugh just yet. Whoever set me up is still out there and will probably try again. I won't get to enjoy that laugh until I figure out who the hell they are, why they're after me, and then stop them.

I down my scotch to settle my thoughts, then pour another when Vivienne walks in.

Not many women can swoop into a room with as much sensual elegance as Vivienne, especially after being roused from sleep. In the light of the single lamp, her black satin robe swirls around her like a moonlit night, her bed-tousled hair brushing her cheek as if each strand takes pleasure in feeling her skin.

"Why are you here again in the middle of the night? And what happened to your trousers? You look like you crawled through a frying pan."

I hold up the sack.

Vivienne looks at it and then looks at me with the surprised expression of a little girl hoping to get the puppy she's always wanted. "Are those my paintings?"

"If they aren't, I've ruined a good pair of trousers for nothing," I say as I pull each painting from the sack and line them up against the wall.

Vivienne joins me in looking them over, examining them for any damage. They've all made it through their adventure in good shape.

"Cantor, how did you—? I mean, you found them so soon.

Cantor, you're—"

"Lucky. Lucky to be alive. Lucky I escaped the cops."

Even straight-arrow civilians have been known to grow alarmed at the mention of cops, and Vivienne Parkhurst Trent— distinguished curator, scholar, receiver of stolen goods—is plenty alarmed now. "What do the police have to do with it? Cantor, the police cannot know about these paintings!"

"They don't, and they won't."

I light a cigarette, enjoy watching Vivienne through the curls of smoke as she settles down, lifts one of the Dutch landscapes, the Aert van der Neer nightscape, and hangs it back on its hook on the wall.

"Where did you find them?" she says. "Light me a cigarette, would you? And what do you mean you're lucky to be alive?"

I take a cigarette from the brass box on a side table, light it, and give it to Vivienne. "The less you know, the better," I say.

"Why? What kind of danger are you in? What kind of danger am *I* in?" She lifts the other painting, the Aelbert Cuyp woodland scene, hangs it back on its hook. She stands back, takes a deep drag on her smoke as she looks with satisfaction at her restored wall of priceless art.

"I don't have the answer for either of those questions yet," I say. "But it's a sure bet that whoever grabbed these paintings isn't finished with me. Their plan didn't work out as they expected."

"And what did they expect?"

"That the cops would find me with a corpse at my feet and stolen paintings in my arms."

The mention of a corpse brings the alarm back into Vivienne's eyes. The smoke from our cigarettes can only blur it, not disguise it.

This time I don't try to settle her down. I want her scared, scared enough to let me do what I need to do to protect her.

I take her carefully by her shoulders, say, "Listen, someone is willing to play rough. They want me out of the way, I don't know why, and they're willing to go through you to do it. You might not be safe here, Vivienne. Whoever pulled this job could come back and raise the stakes. They might not just take your paintings this time. Do you understand what I'm telling you?"

"Just what are you suggesting I do?"

"Why don't I set you and George up someplace where—"

She waves that away before I finish the sentence, shrugging my hands off her shoulders. "I won't be chased from my own house," she says and backs away from me. She vents her annoyance at my suggestion in the way she stubs out her smoke in an ashtray on the coffee table, stabbing the cigarette over and over against the crystal like she's attacking it. "Have you forgotten how good I am with a firearm, Cantor?"

"I haven't forgotten. I know you can plug any prey from yards away. But human predators are meaner, Vivienne, and they don't back off." I move in front of her to make my point. "And the predator who robbed you and set me up for a frame knows how to get into your house without a sound. You'll never see them coming."

Even in the shadowy light, I see the look in her eyes, a look of worry struggling with her natural haughty defiance. "Well, if I'm not safe, you're not safe either," she says. "If someone really is determined to come after you, Cantor, maybe you should be the one to hide. Maybe it's you who should disappear somewhere."

I don't think there's a word in the English language that annoys me more than the word hide. "I don't hide from anybody," I say, "I don't hide how I live my life. I'll take my place in the world whether anyone likes it or not. If I can't take my place in the world, what the hell is the use of living?"

If Vivienne never fully understood me before, I think she's starting to understand me now. I see it in a pinpoint of light flickering deep in her eyes. I'm surprised at the pleasure it gives me.

I place my fingers gently under her chin, lift her face to me, speak softly, "Vivienne, if you won't let me set you up somewhere safe, at least let me stay here with you for a few days. You'll be safer with me around."

The pinpoint light of understanding I saw in her eyes a

moment ago flares into a glint of amusement. "Safe from whom?" she says with a smile that has my number. She slides my fingers from under her chin but holds them for a second or two before she says, "Good night, Cantor."

Chapter Four

There oughta be a law against anyone pounding on your door or pressing the buzzer before noon. And since I'm the type to make my own law if I think I'm getting pushed around, it shouldn't surprise anyone that I'm prepared to give the death penalty to whoever's the moke leaning on my buzzer and pounding on my apartment door, rousing me from my bed at eight in the morning after I've had less than four hours sleep.

The moke turns out to be a guy whose death would bring the kind of trouble that lands me in the electric chair, because when I open the door I'm looking at the stocky build and tough-as-nails face of Sergeant Liam Adair.

He's in a typical cop's getup: badly fitting dull gray coat over a cheap gray suit made by a factory that should be torched for its insult to tailoring. But unlike a lot of his cop buddies, his white shirt is pressed, his green-and-tan tie doesn't have visible coffee stains, and his fedora's at a racy angle.

I'm not as formally attired, wearing only my robe over my underwear. "I'd say good morning, sergeant, but it's too early for there to be anything good about it."

"Well, it might get better if you ask me in."

"I can't say that having cops in my apartment has ever been a happy-go-lucky experience. Especially before I've had my breakfast."

"How about I buy you a cup of coffee?"

"How about you tell me what the hell you're doing here?"

"How about you lose the attitude, Gold, and let me in. I don't do police business in the hall."

He's smiling when he says it. I'm not sure if he's just enjoying our banter or if he's peacocking the power over me he thinks his badge gives him.

In truth, Adair plays fairer than most cops, though that's not saying much. It only means he does a little more homework before he slaps the cuffs on someone. But in my cat-and-mouse game with the Law I'll take whatever fair play I can get, and trust none of it.

I let him in.

I say, "I'd invite you to sit down, Adair, but I don't want to encourage you to linger."

"How long I stay depends on you, Gold. Give me straight answers, and I'll be on my way."

"Suits me," I say with a shrug.

He fingers the brim of his hat, taking the time to let his mind work through the homework he's done on me. Finally, he says, "What were you doing at Hartmann's Warehouse last night? And don't try telling me you weren't there. We ran the fingerprints we lifted from the doorknob. They came up as a match for the prints we have on file for you." He gets a kick out of telling me this, though his smile does nothing to soften the tough set of his face. There's a glint in his eyes, though, when he says, "It seems you got around a lot last night, Gold. There's a fresh entry in your arrest record. You should know better than to hang around in places that get raided."

"Maybe the Law should know better than to raid those places. If dancing is illegal, what's next? Chatting?"

"I guess it depends on who you're chatting with and what you're chatting about."

That idea is so chilling the cold digs all the way down into my marrow.

Adair gives it only a shrug of his own. At least he wasn't

smarmy about it like a lot of other cops and straight-back citizens of my not so friendly acquaintance. "Now suppose we get back to *our* little chat," he says, "and you tell me what you were doing at Hartmann's Warehouse in the middle of the night."

"I can't tell you why I was there because I'm not sure why I was there," I say, "and before you get any more lousy ideas, no, I don't know the old guy who was lying there dead when I walked in, so don't try pinning a murder on me."

"Oh, we know you weren't the shooter, Gold. The guy was shot with a .45, and you're famous for your .38."

"Well, now that we've gotten that out of the way, there's nothing left to talk about. Toodle-oo, sergeant."

"Not so fast. I still need to know why you were there."

I just give him a slow shake of my head.

"Don't be a sap, Gold. Don't you even want to know who the dead guy is?"

"I'll know when you tell me." The conversation is finally swinging my way. I get some information but don't give Adair a thing.

He says, "Does the name Dominic Angeli mean anything to you?"

The name means plenty, and Adair knows it does because I can't keep my eyebrows from rising.

Don Dominic Angeli: an old-time mob boss so powerful a snap of his fingers could bring down banks, topple the city government, have whole neighborhoods leveled to make way for his construction projects, and that was just the legal side of his activities. On the other side, it was said that his operation flooded the streets with dope; ran protection rackets and gambling rings that raked in millions; and used blackmail, hostage-taking and murder as bargaining tools. None of it could ever be proven because the guy cleaned up his dirty money in his legit enterprises, and nobody associated with him would talk anyway. They knew better, or they'd be found in bits in pieces in various vacant lots, if they were found at all. And Angeli was so secretive only a few trusted associates ever got close to him, and only those associates and his family knew what he looked like. He lived his life in the shadows. If a news photographer ever tried to take his picture, the photographer's camera was destroyed and the guy was never seen or heard from again.

But even the most powerful players get old and tired and heartbroken, and after his wife's death from cancer, Dominic Angeli took his sorrow and his millions and retired to a mansion on a big spread upstate twenty years ago, or so they said.

"Yeah, Dominic Angeli," Adair is saying, interrupting my thoughts. "The top Don himself. Who'd have figured such a big timer would end up dead in a crummy warehouse in the middle of the night?"

"Who'd have thought?" is all I say.

"So the question is, why were you brought into it? Listen, Gold, I know you're smart. Smart enough to know the tricky spot you're in. You were in a warehouse with a dead guy, and not just any dead guy, but a crime boss the Law couldn't get their hands on but someone else finally did, got him with a bullet. Someone wanted you to see it; someone wanted you to be in that warehouse over that corpse. Now, show me how smart you are, Gold, and tell me why you were there. Matter of fact, how about you tell me over a cup of coffee? My treat. The offer's still good."

"I'll buy my own coffee, thanks," which is my way of saying I don't accept favors from cops. Adair thinks I'm smart? I'm smart enough to never owe a cop anything, not even a ten cent cuppa coffee.

But he's right about someone wanting me found in that warehouse with Dominic Angeli's body. I can't tell Adair why I was there, not without putting Vivienne into legal hot water about those paintings. But I figure I'd better tell Adair something just to get him off my back and maybe get on the good side of his investigation.

"Listen, sergeant," I say, "it's obvious I was set up, but I don't know why. I'd never met Angeli. I was just a kid when he was the city's big cheese, so I never did business with him, never met any of his people or his family. But there's more than one question about this business. The first question is about who's setting me up and why. The other question might be the real dynamite."

Adair catches on fast. "Like who killed Dominic Angeli."

"Uh-huh. Angeli may have been retired, or so they say, but killing the guy who used to have New York by the balls, and maybe still had a finger tickling them, is either a stupid thing to do, a coldly calculating thing to do, or a desperate thing to do. Look, I'll make a deal with you, Adair. If whoever's behind this tries again or comes after me, I'll let you know. Hell, I won't mind it if the cops solve this and get me out of this mess."

"I bet you wouldn't." He says it through a smile that crinkles his eyes and turns my stomach.

The warm springtime sun is having the time of its life on my street, glowing on apartment windows and sparkling on the chrome fenders and hood ornaments of cars parked at the curb. I'm especially sweet on the way the sunshine brings out the colors of women's swirling coats and glints on their pretty hats as their wearers hurry to work.

These pleasant sights lighten some of the crummy mood left over from my lousy night last night and a never welcome visit from a cop this morning. I actually feel reasonably steady when I arrive at Pete's Luncheonette, my favorite neighborhood chow joint. Doris, the gray- haired, thin-faced waitress who's been behind the counter since they invented counters, serves the best coffee in town, a brew strong enough to set even the most decrepit sufferer of day-after misery back on their feet.

Doris gives me a wave when I walk in just before nine. The cheery wave is replaced by a frown when I slide onto a stool at the counter. Her frown is friendly enough, but with plenty of street savvy behind it. "You look like you had a fight with your bed," she says. "Didn't your mother teach you that beds are for sleeping?"

"Among other things," I joke.

That gives her a laugh, which causes her red lipstick to smear her teeth a little and ride into the creases above her lip. "Is that what kept you up all night?"

"Now, Doris," I say, sliding my finger under her chin, "don't you know you're the only girl for me?"

That gives her another laugh. "Catch me in the next lifetime, sweetie. I've got a well-trained husband in this one. Coffee?"

"And scrambled eggs on a bagel."

She pours my coffee and gives my order to the kitchen. I take a sip of the coffee to kick some extra energy into my sleepless body, then bring the mug with me to a phone booth in the back.

I dial Judson Zane, the bright young guy who keeps my office running like clockwork. Judson knows how to get information from people no one's ever heard of in places no one in their right mind would dare to go. I need him to do a little digging now.

"Good morning, Judson," I say when he comes on the line. "I want you to get everything you can get on Dominic Angeli. You might need a pickaxe to dig deep; the guy was secretive."

"And now he's dead."

"So I guess it's already made the papers," I say.

"And the radio and the TV news. What's Angeli got to do with you?"

"I'm not sure yet. Try to find out if Angeli had any interest in art. I'll tell you more about it when I see you later. I'm at Pete's Luncheonette having breakfast. I'll get to the office in about a half hour or so."

"No you won't. You've got a meeting with Sig Loreale. He called a few minutes ago, said he tried you at home but got no answer. You must've already left for Pete's."

"He say what he wants?"

"Does he ever?"

No. But this time I can guess.

Dominic Angeli might've made everyone's knees tremble in New York's tommy gun days, but Sig Loreale makes everyone's knees tremble now. Sure, Angeli used to own the town, but these days Sig owns not just New York but a good chunk of the rest of America. On the legit side, he's got money in skyscrapers and in those cookie-cutter tract house developments crawling through the suburbs from here to California. Financial markets? There isn't a banker who doesn't jump at the jangle of loose change in Sig's pocket, or a Wall Streeter who doesn't sweat when he phones. And his reach goes deep into dirtier troves of cash too. Murder for hire made him a millionaire even way back in our Coney Island days, when young Sig muscled into the Coney rackets and I was a kid lifting trinkets from beachgoers, scared to death of this new guy knocking off the old-time bosses. Coney Island was the start of Sig's empire. Now his hands are in every racket from gambling to fraud to extortion. His fingers scoop up the cash in City Hall's tills and the politicians' wallets. He's muscled into trade unions on the docks and in the factories. He's got enough cops and judges in his pocket to know everything about anything even before it happens, and to get away with whatever racket he works or murder he orders. His web of informants stretches across the city and clear across the country, even to points beyond. Sig Loreale is the biggest of big shots.

So it wouldn't surprise me that he'd know about the Angeli killing, even if it wasn't all over the news. And there's not a doubt in my mind that he knows I nearly tripped over Angeli's corpse at Hartmann's Warehouse. He probably got the tip from one of the cops he owns.

Sig makes his home in a penthouse in one of his skyscrapers, a sleek tower of black brick topped by golden Gothic arches. By day, the arches blaze in the sun. By night, they glow as if floating, the black bricks of the building disappearing into the night.

The building is on West Fortieth Street, across the street from Bryant Park, that patch of green behind the big library on Fifth Avenue. I've seen Sig taking a stroll in the park from time to time. Never seen him in the library.

The lobby of Sig's skyscraper is an enormous cavern of black tile lit by brass sconces on the walls and gigantic geometric glass and brass lamps hanging from the three-story-high ceiling. The lobby's busy this morning and every weekday morning with businessmen and office workers hurrying to the elevators that will take them to one of the twenty-three floors Sig rents out to legit business tenants. In my blue silk suit, light blue shirt, blue and green striped tie, brown overcoat and cap, I might be mistaken for one of the businessmen walking to the elevators, except for two differences: I favor a tweed cap instead of a fedora, and I enjoy wearing my suit more than they enjoy wearing theirs.

A few of the businessmen and office girls waiting by the elevators give me the side-eye when I arrive at Sig's private elevator at the end of the row. The office crowd knows who they rent from. I guess it scares some of them, but I'm sure it gives others a little thrill, makes for a snappy story to tell the kids at the family dinner.

No doubt I scare some of the office crowd too. They make a show of not looking at me, worried they'd catch my eye. After all, they probably figure if I'm here to see their gangster landlord, then maybe I'm a dangerous killer on my way to getting my next contract. The scars on my face seal the deal.

I also get the usual sneers of disgust from members of the morality mob, those straight-backs who can't handle a dame in a gentleman's suit. Here and there, though, I get a curious glance. I always get a kick out of those. I'm tempted to open my suit jacket and give them the full fashion show, but exposing the .38 nestled in my shoulder rig probably isn't a good idea. Somebody might call a cop, and I've had enough of the Law this morning.

One of the curious glances coming my way is from a cute number in a pastel green coat, her delicately rouged face adorable under a little green hat perched on soft brown waves that embrace her ears. I give her a wink. She turns away fast, hurries into an arriving elevator, misses out on seeing my winning smile.

The muscle guarding Sig's elevator says with a smirk, "Nice try, Gold."

I know the guy, Max Novik, a gorilla in a brown suit. I swear I can hear the scream of the suit's seams straining to cover the bulges of his muscular body. He sports a crew cut to give his big face maximum room to scare the hell out of people. With a hand that gives meaning to the description ham-fisted, he turns the key that opens Sig's elevator door. "The boss is expecting you," he says with a smile friendlier than you'd expect from his brutish face. "They'll take your piece upstairs."

"I know the drill," I say.

The elevator takes me directly to the penthouse floor. The doors slide open to a mausoleum-like hallway leading to the equally deathly big black door of Sig's apartment.

I press the buzzer, and another muscle boy opens the door. He comes at me with the palms of his hands. "I gotta pat—"

I pull out my .38 fast and hand it over. There's no way I'd ever let him or any other guy get his paws on me.

With a jerk of his head, he tells me to go out to the terrace.

The terrace door is on the other side of the living room. Walking through the eerily cozy room of comfortable furniture and peach-colored walls filled with art is an ordeal of memories. Sig and I go back a long way. Our Coney Island days may be behind us, but there are threads that bind us that I can't cut, no matter how many times or how hard I try. This living room is a tangle of those threads, filled with art and antiquities I've obtained for Sig in exchange for fistfuls of cash. Memories of heartbreak and betrayal are tangled up here too: the love of Sig's life murdered on his wedding night, bridal flowers wilting in vases around the room, his broken promise to use his vast web of connections to help me find the kidnapped love of *my* life.

It's a relief to open the French doors to the terrace, step out into the fresh air and clear sunshine.

Sig's terrace wraps all the way around the apartment, affording him a full view of the city he lords over. Atop his tower, the gold-painted arches brilliant in the sun, Sig lives in a glittering world of skyscraper power.

I have to turn a couple of corners around the terrace before I find him. He's seated at a white-cloth'd table loaded with a breakfast feast of a tray of eggs, a bowl of fruit, and a silver urn of coffee. He's attired even more conservatively than his businessmen tenants. Sig's black suit, crisp white shirt, black vest, black tie, a black coat draped across his shoulders, and a homburg on his head give him the appearance of an undertaker. The getup's perfect for a guy who's responsible for putting more bodies in the ground than the gravediggers union.

He puts his coffee cup down when he sees me, his jowly face serious as a lecture, his baggy, hooded eyes regarding me as they always do with a tangled mixture of being pleased to see me and ongoing annoyance.

But it's not Sig who holds my attention. It's the woman seated with him, a classy blonde whose softly waved, chin-length coif frames a perfectly sculpted face which could rival the finest Greek statuary. She looks at me with blue eyes cold as a winter sky.

The rest of her, though, at least what I see of her seated at the table, could warm up even the chilliest night. Her lavender jacket opens to a pink cashmere pullover sweater, which she fills the way a sweater should be filled: completely but with a delicacy that invites my more gentle fantasies.

Sig's gravel voiced, "Good morning, Cantor," and his terrifyingly slow delivery of every word—a habit of speech that's given me the creeps since I was a kid—pulls me out of my lovely fantasies of rolling around with the blonde. "Have a seat," Sig says. "I'd like you to meet Miss Edie Angeli, Dominic Angeli's daughter."

That knocks the last of my lustful daydreams out of me.

Miss Edie Angeli gives me a slow-spreading smile, the type whose pleasure comes from its owner's ability to size up anyone brought into her presence. It's a royal smile. "Won't you sit down?" she says. "We have much to discuss." She doesn't sound like a gangster's daughter. Her creamy voice and silky diction match that royal smile.

I take a seat at the table, start whatever Miss Angeli wants to discuss with the obvious opener, "My condolences for your loss, Miss Angeli," and let her take it from there. I won't know which cards I'll have to play until she—or Sig—deals them.

There's sadness in her lowered eyes and in her whispered, "Thank you," the grief of a loving daughter for her murdered father. But when she raises her eyes again and looks at me, my blood ices in my veins. The woman's sadness is gone; she's Boss Angeli's daughter again, all business now, hard business. "I know you didn't kill my dad," she says, getting back to the raw meat of the murder.

"I know it too," I say. "But how do you know it?"

Sig says, "Because I told her."

"And how do you know it, Sig? You obviously know I was there with the body."

He answers not with words but with a look that says that I should know better.

He takes a sip of coffee, which seems to soften his attitude. "Have some breakfast, Cantor," he says with a wave of his hand across the feast on the table.

"No thanks," I say. "I've already had mine. Now, what's on your mind, Sig? What is it you and Miss Angeli think we have to discuss?"

He says, "Miss Angeli phoned me early this morning and asked if I knew why you were at Hartmann's Warehouse in the middle of the night."

It's impossible to keep the surprise off my face so I don't even try.

It's Miss Angeli who addresses it. "In addition to a considerable amount of money, my father left me with other useful things. Loyal friends in useful places, for instance."

"Like the police department?" I say.

"You're thinking too small," she says. There's that royal smile again, only this time there's genuine amusement in it.

Her amusement is met with my own. I don't bother to hide the smile spreading across my face, even as I take out a cigarette, light it, and offer one to Miss Angeli. She takes it, puts it between her lips and leans forward across the table for me to light it. The flame of my lighter reflects in her eyes. I wonder how much more fire might lurk behind those chilly blue eyes, or how hot that fire might burn.

She hasn't dealt me a lot of cards, but my gut tells me she plays with a stacked deck. Despite her finishing school polish and fancy speech, Miss Edie Angeli is every inch the gangster's daughter, inheritor of her father's remaining loyal and well-placed allies.

Sig takes another sip of coffee, looks at me over the rim of the cup. His eyes are hard, demanding.

Miss Angeli is still smiling, the smoke from her cigarette sliding along her cheek. But the smoke does nothing to soften the iron will inside the smile. "So, why were you at Hartmann's Warehouse?" she says.

"Miss Angeli," I say, "maybe your own informants have already told you, or maybe you heard it from Sig, but I'm sure you know what I do for a living, the world I live in. So I bet you also know that there are rules for surviving in that world, rules no doubt your father understood and even played by in his heyday. If I tell you why I was at the warehouse, I'd be breaking those rules."

She waves that away, sending cigarette smoke curling away from her like wispy snakes. "Listen to me, Gold—"

"Please, call me Cantor. I've just lit your cigarette. That makes us chummy."

"Well, I wouldn't go that far," she says.

I can't resist saying, "How far would you go?"

"Not as far as you'd like."

"Are you so sure what I'd like?"

The royal smile is back as she gives me that size-me-up look again, letting her eyes linger on my suit and tie. "You're asking the wrong question, Cantor. You should be asking what *I'd* like."

"Any time, Miss Angeli, any time."

"You misunderstand," she says, then takes a long draw on the cigarette and lets it out in an equally long exhale that makes me wait for whatever it is she plans to tell me. I don't mind. She's good to look at while I wait, and it gives me the time to let her underestimate my patience, among what other misconceptions she might have about me. When she thinks I've sweated enough, she says, "What I'd like is information about Hartmann's Warehouse and what you were doing there."

It's my turn to take a pull on my cigarette. My exhale's more direct, sending blown smoke between us. And then I smile a chilly smile. So does Miss Angeli.

It's not lost on me that Sig has said nothing during my back-and-forth with Miss Angeli. I give him a glance to check his mood.

He doesn't seem to have much of a mood one way or another, content to let whatever's between me and Miss Angeli play out. Smart move. Out of respect for her father's legacy, Sig's already done the favor the woman's asked for by bringing me here. If I fork over with information, she'll be in Sig's debt. If I don't, it's her problem, not his. If the business of the Dominic Angeli murder gets messy, Sig has ways of cleaning it up. He doesn't need me. He doesn't need Dominic Angeli's daughter.

And I don't need her either. I've restored Vivienne's stolen paintings.

I get up from the table "It's been nice meeting you, Miss Angeli. Maybe I'll see you around some time," I say as I start to walk away.

Her creamy voice calls after me, "Who are you protecting, Cantor?"

I want to turn around, look at her face, see the savvy in her eyes, the sharp smarts she learned at the knee of her gangster father. But I just keep walking. I'm usually a sucker for smart women, but Edie Angeli has dangerous smarts, the kind that can get Vivienne killed.

If you walk by the little nondescript corner building across the street from the Hudson River's midtown docks, in the shadow of the elevated West Side Highway, you'd never guess that inside is a high-money smuggling operation, or that the basement vault contains treasures cooling off before they're delivered into the grasping hands of their new owners. My office is known only to the few who need to know and the even fewer who have the power or connections to find me, people like Sig. Among the people who don't know about my little building—and I make sure they'll never know—are cops or other busybodies of the Law. My lawyer buried the ownership trail in so many layers of paperwork you'd need a steam drill to dig down to the bottom of it all and you'd still never find the name Cantor Gold.

You can't get into the building by the front door either since there's no front door, just a steel slab that gives the place the appearance of being locked up and abandoned. The only way in is through the maze of alleys behind the buildings lining this block of Twelfth Avenue.

The shadowy alleys are another layer of protection against exposure of my business. If you don't belong here, the down-and-outs who live in the corners and crevices will quickly relieve you of your wallet, your coat, your shoes, maybe even your life. And you'll never hear them coming. They know how to blend in with the whoosh of traffic on the highway and the avenue below, their footsteps muffled by the music of the waterfront: the clang of buoy bells and the deep bellow of ships' horns along the river.

I'm safe here in the alleys. Its denizens know me.

The waterfront music follows me into my little building, muted only when I close the sliding steel door behind me.

Judson is at his desk in the outer office, the sleeves of his yellow shirt rolled up to the elbow, a pack of cigarettes in his shirt pocket. He's going through the coded entries in the office books, his boyishly angular face all business behind his wire-rimmed glasses. The city's coeds are wild about Judson. They think he's adorable behind his wire rims.

Judson's a detail kind of guy. Besides his talent for digging out information from even the deepest holes, he's good at organizing things, things like keeping track of which client has paid up, which client hasn't, and who gets what from the vault downstairs. Plucking him from his teenage street gang ten years ago was one of the smartest moves I've ever made.

He looks up when he hears me come in. "I got some dope on Angeli, like you asked. And you're right, it wasn't easy. The guy was a shadow, even when he was alive."

"Yeah, he was famous for it," I say. "You get anything useful?"

"You tell me. He started out as a pushcart peddler down on Elizabeth Street when he was an immigrant kid of fourteen or fifteen. He barely spoke any English yet." Judson leans back in his chair, puts his feet on his desk, revealing the uniform of his generation: cuffed blue jeans above the ankles of his high-top sneakers. Relaxed, he continues his spiel. "Angeli's pushcart operation sold everything from apples to silk stockings, all of it stolen. But he didn't stay on the streets for long. By the time he was in his twenties, he was a full-fledged gangster, leading a nasty bunch who broke heads if anyone balked at paying up."

"That's how they did it in those days," I say. "Fists first, conversation later. Smart operators like Sig wised up, though. He'll only kill you if you don't like his conversation."

Judson says, "Angeli wised up too. He learned to work quiet, and he always stayed in the shadows. He never went for the flashy stuff, never wanted to get his name in the papers. He didn't mingle much either. The guy made a fortune, but he rarely went to the better restaurants, almost never went to the theater unless his wife insisted, and even then he'd only sit in the balcony, out of the limelight of the high-paying orchestra and box seat crowd whose pictures end up in the society columns."

"So I guess he didn't go to museums or galleries much either, and never bought or stole any art?"

"Nope. There's nothing like that in anything I could get on him. For a crime boss, he led a pretty dull life."

"Except when he was robbing you blind or having you killed."

Judson gives that a shrug and a smirk, then says, "So what's Dominic Angeli got to do with you? The guy's been out of the rackets for years."

I give Judson the story, tell him all about Vivienne's stolen paintings and the note that sent me to Hartmann's Warehouse, only to almost fall over Angeli's body. And then I tell him about my meeting with Sig and the very surprising presence of Edie Angeli.

That sits him up.

"Yeah," I say, "she's every inch her father's daughter. Icy as they come but in a package that could heat up the coldest bedsheets."

Judson takes a smoke from the pack of Luckies in his pocket, lights it, and gives me a hard look that's part scolding, part pity. "Just make sure you don't get burned, Cantor."

The guy knows me.

I give him an amused nod and walk into my private office, take my coat and cap off, and sit down at my desk.

My office is more than just my place of business. It's my refuge when I need to lay low. I've outfitted it with plenty of comforts: an oxblood leather couch cozy enough for sweet dreams when I sleep here; a pale green club chair soft as a woman's embrace; a shower stall; a closet with changes of clothes; a small but well-stocked refrigerator and a hot plate so I don't go hungry. There's a radio when I need music to soothe me, a television set when I need a laugh or want to catch an old late-night movie, and a hefty supply of booze to keep me companionable company. I didn't spare any expense on the place. Why should I? I risk my life every day to live the way I want.

I light a smoke and think about Edie Angeli, how she pegged me about protecting someone. She doesn't know who that someone is, and I'm determined to make sure she never does. I kick back in my chair and consider what to do about the smart and dangerous Miss Angeli. And I think about who might be in back of last night's grab of Vivienne's paintings as the setup for a murder frame. I think about these things, try to figure my next move, when the phone rings, jangling into my thoughts.

The phone stops ringing when Judson picks up the call. A second later he knocks on my door, opens it, and tells me that

Esther Sheinbaum's on the line. "You want to talk to her?"

Talking to Esther "Mom" Sheinbaum is like talking to a mother who can't hide her disappointment in you but can't cut you off either. At least, that's what it's been like since the night she spilled her disapproval of me, my love life, my style of clothes. But money talks louder than disappointment, so we still do business. The Mom moniker, though, isn't particular to me. She's called Mom by everyone on both sides of the Law because she's been around since the city's gaslight days. She's the most successful fence and purveyor of stolen goods New York has ever known. She's supplied diamond trinkets to clients as varied as gamblers, gangsters, city councilmen, and mayors to keep their wives or mistresses happy.

Mom and I have a history that goes back almost as far as my history with Sig. And Mom even figures in the tangle of threads connecting me to Sig: that love of his life who was murdered on their wedding night? Mom's daughter Opal.

I nod to Judson and pick up the phone. "What's on your mind, Mom?"

"*Mommeleh*," she says in her Lower East Side singsong, "I just got a very bad telephone call from someone who sounded like they were talking through a hankie or a paper bag or something. Or maybe it was a ventriloquist. Anyway, a phony voice. The caller was talking about you. It seems you annoyed somebody, and now this *momzer* wants to annoy me. I don't like being annoyed, Cantor"—in Mom's immigrant accent, my name comes across as *Kentuh*—"and I don't trust smart aleck *pishers* who try to put one over on me by giving me a phony voice."

This phone call's making my spine itch, like ants crawling between every bone. "What did he say?"

Through a *tsk*, Mom says, "The *yutz* gives me a warning. Me. Gives a warning to *me*. Such a nerve."

The guy's got plenty of nerve. Either that or he's clueless about who he was talking to. Mom Sheinbaum's a powerful player, the longtime Empress of the Underworld. Only a fool, a *yutz*, would try to rattle her.

I say, "What did he warn you about and where do I figure into it?"

"The *momzer* says I should tell you that you made a mistake giving those paintings back to that woman, and that next time you'd better wait for instructions or the body on floor will be me. Cantor, who does this SOB think they are, threatening me? Anyway, I says to the *schnook*, 'Why don't you ask her yourself?'"

Good question. "What did they say?"

"Nothing, just laughed. You shoulda heard it, a real mean laugh. Cold. And that silly voice made it worse."

"Did you get a name?"

"Nah, they just laughed that nasty laugh and hung up before I could ask. But y'know what? Now I think about it, the voice maybe sounds familiar. I can't put my finger on it but—*oy*, maybe it just sounds like every other smart aleck. And that hankie or paper bag or whatever it was disguising that voice didn't help."

"Young? Old?"

"Smart alecks all sound the same. Listen, Cantor, you gotta take care of this. I'm in no mood to wind up dead."

Chapter Five

The question gnaws at me: why didn't the guy who called Mom talk to me himself? This is the second time he's walked around me: first the business with Vivienne's paintings, and now by threatening Mom. The guy never said Dominic Angeli's name to Mom, never said it was Angeli's body on the floor, or at least Mom didn't mention it to me, which she would have. It wouldn't surprise me if Mom and Don Dominic Angeli had crossed paths back in the old days, might've even done a little business. So why didn't the guy bring up Angeli's name to Mom?

And how the hell did the guy even get to Dominic Angeli to kill him and dump him in Hartmann's Warehouse? The old Don was probably one of the most insulated guys in the world. He's been tucked away behind the walls of his country estate for years. And I'll bet those walls weren't just pretty architecture; they probably had guys with guns backing up the fancy stone.

And then there's the little matter of how the killer got Angeli off the estate and into the city. What would it take to lure the reclusive Dominic Angeli out of his mansion and into a Manhattan warehouse? Or if Angeli was killed in the mansion, then getting the corpse into the city and dragging it into the warehouse without anyone noticing must've taken some doing.

I hate to say it, but hats off to the guy for pulling off an impossible job.

Mom said the voice on the phone sounded familiar. Well, that could be anybody. Mom's dealt with a lot of people over the years. What I've got to figure out is who does she know who can get to Dominic Angeli and who's also connected to me? And why the hell are they coming after me anyway?

I pick up the phone again, dial Sig. When I get him on the line, I say, "Is Miss Angeli still at your place?"

"No, she is not. She left shortly after you did, Cantor. Why?"

"Listen, someone's playing deadly games. I can't tell yet if they're just deadly games or stupid and deadly games."

"What would lead you to believe they're stupid games?"

"Because whoever's playing them just called Mom Sheinbaum with a message for me and threatened to kill her if I don't do what they want. So you tell me, who would be stupid enough to threaten Mom Sheinbaum?"

There aren't many people Sig Loreale respects. At the top of that very short list is Mom. And not just because he wanted to marry her daughter. He respects Mom's smarts, her gristle. He respects the history she carries inside her, a history of scratching up from the immigrant gutter to the top of the criminal world and staying there. It's a history that matches his own, only her journey, as a woman, was tougher, and he knows it.

I hear only the sound of Sig's breathing, deep, long breaths riding on thoughts I'm probably better off not knowing. Otherwise, he's silent, a silence that passes slow as a lifetime until he says, "I will see to Mrs. Sheinbaum's safety. Now, I take it you wish to speak to Miss Angeli?"

"Yeah. She might be the chess piece I need to checkmate this guy. How do I get in touch with her?"

He gives me an address I don't expect.

I have a rented space in Louie's Parking Garage, down the street from my office, because I can approach the garage from the alleys and drive in through a back door. It gives the cops less chance of tailing me. They don't see me drive in; they don't see me drive out.

The drive to Edie Angeli's place is pleasant on this spring afternoon. I've got the convertible top down on my car, enjoy the breeze on my face and through my hair.

The car's a recently delivered burgundy '55 Buick Roadmaster. The lines on this baby are sleeker than the previous models, a little more futuristic, a little less earthy. I like it, though I feel a bit wistful for the old curves.

The sunny day lends a nice patina to the car's burgundy body and glints on her chrome accents on the dashboard. In the cool breeze, the bright sun, with mellow tunes on the radio, and midday traffic that's actually moving, I feel pretty good for someone who's being hunted by a killer.

Charles Street in Greenwich Village is the last place I'd expect to find Edie Angeli. In addition to the lunch pail families who've populated the Village for generations, the neighborhood's often been home to artists, musicians, writers, and other free thinkers. These days, it's the Beat crowd; poets, novelists, musicians and artists who are giving American culture an overdue thrashing.

There's a noontime stickball game noisy with boyish shouts of "Let 'er fly, Frankie!" and "Watch it! Watch it!" going on in the street. When I get out of my car, I have to dodge the flight of a pink Spalding rubber ball—pronounced Spald*een* in New York street parlance—headed straight for me. A kid in dungarees and a white T-shirt, his dark hair flopping around on his head as he runs, makes a dash to the sewer drain serving as first base. He slides. He's safe. *Good play, kid.* Maybe he'll make the Yankees someday if he dreams big enough.

The address Sig gave me is an ornate, slightly crumbling three-story brownstone in the middle of the block. New York is full of old buildings like this one, tenements tricked out with gewgaws reminiscent of Old World architecture remembered by the Old World immigrants who moved in with their suitcases and their New World dreams. It seems an unlikely address

41

for a wealthy gangster princess. Then I think maybe she owns the joint. Maybe she inherited it from her father and she's just here today collecting rents. Maybe it's a legit front for the dirty Angeli money.

There's no name listed beside the buzzer for apartment 3-A, not that I'll ring anyway. I want to get into the apartment, even if Miss Angeli's not home. You can learn a lot from people's apartments. You can learn what matters to them, even what trouble they're in. You can learn who they really are.

I pull out my case of lockpicks from my inside jacket pocket, quickly finagle the street door lock. In less than a minute I'm through the door and inside the first-floor hallway, a shadowy place with dust motes swirling under the single ceiling light. A wistful melody on a jazz trumpet from an apartment at the end of the hall mixes with the wail of a crying baby from an apartment nearby. I wonder who's influencing the other in this New World symphony.

Other sounds from other apartments drift around me as I climb the creaking wood uncarpeted stairs to the third floor: a guy laughing, pots and pans clanging, the television audience applauding the winner of the *Strike It Rich* sob story game show, a toilet flushing. When I reach the third floor, Chuck Berry is rocking "Maybelline" on the radio in one apartment, doing battle with Sinatra's melancholy "In the Wee Small Hours of the Morning" in another. I call it a draw.

The Sinatra tune's coming from apartment 3-A, Edie Angeli's place. I start thinking better of her.

I press the buzzer, stand back a little bit to let her get the full picture through the eyehole.

A minute later, Sinatra stops singing, the door opens.

"Miss Angeli," I say.

The surprise on her face fades fast. If she wonders how I got into the building without buzzing the street door, I guess she quickly remembers how I make my living.

She's still wearing the pink pullover sweater, which catches my attention much as it did at Sig's place. But now that she's not seated at a table, I can enjoy the full length of her. Her lower half is a sinuous flow of gentle curves in a slender pair of black toreador pants. She's barefoot, her toenails painted red.

She says, "You must be pretty tight with Loreale if he told you where to find me."

"Let's just say we have a mutual interest. Are you going to invite me in? Or do you want to do business in the hall."

She cocks her head, gives me the same size-me-up look she gave me when we were introduced at Sig's. This time, after taking my measure from head to toe, she gets it that I'm not leaving until I get what I came for. She steps aside and nods for me to come in.

If I was shocked at meeting Dominic Angeli's daughter in the first place, shocked at the unexpected aristocratic bearing of a gangster diva, shocked at the down-at-the-heel address where I find her, none of those shocks match the shock I feel now because of what I see in her apartment: a paint-spattered apron tossed on a paint-spattered chair; paint-encrusted palettes on tables covered in colorful drips and dots; tubes of paint; cans and jars of brushes; cans of turpentine; sketches and handwritten notes tacked to the walls; a battered, paint-stained desk; equally paint-stained wooden file cabinets; and paintings, lots of them. Two on easels, others, unframed, hang on the walls around the large room, several more lined up along the floor. All of the paintings are abstractions of shapes and color: brilliant colors, dark colors, all swirling in emotional encounters that thrill you or break your heart.

Well, whaddya know: Miss Edie Angeli is an artist. A good one.

The surprise on my face probably fades a lot slower than hers did when I arrived at her door. She says, "Did you expect me to come to the door wielding a tommy gun?"

"I'm sure it would be unforgettable," I say. I wander over to a wall of paintings, drawn to one in particular with twisting arcs of reds and blacks and a deep brownish orange against a mottled dark gray ground. The painting's mood feels proudly boisterous and inconsolably sad at the same time, the way you feel when life smiles on you while it kicks you in the ass. I linger over the painting, get a good look at the brushwork, at the confidence of the hand that made the strokes. Edie Angeli is no empty-souled dilettante.

And then I notice the signature at the corner of the paintings: E. Dumont.

I turn to look at Edie. No doubt my puzzlement is all over my face.

"Yes," she says, "Edie Dumont is me. I use the name because a lot of art buyers won't do business with a gangster's daughter."

Considering all the clients who hire me to get their treasures any way I can and then either look the other way or maybe even get a thrill from it, Edie's remark gives me a chuckle.

She catches on. "Well, okay, they might," she says with a sly smile, "but not the way I'd want them to. The Angeli name would get in the way of the artwork. Look, I'm aware you know a lot about art, but let's skip the art appreciation session for another time, and just tell me why you're here."

She takes a cigarette from a pack of Camels on a table crowded with art supplies, holds it to her lips.

I get the message as much now as I did on the terrace at Sig's place. I take out my lighter, light her smoke, then pull out my pack of Chesterfields and light one for myself.

"I'm here," I say through the smoke, "because a mutual acquaintance of mine and Sig's was threatened over the phone. The caller was very likely the guy who killed your father. Now, Dominic Angeli was not an easy guy to get to, so I figure maybe you could shed some light on who might have had access to him."

"Why would the caller threaten your friend? Did your friend know my father?"

"Possibly, in fact likely back in the old days. But the guy never mentioned Dominic Angeli on the phone. This whole business, including your father's murder, looks like a play to get to me. They want to toy with me like a cat torturing a mouse before it eats it. I don't know why, but someone has it in for me."

That seems to amuse her. A little smile creeps toward the corner of her mouth. "I can't imagine why," she says.

"Try harder. Somewhere there's a connection between me and Dominic Angeli."

"And you think if I can get you some names, maybe you can connect one of them back to you?"

"That's what I figure. Anybody ring a bell?"

She stubs out her cigarette in a cheap brass ashtray. "Come with me," she says.

"Where are we going?"

"Lunch. I'm hungry."

Café Lorenzo is one of those dark little joints that's been serving zesty food, light-as-air pastries, hearty wine, and strong coffee since the gaslight days when the Village was an Italian enclave. It's the kind of eatery cherished by longtime locals as well as the more recent Beat crowd, the latter appreciative of the kick of the coffee and tongue-loosening wine at cheap prices.

Cozy place, but I wish Edie had brought us somewhere else for lunch. The shadowy café, with its pools of soft light from small lamps on the tables, dredges up a memory I have a tough time living with, the memory of the first time I saw the woman who claimed my heart and soul, the woman at the center of that wound that won't heal. It was in a joint just like this, in this very neighborhood, that I first saw Sophie, Sophie de la Luna y Sol. She was in a booth, reading a newspaper. The sight of her floored me, not only because she was beautiful but because I had a feeling deep in my gut that we'd been waiting for each other in that café all of our lives.

Six months later, she was gone, stolen from me, kidnapped, sold into sexual slavery. I searched for her. I found her. She went down in a hail of bullets on a street in Havana.

This café is bringing it all back.

"Cantor?"

The sound of my name crawls inside me, then drags me out of my reverie. I look at the woman sitting across the table from me, the stunning woman who is not Sophie.

"Cantor?" the woman says again. I hear, too, the murmur of other diners, the clatter of plates and silverware. I'm back in the present, looking across the table at Edie Angeli, who's smiling at me, sort of. "You'd gone away for a minute," she says.

"I'm here now," I say.

She leans back in her chair. The light from our table lamp glows on the pink sweater she fills so nicely, rolls along soft waves of her perfectly coiffed blond hair, and catches a gleam in her eyes. She's doing her appraisal number on me again, probing into places I don't want her to go, looking for secrets, looking for where I was before she pulled me out of my memories.

The artist in her might be sensitive, even profound, but the gangster princess part of her is dangerous. I don't dare let her see anything deeper than the scars on my face.

I bring us back to business. "Miss Angeli," I say, "since I'm the one with the questions, lunch is on me."

"My, but you are courtly. I believe that earns you the right to call me Edie."

I hail the waiter. Edie orders an insalata and a small cheese platter. I go for grilled calamari. The waiter suggests a light white wine. Edie says, "Just coffee afterwards for me." I go along. Light white wine is for lazy afternoons, not conversations about murder.

When the waiter goes away, I say, "Well, then, you figure you can help me out?"

"What's in it for me?" she says.

The woman who asked that question is not the woman who lives in an art studio filled with paintings. The woman who asked the question is the savvy inheritor of her father's ruthlessness and an eye for power plays.

Two identities live in the same woman. My best bet may be to wriggle my way into the line between them.

I say, "All those paintings I saw at your studio. They're good.

They go deep. They tell me who you want to be. But the Angeli connection threatens that."

"Are you telling me to cut off my family heritage? That's insulting."

"I'm asking you to use that family heritage. You asked what's in it for you if you help me. Well, if we work together to figure who killed your father, then Edie Angeli, the crime boss's daughter, might be able to free the artist Edie Dumont from the Angeli associations and its current murder problem. You could help the artist take her own place in the world."

I've struck a nerve. At least I think so. Edie's still looking at me, but the look in her eyes isn't sizing me up anymore. Something in her eyes is pulling away from me, focusing on nothing in front of her while some inner thoughts take over.

"My father always kept to himself," she says, slowly coming back into our conversation. "It's why the Law could never bring him down. Whatever he did, he did on the quiet. The police, the prosecutors, they could never attach his name to anything. After my mother died, he became even more secretive."

"That's when he moved upstate full time."

"Yes. He really missed my mother. He was an old-fashioned Old World guy and he loved my mother with all his heart. He was terribly lonely without her. My own heart ached for him." And aches still. I hear it in her voice. I guess Edie Angeli was at heart Daddy's girl. "And besides that," she says, "my mother was his most trusted confidante."

Well, well. So Momma Angeli wasn't just the devoted little woman stirring pasta in the kitchen. It turns out Edie Angeli, gangster princess, is the daughter of a gangster queen. How about that.

The waiter brings our lunch.

Edie picks at her insalata. I down a forkful of calamari while Edie silently wanders through another line of thought.

Finally, she says, "My father always hated my life as an artist. He was afraid it would bring too much attention to the family. But he never tried to stop me, and you know he could have."

The way she says it sends a chill across the table.

She lets whatever she meant hang in the air as she chews a cube of cheese. Then she says, "But he loved me. And I loved him."

"So avenge his murder. And you don't have to do it alone."

"Don't you think I could?"

"I think Edie Angeli knows how to make use of those loyal friends in useful places she mentioned this morning. So sure, I think you could do it without me."

"It would leave you out in the cold if I did."

"It might leave me stiff and cold too."

She greets that with a cock of her head and an expression of curiosity. "Then maybe someone really is out to get you. I thought they were only trying to frame you."

Everything inside me tightens up so fast the calamari almost gets stuck in my throat. I force it down as discreetly as I can, then give Edie a smile. "If you know that, then you've already been tapping those loyal friends in useful places."

She acknowledges that with an easygoing shrug, leans back in her chair again and returns my smile with one of her own; the royal smile, but this time with a bit of her father's gutter savvy under it. "And what about the person you're protecting?" she says. "It's a woman, isn't it." She presses the point by looking at me as if she's examining every thread of my blue suit, the cut of my jacket, even the fold of my light blue pocket square.

Judging by the change in her smile to something less high and mighty, I think the suit's met with Edie's approval. Maybe its wearer has too.

The idea has its charm, the kind that can kill me. I back away from the lure of any Edie Angeli fantasy, just say, "There are very few men I'd go out of my way to protect."

"And not many who'd protect you," she says. "Except maybe Sig Loreale."

My short laugh is more of a grunt. "You overestimate his opinion of me. If Sig protects me occasionally—and believe me, you could count on the fingers of one hand after a bad accident how many times he's so-called protected me—it's because at that moment I was worth more to him alive than dead. Sig Loreale's loyalty is reserved only for Sig Loreale. He bows to no one."

Edie says, "He bowed to my father. Oh, didn't you know? I remember Loreale visiting our country place when I was a kid. He was always very respectful. And when my father decided to give up the reins of power, Loreale asked my father for his blessing in allowing him to take over."

No, I didn't know, but I'm not surprised. Sig didn't need Boss Angeli's blessing to take over. Sig was already taking control of New York. But making a show of respect for the old Don was a smart move. It avoided hard feelings among Angeli loyalists, stopped any disgruntled Angeli triggerman from going after the new boss. Sig could've handled whatever blowback might've come his way if he'd just moved in on the old boss's rackets, but kissing the Angeli ring avoided all that trouble.

So Edie read it wrong. Sig wasn't showing fealty to Don Dominic Angeli. Once again, as always, Sig's move was in service to himself.

Still, Edie's interpretation of the event allowed her to contact Sig in order to get to me. And Sig went along because it kept the remaining Angeli loyalists friendly. Chances are Sig couldn't care less about Edie except for her last name and the possible annoyances it could summon, annoyances he avoided with a simple invitation to breakfast.

I push the rest of my calamari away. "Listen, Edie, this stroll down your memory lane with Sig and your father is all very interesting. I'm always up for a history lesson, but it doesn't get us anywhere in solving your father's murder or getting me out from under it. So, what have you got for me? Can you think of anyone who might have even a distant connection to me and your father? I'd never met Dominic Angeli, but I bet I know people who had."

"Well, there's Loreale," she says, dismissing the idea the minute it comes out of her mouth.

"Sure, but forget Sig. He has no reason to put me in a tight

49

spot. At least not this time. Who else?"

I signal the waiter to bring our coffee as Edie runs through a list of names of old Angeli loyalists. Some I'd never heard of. Others, whose names I've heard here and there, I'd never met and had no personal connection to. The few I'd met are mostly geezers now and out of the game.

None of this is any help.

We're finishing our coffee, a terrific espresso with plenty of punch that avoids a bite, when Edie says, "It's a good thing you never met my father. He wouldn't have approved of you. He would have thought you were, well, the wrong sort. But then again," she adds with a little laugh, "he never liked the boys I dated either. No one was ever good enough for his princess. It's why he sent me off to finishing school in Switzerland; you know, those places where snooty society girls are taught the proper way to pour tea for their father's diplomatic career."

A new idea slides through her words. "Wait a minute," I say. "Maybe that's it."

"What's it? What are you talking about? What does my old school have to do with you?"

"Not your school. The boys, and then the men. I guess your father thought the men were never good enough either. Who did you run around with, Edie, who I might know?"

The way she looks at me you'd think I'd said that I'd defend to the death the belief that the moon really is made of green cheese.

"Listen, sweetie," I say with a trace of a sneery tone I don't bother to hide, "my racket brings me into the parlors of some of the most high-hat people in town, so don't give me that look that says you and I would never mix in the same circles. We both come from lowbrow Old Country stock, our families right off the immigrant boats. And believe me, the town's high hats would toss us both to the gutter if we gave them even the slightest reason to. You know it as well as I do. That's why you sign your paintings Edie Dumont. So take off your finishing school gloves, stop pouring weak tea, and tell me about any fellas who professed their undying love for you."

She takes a sip of coffee longer than the little cup would suggest, and looks at me over the rim. The light from our table lamp catches her eyes, shows me the conflict of scorn and hurt pride inside her. "All right," she says when she puts the cup down. "Here's the rundown on the love life of Edie Angeli."

"And don't forget Edie Dumont. I'm in the art game, remember? Our circles might have bumped into each other."

That earns a reluctant nod. Then she starts talking.

None of the names in her long list of suitors means anything to me, except two. One makes me laugh. The other makes me cringe.

Chapter Six

It's just a short drive from the Village to Mom Sheinbaum's place on the Lower East Side. Instead of the aromas of red sauce and wine savored in Edie's neighborhood, down here the air is tangy with corned beef, pastrami, and briny pickles.

I park in front of Mom's Second Avenue brownstone, one of the last private residences on a fast commercializing street. The world Mom ruled over is disappearing house number by house number. A few remaining pushcart peddlers still cluster at the curb to hawk their wares. The pickings of fruits and vegetables, used kitchen appliances, and old clothing aren't as plentiful as they used to be back when I was a kid coming to Mom with my Coney Island contraband for her to fence, and for her to mentor me in the ways of thievery. The Lower East Side, home to generations of immigrants who saturated the neighborhood with their hopes, their dreams, their sweat, their crimes, is changing as fast as the rest of the country. The old ways are vanishing, swallowed up by supermarkets and appliance stores, and all the shiny new ways promised by the latest buy-now-pay-later TV commercials.

In the meantime, Esther Sheinbaum is still a star of the underworld, still the best mover of stolen goods in the city, probably the whole country too. Mom knows who's who, who's where, and who's got what. Among all those who's who, maybe the voice that sounded familiar to her on the phone this morning was one of the guys Edie mentioned.

I sit in the Buick for a minute before getting out. It's not always easy for me to visit the old woman. There's a trickle of bad blood between us, a betrayal of trust since she broke my heart the night she told me that she doesn't approve of my style of dress or my romantic predilections, that she thinks I'm unnatural.

But there's too much history that binds us. And there's still money to be made between us. So we don't cut loose of each other. We can't.

I get out of the car.

I make it quick up the front stairs, ring her doorbell, straighten my tie, run my hand through my hair to flatten it best I can, and adjust my cap while I wait for Mom to answer the door.

She greets me with a sidewise grin and a narrowing of her small button eyes that lets me know she's not surprised to see me. "Took you long enough," she says. The white stripes of her green housedress stretch in bulbous curves around her prodigious bulk. Sunlight from the street shimmers in the tight waves of her short silvery hair, creating an aura around her pudgy face.

"It's only been a few hours, Mom, since we talked on the phone. What's your hurry?"

"I'm in a hurry not to get killed by some smart aleck *momzer*," she says. "You get things fixed yet?"

"I'm working on it."

"Well, work faster, and don't stand out there on the steps. You're letting in a draft. Come inside and tell me why you're here."

The neighborhood may be changing, but Mom's house isn't. The living room is still furnished in the overstuffed and fussy manner of the early days of the century, when Mom and her now deceased husband first moved in. Same story in the dining room. It's where Mom and I have had our meetings since I was a kid bringing her a satchel of purloined trinkets. The mahogany dining table and heavily carved sideboard are polished to a shine, as always, and there's a loaf of honey cake on a silver tray on the table, along with a floral teapot and a cup and saucer and cake plate, as always.

"Want some tea?" she says, and sits down at the head of the table.

"I'll pass." I take off my coat, drape it over a dining chair. I take off my cap and start to put it on the table, but take it back and put it on the chair with my coat when Mom gives me a look that's as scolding as a wagging finger.

"Tables are for eating," she says. "Only a bum puts a hat on a table. So tell me, why are you here?"

I take a crystal ashtray from the sideboard, bring it to the table, sit down, and light a cigarette. "You said the voice on the phone this morning sounded familiar. You able to pin a name to it yet?"

"Nah," she says. "Why? You got a lead?"

"Maybe. You know a guy named Mel Birnbaum?"

"Never heard of him."

"Maybe you know him as Mel Burns."

"Still never heard of him. Who the hell is he?"

He's the guy whose name made me laugh. "He's an actor," I say. "A bit player, lives in my neighborhood. I've met him at card games now and then."

"I should know a bit player? I got actor clients, big Broadway types, even showgirls who like to turn the jewelry from rich admirers into quick cash. That's all you got? Some *schlemiel* I never heard of?" She picks up her teacup, the rings on her plump fingers catching light. She takes a sip of the tea, her eyes dismissing my less than stellar offering.

"All right," I say, "what about Dave Handy? Could the voice on the phone have been his?"

Mom puts the cup down, starts chuckling. The chuckle grows into a laugh that shakes her body, causing the stripes on her green housedress to wriggle over her bulk. "Handy Dave Handy?" she says through a snort. "The once-upon-a-time fixer?" Mom may be laughing, but it was Dave's name that

54

made me cringe.

"Think," I say. "Maybe it was Dave's voice?"

She gives that a shrug. "Like I told you, the idiot was talking through something, maybe a hankie, maybe a bag, maybe something else or nothing else. I couldn't tell you. So yeah, coulda been Handy Dave, or maybe not. But Dave would know better than to put the knuckle on me. The guy's a *schlemiel*, but he's been around and knows the game."

Mom's right. Dave Handy knows the game. He's the guy a lot of people used to go to if they needed something fixed, like getting a debt written off, or getting a booze license for a neighborhood bar, or getting someone dead. He used to be a top player not long ago, but something went wrong and he lost his edge. Handy Dave Handy's not so handy anymore. Like Mom says, he's just a *schlemiel* these days, but a *schlemiel* with connections. Connections like the Angeli father and daughter.

Mom says, "Anyway, you think Dave's got it in for you? Did you ever annoy him, Cantor?"

"I don't know, but you can bet I'll find out. Listen, you ever hear that maybe Dave might've been a break-in artist?"

"Never heard that about him. Far as I know, Dave was strictly an operator—y'know, a back slapper and hand pumper. Maybe a little blackmail on the side to make sure he could fix whatever somebody wanted fixed. Why? Is there a break-in mixed up in this?" She starts to cut herself a slice of honey cake, but stops, eyes me. "What aren't you telling me, Cantor?"

"Have you seen today's paper? Or the TV news?"

She gives me a questioning look; then her fleshy face turns rock hard, her lips a tight line. If I didn't know better, I'd say there's worry in her eyes. But I do know better. Mom Sheinbaum stopped worrying about me years ago, if she ever worried at all. "The Angeli killing," she says in her singsong immigrant speech. "You're mixed up with Domnic Angeli's killing?"

I stamp out my smoke, go to the sideboard to pour myself a scotch, and start talking as I take the drink back to the table. I give Mom the whole story, from Vivienne's midnight call, her

55

stolen paintings, the scene in Hartmann's Warehouse, meeting Edie Angeli at Sig's, and her revelations at lunch about dating Dave Handy and Mel Burns. "The thing is, I can't figure how the hell the killer got to old man Angeli. The guy lived in a fortress with an army of loyalists to keep threats away from him."

Mom gives that a flick-of-the-wrist wave. "Don't kid yourself, Cantor," she says. "There's always a way to get to somebody. And I been hearing that those loyalists weren't so loyal anymore. Listen, when old Dominic left the action for that castle of his upstate, his muscle boys didn't have a whole lot to do. The only money they saw was what Dominic paid them. Y'know, a salary. And Dominic could be a cheapskate, so I bet he paid his boys *bupkis*. The big dough they used to make from kickbacks, bag carries, contract hits, all that was out the window. Money talks, Cantor, and Dominic Angeli's wallet wasn't doing very much talking lately."

"You saying one of the boys could've been bribed to let someone get to the old guy?"

"Wouldn't surprise me," she says with a shrug. "What about the Angeli girl? Was she close to her father?"

"Yeah, so she says."

"You gotta be careful about family, Cantor. They keep secrets better than the—whaddya call it?—the CIA. So now, okay, what about that other guy you asked me about, the actor?"

"Mel Burns."

"Yeah, him. He got something on you?"

"I can't think of anything. The guy's sort of a joke."

"Well, would this actor be stupid enough to think he could put the knuckle on me? Hell, would the guy even know me?"

Mel's name gave me the laugh because the guy's a loser. I can't figure any reason why Edie would ever run around with him. Well, maybe one reason: Mel's handsome as a matinee idol with a voice smooth and warm as a hot toddy. Blue eyes, sculpted jaw, and a wallop-wattage smile. He's got the face to be a big star. Trouble is, he hasn't got even a thimble's worth of talent. Best he ever gets are bit parts when they need a pretty face.

Good card player, though.

Dominic Angeli wasn't part of Mel's card-playing crowd. So how did pretty boy Mel get to Angeli's daughter?

I'm batting zero here. I can't come up with any reason why either Dave Handy or Mel Burns would come after me. And neither guy would threaten Mom. Dave, because he knows better, and Mel, because he doesn't know Mom at all.

But these two guys are the only threads connecting me to Edie Angeli. I've got to pull those threads.

Mom finally cuts that slice of honey cake, puts it on her plate, then takes up a forkful. Before she puts it into her mouth, she says, "It's from Weinstein's on Rivington Street. They make the best. I want to live long enough to enjoy Weinstein's honey cake while they're still in business. You understand, Cantor?"

I answer with a nod, put on my cap and coat, and leave the house.

Outside, seeing all the changes in the neighborhood, I wonder how much longer Weinstein's will be around.

The only things Handy Dave Handy's fixing these days are drinks at the Happy Hour Saloon on Ninth Avenue in Hell's Kitchen, a midtown neighborhood that earned its name about a hundred years ago and has lived up to the moniker ever since.

The Happy Hour Saloon is the kind of dimly lit, stale beer stinking place where the cigarette and cigar smoke is thick, the serious drinking starts in the morning, and by nighttime the drinkers are either passed out or world class philosophers.

It's a quarter to three in the afternoon when I walk in, so the half dozen regulars drinking at the bar are only halfway to their endgame. Four of them are guys in shabby overcoats and beat-up fedoras or caps. They started drinking twenty years ago to kill the pain when they lost their jobs in the Great Depression, stayed drunk when the Depression ended with the Second World War, and now drink to rhapsodize about the good ol' days. The other two drinkers are women whose best years never had best years and now have only a bottle in which to drown their lousy years. None of the six has passed out yet, and the conversation is still light around the edges. The guys talk mostly about sports. The two women aren't talking at all, though one of them gives me the nasty eye, and the other one doesn't bother.

Dave's behind the bar, a bar towel slung over his shoulder, a shot glass in his hand. He's holding the glass over a pyramid of shot glasses, lowering it slowly until it tops off the pyramid.

He sees me come in, gives me a smile, the kind that's somewhere between recognition of a familiar face and what the hell are you doing here. There's a slight sneer in Dave's smile. There's always a slight sneer in Dave's smile. He's famous for it. It gives personality to his otherwise bland face whose pasty complexion matches Dave's dough-blond hair.

"Well, look what the wind blew in," he says in his snickering style. "If it isn't the classy Cantor Gold. Aren't you a little out of your alleyways?"

"And which alleyways would those be, Dave?"

"The secret ones. The no boys allowed ones. No real boys, that is." The sneer's not so subtle now. He takes the glass from the pinnacle of the pyramid, flips it, catches it in one hand, while never taking his eyes off me. "So what are you doing here?"

"I came in for a drink and a chat."

He puts the shot glass in front of me. "Name your poison."

"Chivas."

"Wrong joint. Our clientele's not so choosy."

"Then whatever scotch you've got." I put a buck on the bar. "Keep the change."

He puts the buck into the cash register, pockets sixty cents, then pulls a bottle of some firewater brand from the line of booze behind the bar, pours me a shot. I down it quick, get the rotgut bite over with.

Dave leans against the back of the bar, crosses his arms, and gives me another of his sneery smiles. "So, what do you want to chat about?"

"Edie Angeli," I say.

It's the only time I've ever seen any color in Dave's pasty cheeks. "What about her?"

"You two used to be an item, or so I hear."

"Yeah? Heard it from who?"

"Oh, you know, word gets around. Like the way word got around that your Handy Dave handyman days are done and you're pouring drinks for drunks in Hell's Kitchen. What happened, Dave? I never did get the story."

There's menace in his short laugh as he leans forward, puts his elbows on the bar, looks straight at me. "You want the story? Okay, sure. I was stabbed in the back. After all the favors I did for all those big shots, after all the fixes I made so they could lah-dee-dah their way to riches, well, make one tiny mistake, make one fix that didn't work out, and you're through. Left me wide open for someone to stab me in the back. My phone stopped ringing. My bank account shrank to nothing. No one even shook my hand. I was big time poison."

"You figure who stabbed you?"

He gives me his sneery grin. "You mean, was it anyone you know?"

"I know a lot of people," I say. "Matter of fact, I meet new people every day. Some of them friendly, some not. Some even make trouble. Maybe it was one of the troublemakers who stabbed you."

"That'll be a long list," he says.

"Let's shorten it," I say. "Was it someone connected to Dominic Angeli? Or his daughter Edie?"

Dave's grin disappears. Instead, he looks like he's sucked a lemon dipped in curdled milk. "You trying to connect me to the Angeli killing? Yeah, I heard about it. Everybody in town's heard about it. It's all over the news. There's nothing like a big shot found dead in a crummy warehouse to make the front page."

"How do you know the warehouse is crummy?"

"Aren't they all?"

He's getting too comfortable in his slippery answers. It's time to trip him. "What do you know about fine art, Dave?"

He smiles again. The famous Handy sneer at its edges gives it added threat. "Art's your racket, Gold. You stick to your racket, and I'll stick to mine," he says.

"Just what is your racket these days, Dave?"

He flips another shot glass from the pyramid, catches it in his hand as skillfully as a circus juggler. "You've had your drink, now get lost. Nice seein' ya."

Chapter Seven

Dave didn't give me much, but he gave me a few useful things, things like making it clear he doesn't like me, maybe never did. Things like something about Edie makes him tighten up, and something about the Angeli killing makes him edgy.

But not liking me doesn't mean he's out to get me. And tightening up about ex-girlfriends isn't a crime. Hell, I can sympathize. And the Angeli killing could be making the whole underworld edgy. Anyone who's ever had anything to do with Dominic Angeli is probably cringing in their underpants.

Two things about Dave, though, are making my skin prickle. One is that bit about whoever it was who stabbed him in the back. He didn't say the stabber was connected to me, but he sure let the idea dangle. Maybe he was just playing around with me because he doesn't like me. Or maybe he was toying with me like that cat torturing the mouse before it eats it.

The other thing that's itching me is how handy Dave is with his hands. He flipped those shot glasses with the finesse of the best lightfingers in town. I'd never known Dave to pull heists or break-ins, but you never know. Watching his hands work convinced me he could've pulled off the heist of Vivienne's paintings.

Well, I gave him plenty of rope. Let's see what Handy Dave Handy does with it. Maybe he'll try to hang me. Maybe he'll end up hanging himself. Meantime, I'll pay a visit to the guy whose name made me laugh.

The Baronet is one of those cheap but clean enough Theater District hostelries that offers weekly and monthly rates to young actors full of hope of making it on Broadway, old actors clinging to faded or imagined glory, and actors not very young but not very old still holding on to dreams of their big break. Mel Burns is among the latter.

The desk clerk, a skinny guy who blends in with the dust in the air, tells me Mel isn't in.

"Any idea where I can find him?"

"How should I know?" the guy says. "What am I, his agent?"

"Who's his agent?"

"Some bottom drawer ten-percenter over on Forty-second Street. Name might be Binsky or Blinsky, or something like that. I don't pay much attention to Mel's big talk."

I head across the lobby to the row of public phone booths, pick the booth that has a Yellow Pages directory. I check the listings for Theatrical Agents, find an Irving Linsky at a Forty-second Street address, dial it up.

A guy answers, "Irv Linsky here. You need talent? We got talent. Whaddya lookin' for?"

"I'm looking for Mel Burns."

"What's the gig?"

"I, uh, I need to interview him for a little show I'm putting together."

"Yeah? What kind of show?"

"The kind that pays agents ten percent."

I hear a *tsk* between his teeth, the sound indicating a shuffle of thoughts. He finally says, "He's over at the McClure & Fineman ad agency recording a television commercial."

I hang up, check the phone book for the address of McClure & Fineman.

The midtown blocks of Madison Avenue have been home to the American advertising hustle since the heyday of radio, when jingles for everything from dish detergent to toothpaste to cars replaced ponderous paragraphs in newsprint. These days, the street's ad agencies are rolling in dough from television commercials. You can't turn on a TV set without some guy pretending to be a doctor selling you a vitamin tonic, or some dame pitching something to make your lips brighter, your skin creamier, your hair shinier, or your dishes cleaner—the first three in hopes of snaring a man, the last in service to pleasing him. It's the perfect medium for Mel Birnbaum, a.k.a. Mel Burns. He might not have much acting talent, but I guess his pretty face and smooth-as-velvet voice are just what the purveyors of American schlock are looking for to convince the new keep-up-with-the-Jones's set to part with their cash.

The McClure & Fineman Advertising Agency is in one of the sleek new skyscrapers sprouting up along Madison. This one's white brick, with long horizontal bands of windows that break up the building's bulk. The directory in the black-and-white marble lobby says McClure & Fineman's offices are on the eighteenth floor.

The elevator, a white marble and mirrored box, moves up fast and opens at the eighteenth floor onto a reception area decorated in blocks of color and framed posters of some of the agency's ad campaigns for clients' products. The McClure & Fineman agency is clearly a fan of the new fad of using America's fantasies to sell stuff. I get a laugh over an ad for a men's deodorant that shows a dame in a bathing suit, and an ad for a '55 DeSoto featuring a woman wearing an evening gown with so much swirling taffeta she'd never be able to get into the car.

There's a brunette at a typewriter behind the long, ultramodern white desk. Her fingernails tap a light clack on the typewriter keys. She's wearing a business suit, a charcoal gray number with a long line of red buttons down the front. I guess the suit's supposed to make her look efficient, but those buttons send out their own invitation.

Her eyes cancel the invitation, though. The way she looks at me as I approach the desk makes me think she's considering calling the authorities, or maybe just her boss. I tip my cap out of respect, or at least to have a little fun with her. "I'm looking for Mel Burns," I say. "I understand he's here recording a television commercial."

She's still staring at me while she fumbles for a clipboard on her desk, finally looks at the clipboard, turns a few pages, then says, "Uh, sure, he's here. Just a minute." She picks up the phone, dials a two-number extension, gets someone on the line. "There's a—there's someone here to see Mel Burns. He still recording?" There's a pause at her end of the conversation, then, "Uh-huh, okay, hold on." She puts the receiver against her shoulder, says to me, "What did you say your name was?"

"I didn't say, but it's Cantor Gold."

She repeats my name to whoever's on the line. There's another pause, and then she hangs up. With a smile that has all the warmth of nighttime in the Arctic, she says, "Recording Studio Two. Through that door and along the hallway," and points to a door across the reception area. "Don't go in if the red recording light is on. Wait for it to turn off."

I give her another tip of my cap, say, "Yes ma'am." She doesn't like it, but I smile anyway as I head in the direction of the door.

Inside, the hallway is wide and shadowy, with four steel-fronted doors, two on each side of the white-painted hall, the linoleum floor shiny white. Each door has a black number on it and a light at the top. Door Two's light is still red. When it goes off, I open the door and walk into a control room where a balding guy whose back is toward me sits at a panel arrayed with lights, dials, switches, and a microphone on a swing-arm. The whole contraption is in front of a glass wall and next to a door to the small recording studio beyond the glass wall where Mel Burns stands at a lectern below a suspended microphone

Mel's gone all Hollywood in a brown tweed sports jacket,

yellow shirt, no tie, and brown trousers. He's holding the earpiece of a headphone against his ear, the better not to muss his perfectly combed light brown hair. He doesn't see me come into the control room.

The guy at the control panel says, "Playback." Then I hear a silly little jingle followed by Mel's smooth voice giving a spiel about the superior holding power of Liquinet hairspray.

But the voice saying, "Hello, Cantor," isn't Mel's. It's a female voice, though not a particularly feminine one. It's a voice I haven't heard for a year or so.

"Ike Martindale," I say to the woman who's now standing beside me. "It's been a while."

"Shhh." She takes me aside, out of earshot of the guy at the control panel. "I use the name on my birth certificate, Ivy, around here," she says, in a back-alley whisper.

Her sandy hair is still cut short, but it's brushed up more feminine than it used to be, and the snappy tailoring I remember has been replaced by a green skirt and a white blouse that should be worn by someone else. I get the picture. Ike is hiding behind Ivy just to earn a living. So many of us do.

I say, "I had no idea you work here."

"Yeah, I work here. That's why you're allowed in. I knew you wouldn't take no for an answer, and I didn't want the doors busted down and the furniture broken. What do you want with Mel?"

"I need to talk to him."

"He in trouble?"

"Why would you say that?"

"Because of who's asking." Still talking low, Ivy takes us farther away from the guy at the control panel. "Look, Cantor, I'm a production manager, one of the very few women around here who isn't a secretary, a receptionist, or some account executive's pillow talk. I like my job, and I worked like a dog to get it. I don't need trouble. And you bring trouble. You always did. It was fun once, getting into scrapes with you, but I don't need that kind of trouble waltzing in here. I have to earn the rent."

Ivy's got a good gig, but it comes at Ike's expense. I'm not sure who I'm nodding to, don't know who's this person pinning me in the corner of the room, Ike or Ivy, but my nod feels sad, my head heavy.

"So I ask you, Cantor," she says, "are you here because you've got trouble with Mel?"

"I don't know yet. I won't know until I talk to him. If there's nothing to worry about, I'll be on my way. If there's trouble, I'll make sure you're not roped into it."

The woman who calls herself Ivy stands stiff as a prison guard, making sure Ike Martindale stays locked away. After a quick purse of her lips and a short sigh, she says, "I probably owe you a favor or two from back in our rowdy days." She turns to the guy at the control panel. "Is that a wrap, Gus?"

He says, "Yeah, I think so. We'll run it by the client tomorrow. You can cut Mr. Blue Eyes loose." It's the first time he's turned away from the control panel, so it's the first time he sees me. His eyebrows go up about a mile.

Ivy says, "Okay, Gus, tell Mel to come in here. You can go home too. It's after four-thirty, near quitting time anyway."

With a last look at me, Gus turns back to his control panel, flips a switch, pulls the swing-arm microphone to his face, and says, "That's a wrap, Burns. Boss lady says you should come in here." Finished with his message, he walks out of the control room.

The boss lady label makes my teeth grind.

A minute later, Mel walks into the control room through the studio door.

Seeing me, Mel gives me his hundred-watt smile through his Greek god sculpted lips, the smile that makes his baby blue eyes twinkle, the smile Edie Angeli no doubt fell for.

Ivy says, "I'll leave you two alone." She throws me a fast look, a pleading look, on her way out the door.

"Cantor Gold," Mel says, all bright and cheery. "Haven't seen much of you in the card rooms lately. A pity. I've been studying up on strategies. Getting real good at handling the cards too. Bet

I could empty your pockets." The idea amuses him.

"You know how it is, Mel. Life gets busy."

"You said it. I'm finally making some real dough. Booked up for months with this TV stuff. I tell you Cantor, forget about Broadway. Television money is fast and there's buckets of it. I'm doing spots for everything from laundry soap to pricey cars. Did you catch my Cadillac spot? Very classy."

"Well, I'm happy for you, Mel. You've been scratching it out at the theaters for a long time."

"Don't remind me," he says with a sneer that could only look good on a face as pretty as his. "Buncha Broadway snobs. But hey, how'd you know where to find me?"

I ignore the question. "Listen, Mel, I had lunch with Edie Angeli today, paying my condolences, you understand."

"Yeah, I saw the bad news about her father. Lousy business." Raising one of his perfect eyebrows, he says, "I didn't know you know her."

I ignore that too. I'm not here to talk about my involvement with Edie Angeli. I'm here to get a line on Mel's connection to the Angelis and what it might have to do with me. I say, "Edie mentioned you two were an item once."

He smiles at me again, but this time the smile has no cheer in it. It's barely friendly. "She thought of herself as an artist. Had more time for her paintings than she had for me. That's not a way to please a guy."

The memory scratches him. Maybe I can scratch deeper. Maybe I might even peel back some skin. "By the way, you know a woman named Vivienne Parkhurst Trent?"

His smile becomes a television grin. A laugh even grows out of it. "Cantor, what is this? A competition for women? We don't hunt in the same forest!" His laugh is almost boisterous now, accompanied by a buddy-buddy slap on my arm.

"Just curious," I say with a shrug to signal it was just an idle thought.

"Why? Does Edie know this, uh—what did you say her name is?"

"Vivienne Parkhurst Trent."

"Oh yeah. So you say Edie knows her?"

"Their circles overlap," I say.

Mel takes a pack of Viceroys and a book of matches from his shirt pocket. He lights a cigarette, takes a long drag, blows out the smoke through a tighter version of his TV smile. "That could be dangerous," he says.

"Yeah, the art game can be pretty cutthroat," I say.

"Well, you'd know more about that than I would. I'm talking about Edie's father. Edie takes after him more than you know. Or maybe you do know." He takes another drag on his smoke, says on the exhale, "Just why are you here, Cantor? Never known you to take an interest in my career, and I know you don't give a damn about my love life. So what gives? What's with you and Edie?"

It's my turn to give a buddy-buddy clap on the shoulder, and I give it to Mel like an old pal, proving I'm a better actor than he is. "She's just had a death in the family. I figure that helping her out is the chivalrous thing to do."

"Is that what you're doing? Helping her out?"

"What do you think I'm doing?"

"I don't know, but maybe you should be careful, Cantor. I know you think I'm just a two-bit actor—"

"You've got it all wrong, Mel," I say. "I'm just throwing out a lifeline on behalf of a grieving friend. You know, some rope."

I call Judson from a phone booth on the corner of Madison and Fiftieth, catch him before he leaves the office for the night. "I need you to do a little deep digging, Judson. Sorry if I'm walking all over your evening plans."

"What's the job?" is all he says. Judson's not one to let his personal life spill all over the place. Unlike a lot of young guys his age, he's not a braggart Romeo.

"Two jobs," I say. "First one: you remember Dave Handy? Used to be a fixer."

"Handy Dave. Sure."

"I need the story on his fall from the big time to a bartending job at the Happy Hour Saloon, a dive over on Ninth Avenue. He says he was stabbed in the back after he fouled up a fix, but he was tight-lipped about who stabbed him. Do what you can to get that story. Maybe he thinks it was me. I don't remember ever crossing him up, but maybe I insulted his poor old mother once."

That gets a chuckle from Judson.

"The other job," I say, "is getting all you can on Mel Birnbaum, goes by Mel Burns. The guy's a failed Broadway actor, but he's raking in cash these days doing TV commercials. Both Dave and Mel used to run around with Edie Angeli. See if you can find links between me, them, and the Angeli family."

Judson lets out a low whistle between his teeth. "This could take a little time," he says. "That's a wide alley to dig around in, and old Dominic Angeli kept the family's lives wrapped tight and their secrets buried deep."

"Just dig as fast as you can, Judson."

I hang up, drop another dime down into Ma Bell's lap, make another call. When the call's answered, I say, "Are you free tonight?"

Chapter Eight

An hour later, after I've showered and changed clothes, all decked out in a dark brown silk suit, pale green shirt, brown tie with small peach-colored chevrons, and a pale green pocket square, I say, "Good evening," to Vivienne's butler George as I walk through the mansion door. George takes my coat and cap. A chef's apron has been added to his butler's getup.

"Miss Vivienne will join you in the dining room," he says.

Dinner service for two has already been laid out when I walk in. Vivienne's impeccable taste is in every plate and fork. The chinaware, eighteenth-century Royal Delft in a blue and white floral pattern, is perfect against the rich brown patina of the walnut dining table. I'm pretty sure the silverware is nineteenth-century English, judging by the style of the carved grape and vine decoration. The whole setup glows in the soft dazzle of a crystal chandelier. The light flows across the well-appointed pale blue room and sparkles on enormous paned windows framed by dark blue drapes held open by gold cords. You could sign peace treaties in here.

There's a good chardonnay open and breathing on the table. I'm about to pour myself a predinner taste when Vivienne walks in. Her perfume, a delicate spice with a teasing whiff of sweet, is expensive, tasteful, alluring, just like Vivienne.

She's in a sleeveless red knit dress that clings in all the right places as it makes its way down her body to just below the knee. The dress has a shawl neckline that drops just low enough to tease about what lies beneath. My eyes take the scenic route down along her legs, ending at a pair of red ankle-strap shoes with gold buckles, expensive and sexy, just like Vivienne. The outfit might look tawdry on another woman, but Vivienne pulls the whole ensemble off as the classiest thing since the invention of the wine list.

She completes the elegantly seductive picture with a lush red lipstick, equally lush red nail polish, and simple earrings of a round ruby surrounded by tiny diamonds. The earrings play hide-and-seek through the brunette waves of her hair. I know the rubies and diamonds are the real McCoy because of who's wearing them.

This vision of Vivienne is certainly delicious, but I wasn't expecting it. Vivienne is always well dressed. She's always up on the latest haute couture, and can certainly afford it. But elegant vamp is something new, at least to me. I wonder if any of her other dinner companions have been lucky enough to have had the pleasure.

"I hope that's a smile of approval," she says, playing with me.

"You don't need my approval, but you've got it anyway," I say, playing back. I give a nod to the fancy spread on the table. "I didn't know we were dining formal tonight."

"Well, after last night's frightening adventure, I thought it might be nice to treat ourselves to a special evening, and to celebrate the return of my paintings."

"All right, I'll drink to that." I pour us each a glass of wine. "Cheers," I say.

"Cheers," she says, nearly whispering.

We sip our wine. We look at each other over the rim of our glasses, until Vivienne looks away.

Sure. That's the Vivienne I know, the one who sometimes walks me to the edge of the pier to admire the sunset, then pushes me off.

Right on time to save the moment from drowning me,

George walks in with a rolling cart containing the evening's fare: poached salmon with a drizzle of hollandaise, a light cucumber salad on the side, and a selection of rolls on a warmer.

We take our seats as George serves the meal, refreshes our glasses of wine, and then does his discreet disappearing act.

Vivienne says, "I thought light springtime fare would be suitable tonight, Cantor."

"Fine with me," I say. "We have things to talk about, and we wouldn't want the weight of dead livestock in our bellies to slow us down."

Well, at least I made her laugh.

The salmon is perfect, of course, the hollandaise like liquid silk on my tongue. The cucumber salad cuts through with the crispness of an early spring breeze.

So uh-huh, the food's perfect, the wine's perfect, the woman across from me at the table is divine. Before I'm smothered by the sensuality of it all, I'd better finish this fancy meal and get down to business.

I say, "Listen, Vivienne, I asked to see you tonight because I have news you'll want to hear. I may have made some headway in tracking down the thief who stole your paintings."

I figured she'd be happy about the news, or at least interested. Instead, she's looking at me as if I'd insulted her.

Whatever's bothering her, she covers it quick with a sip of wine.

I'm tempted to ask what I've said or done that's ruffled her, but it's pretty clear she doesn't want to talk about it. Probably best to move on anyway. I've got a killer to find. "Do you know anyone named Dave Handy, or Mel Birnbaum? Mel also goes by the name of Mel Burns."

Vivienne picks up her last forkful of salmon, swallows it, then says, "The first one, Handy, no I don't know anyone by that name." Her voice is flat. "The other one, Mel Burns? I'm not sure. Sounds familiar."

"He's an actor."

"Oh. Maybe that's where I've heard the name. Cantor"—she

abruptly changes gears, her disappointment about, well, I don't know what, is gone—"I hope you find the thief, I really do, but talking about it isn't why I arranged this dinner tonight. When you phoned to ask me if I was free, I thought, well—"

There's a knock on the dining room door. George walks in. "Shall I clear the plates and serve dessert and coffee now, Miss Vivienne?"

"Yes, please, George," she says. "You're a dear."

I light a cigarette for Vivienne, another for myself. We sit and smoke, saying nothing while George brings in a pastry cart and coffee urn, clears our dinner dishes, and pours our coffee. He even puts two crystal ashtrays on the table, one near each of us. In a dinner of perfection, even George is perfect.

When he's gone, I say, "What's wrong, Vivienne? It's like you've been a few different people all evening. Who am I having dinner with?"

She stubs out her cigarette, takes a sip of coffee. When she puts the cup down, there's yet another Vivienne, another woman I've never met before, an uncertain woman. If it wasn't for the red lipstick and provocative red dress, I'd say the expression on her face is almost childlike. "Last night, you joked about the danger of taking me dancing."

"It was no joke. I wound up getting smacked with a billy club and spent an hour or so in jail just for dancing. The cops bloodied me," I say, indicating the bruise on my head. "Bloodied a lot of us when they raided the place."

"Yes, I've read of such raids," she says, her naïve expression gone, her rich, silky voice returned. "Do they happen often?"

"Not every day, but often enough. Why?"

"Because I'd like you to take me dancing."

I can't tell if I've just been stroked with a feather or slammed by a boulder. I feel both. "Well, that's a new one," I say, "you asking me for a date."

"Don't make fun of me, Cantor," she says, her voice dissolving into a near whisper. "It wasn't easy for me to ask."

"I'm not making fun of you. I'm just surprised. And worried."

"Worried? Oh, are we back to protecting me again?"

"I'm worried you'll regret going dancing with me, Vivienne, like the way you regretted the night we spent together."

She lifts her coffee cup to her lips, but puts the cup down again without drinking, as if she's afraid the coffee might get stuck in her throat. Or maybe she's worried that something she wants to say might get stuck in her throat. She finally speaks, but so quietly I barely hear her. "What makes you think I regret that night?"

"Because you avoided me for weeks," I say as sympathetically as I can, "and whenever I did see you, you avoided the subject altogether. You treated that night like it was a mistake, like I'm a mistake. Well, I'm not anyone's mistake. I won't live that way. Listen, Vivienne, nothing would make me happier than to take you dancing, but you've got to tell me why you want to go. And I've got to believe you."

Her nod is thoughtful; whatever thought is behind it is truthful. "All right," she says, but whatever else she starts to say is interrupted by another knock on the dining room door and George entering the room.

My frustration at being left at the barn door once again is clobbered by my alarm at George's countenance. His face is pale and pasty, his features tight. He's holding an envelope with my name on it. "I found this on the hall table just now, on my way here to clear the coffee service." He hands me the envelope, then leaves quietly again, shaky on his old man's legs.

Vivienne's face has gone pale as her butler's. I feel the blood drain from my face, too, feel the chill of being stalked by an unknown enemy who knows not just how to track me but knows who matters to me, or is making it their business to find out. And they have the stealth to enter this house, put the envelope on the hall table and leave silently as a cat. It's got to be the same person who broke in last night and stole Vivienne's paintings.

Smart and stealthy. Someone's playing dangerous moves with me and I don't even know the game.

I open the envelope, read the note inside. It's got the same blocky capital letters, the same mocking tone:

> I HOPE YOU AND MISS PARKHURST
> TRENT ARE ENJOYING YOUR EVENING.
> SORRY TO CUT IT SHORT. INSIDE
> THE SHED ON PIER 32 UNDER THE
> MANHATTAN BRIDGE IS A SURPRISE
> FOR YOU. IF YOU DON'T GO, THE
> SURPRISE WILL BE WORSE.

I say, "I need to make a call," and pocket the note.

"There's a phone in the living room. What's in the note, Cantor? Don't keep it from me. I'm as much a part of this as you are."

I hate getting her more involved. The danger is too great. But she's right. She's already part of the action. I hand her the note. After she reads it, she says, "I'm going with you."

"The hell you are. We're dealing with a killer, Vivienne. Not exactly your crowd."

"Tell that to the game I've brought down."

"Deer don't sneak into your house and threaten murder."

She can't argue with that, so she doesn't bother.

We leave the dining room for the living room.

I go to the phone on the bar behind the sofa, dial Red Drogan's number.

Whoever's stalking me picked a good spot for the next move in whatever game we're playing. The shed running the length of Pier 32 is well hidden in the shadow of the Manhattan Bridge, the middle of the three bridges spanning the East River from lower Manhattan. Across the river, electric signs glow on the rooftops of Brooklyn. The signs tint the night mist with neon advertisements for everything from beer to tires to floor tile.

I scan the river, take a look at the maritime traffic that runs all night in the city's busy port. Somewhere among the

75

freighters, barges, ocean liners, and tugboats is Red Drogan's tug. I told Red there's a C-note in it for him if he'd hover near the pier in case I find myself in a tough spot inside the pier shed. He told me to keep my money. I won't. His knowledge of the city's waterways and what goes on in the port is worth every dime. His friendship, though, is priceless.

Before I go into the shed, I pull out my .38, check the chambers. All six are full. I've got extra rounds in my trouser pocket. I'm ready for whatever dangerous game the player's got in mind.

I use my pocket square to open the door to the shed. I won't leave any fingerprints this time for the cops to find.

It's damp inside, empty and dark except for the dim glow of a lantern on the floor at the far end of the shed. There's a silhouetted shape next to the lantern, a large lump of some sort, like a mound of dirt.

I guess it's the dampness that eats through me, or maybe it's the cold sweat that's biting every inch of my skin the closer I get to the lantern and that mound.

The shape comes into view. It's not a mound of dirt. It's a burlap sack.

That cold sweat just got icier.

I don't scare easily, but the player's got me plenty scared, scared I left Vivienne's place too soon, scared I left her alone, scared I gave my stalker time to get to her, scared of what's in that sack. By the time I'm standing over it, my hands are shaking.

There's nothing but a bit of string tied loosely at the top of the burlap. My hands shake so much I fumble the string twice before I finally get it open.

My body's clammy but my lips and tongue are dry and scratchy as I open the sack. The stench of death, of a body's lost juices, drifts up to my face, burns my nostrils, catches in my throat.

I want to scream but I can't. Everything inside me, from my belly to my throat, twists into a knot. The only sound I can make is a grunt so raw it hurts.

And then I'm on my knees, coughing, gagging on a sob that's trapped inside me as I look at the bloodied face of Edie Angeli, her dead eyes staring up at me from inside the burlap sack.

Chapter Nine

I hear the low bellow of ships' horns on the river. They merge with the slow clang of buoy bells, the chug of ships' engines, the slap of water against the pylons below the pier, into a waterfront dirge flowing into the shed.

But I don't hear the sirens of cop cars or the boats of the river police.

I'm not being set up. I'm being taunted.

But why taunt me by knocking off Dominic and Edie Angeli? Before today, I'd never met either of them. They meant nothing to me.

These unanswerable questions, questions about the Angelis, about who has a murderous grudge against them and me, buzz through my mind like bees on a rampage. I have to push the buzzing questions away, figure what I need to do right now. There might not be any cops on the way, but tomorrow morning someone's going to walk into this shed and call either the Law or the waterfront bosses, so I can't leave any trace of me behind.

I don't touch the lantern, I take the string from the sack and put it into my pocket. And then I see it, the bloody edge of paper sticking out of the collar of Edie's pink sweater.

I use my pocket square to pull out the paper and unfold it. It's another note, written in the same crazy block letter style:

How do I goddamn feel? The murdering sonuvabitch wants to know how I *feel*? Sick. I feel sick so deep in my gut my stomach's making plans to bolt and take any nearby organs with it. Even my heart feels sick, too sick to keep beating. And I feel angry. I feel like I want to tear the killer apart, bloody the monster who's using murder to tear *me* apart. I want to break the bones of the stalker who's a step ahead of me, taunting me. Scaring me.

My skin, already clammy, has gone icy cold, the kind of cold that seeps deep and could numb all movement if I let it. But I don't dare let it. I have things to do to if I want to stop this guy from killing again, things to do if I want to stay alive.

The first thing I do is pocket the note and leave the shed. I go the end of the pier and give Red our prearranged signal: two flashes with the flame of my lighter.

Within seconds, I see his mast light flicker through the river mist, hear the chug of his engine, and in less than a minute he pulls his tug up to the pier.

I hop aboard.

He says, "Where we goin', Cantor?" His friendly face, wrinkled from years of river wind, and his voice, splintery as old driftwood, are welcome and comforting as a shot of booze, which I take from his offered bottle of rye.

"We're not going anywhere," I say. "I need you to get some information from your contacts along the waterfront, ask if anyone saw somebody carry or lug a big burlap sack into 32's pier shed tonight."

"Sure. What's in the sack?"

I need another pull on the rye to answer Red without stumbling all over my shattered soul. "A dead woman," I say. "Name's Edie Angeli."

He takes the bottle from me, takes a long draw of his own, then says, "Angeli? Any relation to that gangster fella who bought it yesterday? Heard it on the radio."

"His daughter. Don Dominic Angeli's daughter."

"Someone knocking off the Angeli family? Bad business. What's it got to do with you?"

"I wish I knew, Red. I wish I knew," I say, and press two fifty-dollar bills into his palm.

I walk back to my car, parked in a shadowed alley between two clam bars under the bridge, then drive around the waterfront neighborhood looking for a phone booth. If my stalker's following me, I'll just have to take that chance, but I've got to make some calls, and I don't want to lead the stalker back to my apartment. I don't want him to know about the alleys behind my office, either, if he doesn't already.

I find a booth under a streetlight at the corner of Water and Catherine Streets. There's nothing around here except marine supply shops closed for the night, and old brick warehouses that hold goods brought from the piers or waiting to be shipped out to sea. And as if life and work on the waterfront isn't tough enough, the warehouses also host the dirty deals between waterfront mobsters, dirty cops, and even dirtier politicians. Corpses sometimes turn up tucked away in the warehouses' nooks and crannies, too, usually the bodies of poor schnooks who've crossed the mob or were late once too often with their loan payments or protection money.

My first phone call is to Vivienne. I tell her that Edie Angeli is dead. "Things are getting dicier, Vivienne. It's time to consider leaving your house for someplace safer."

"I told you," she says, "I don't care how much this guy tries to scare me, I will not be chased from my own home."

"Then make sure all the doors and windows are locked—"

"That didn't stop the intruder before," she says.

"No, but maybe your skill with firearms will. Keep a weapon close, Vivienne."

"Yes, all right. Cantor? When will I see you?"

"When it's safe to take you dancing."

80

My next call is to Sig.

When I get him on the line, I tell him about the stalker finding me at Vivienne's and the note sending me to the pier. I tell him about finding Edie dead in the pier shed and the note I found in the neck of her sweater. "Someone's on the hunt for me, Sig. And if they've been following me all day, then they know I was at your place, probably know Edie was there too."

I don't have to say any more. Sig's smart enough to figure the implications. Whatever my stalker has in mind for me, Sig doesn't like it getting so close to him.

He says, "Cantor, here is what I want you to do," in his slow, drawn-out way, each word sharp as a knife. "There is a garage on West Eighteenth Street near Tenth Avenue, the Metropolitan Garage. Drive in and leave your car there, but don't walk out onto Eighteenth Street. Have your cabbie friend—you know the one—"

Yeah, I know the one. He means Rosie Bliss, the woman Sig held hostage six years ago until I solved one of his problems.

He says, "—have her meet you at the back door of the garage, the Seventeenth Street door. Tell her to bring you here." He hangs up.

I make one last call, dial Judson at home. "It's me," I say, when he picks up the call. "I need you to get through to Rosie's cab, have her come pick me up at the back door of the Metropolitan Garage on West Seventeenth. I'll fill you in later. Meantime, did you get anything on Dave Handy's fall from grace? Like what fix did he screw up and who did it annoy? And what about Mel Burns? Any connection between Burns, the Angelis, and me?"

"Whoa, slow down," Judson says. "I did some deep digging, but information on Handy is sketchy. It seems he knew a lot about a lot of people when he was on top, and now those people don't want to talk about his fall. Mouths are closed tighter than a banker's fist. But I did turn up something interesting in his love life. It seems he ran around with Edie Angeli."

"Yeah," I say, "she told me about it."

"Okay, but did she tell you the rabbit died?"

81

That's the sort of news that raises your eyebrows and makes your tongue curl. It takes me a minute to say, "No, she didn't," though I'm not surprised that neither Edie nor Dave mentioned it. Out of wedlock pregnancy isn't the sort of thing a woman talks about if she wants to avoid the social equivalent of stoning, and the daddies have been known to run in the other direction. Plus, I don't peg Dave Handy as the marrying kind. Or Edie either, for that matter, certainly not to the likes of Dave. "What happened to the kid?" I say.

"Well, I can't find anything about her having the baby or giving it up for adoption, so I guess she must've gone under the knife. Pappa Angeli could likely have set her up with a willing doc, or held a gun to the head of an unwilling one. But I don't see where any of that connects to you."

"Me neither," I say. "But keep going on it, Judson. I know it's a long shot, but see where it goes and who else it goes to. Okay, what about Mel Burns? Anything there?"

"Only that you and Burns frequent the same card rooms. I hear he's a pretty good card player."

"And getting better, or so he says."

"Card counter or fast fingers?"

"Good question. Keep digging, Judson."

I stand in the shadowed back door of the garage, well back from the sidewalk and the light of a streetlamp at the curb. My eyes dart back and forth along Seventeenth Street, a block of old walk-up apartments and garages like this one that used to be stables fifty years ago. I look for cars out of place among the low-end heaps parked along the curb. I check for movement that doesn't belong; maybe someone's walking too slow, or someone's walking too fast, or maybe someone's not walking at all.

But all I see on the street is a guy zipping his jacket under the streetlamp while his dog takes a leak against the tire of a beat-up DeSoto. Across the street, there's a guy in a fedora walking arm in arm with a woman wearing a light-colored headscarf, the couple all lovey-dovey before they go into one of the brownstone walk-ups. A woman wearing a bulky overcoat struggles with two bags of groceries while she fumbles for a key to the tenement next door to the garage, her flowered hat threatening to fall off her head. I'm tempted to give her a hand, but that would mean leaving my shadowy spot, maybe giving myself away if my stalker's somehow managed to follow me.

So I stay in my shadowed hiding place, and feel crummy about it. Hiding is something I never took to. But now here I am, slinking in a shadow, giving up my place in the world.

The hell with that. Stepping out might be dangerous, but it's better than feeling like a trembling insect afraid of getting stepped on.

I'm not stupid, though, and I check the street once more, satisfy myself that no one's got eyes on me before I walk the few steps to the woman at her door. "Let me help," I say, and take her key, open her door.

"Thanks, mister," she says, noticing only my overcoat and cap. I don't correct her. Why bother? Either she'll be offended or she won't get what I mean. It doesn't matter.

A pair of headlights slows down as they near me. It's Rosie's Checker cab.

I get into the back seat.

Rosie drives away, streetlight catching the silvery blond mist of her hair curling out from her cabbie's cap. Even in her driving duds, and even seen from the back seat of the cab, Rosie Bliss is a woman who can rouse all those places that like to be roused. She used to let me indulge those places from time to time until she got tired of waiting for me to get over that wound that won't heal.

So she withdrew her heart from me, but she didn't withhold her skill behind a wheel. Rosie handles the cab like a jockey with good hands, taking the streets and rounding the corners as if she owns them. She can cut through traffic like a sharp knife slicing a knot. There's no one better than Rosie when I need to get from one place to another quietly, secretly, out of sight of cops and other busybodies. When Rosie ferries me around, I'm just another of New York's millions of passengers in the back seat of a cab, of interest to nobody, not even the Law.

She says, "So where we going, Cantor?"

"Sig Loreale's place on Fortieth."

She pulls over as we head uptown on Tenth Avenue, then turns around to look at me. Her usual soft-as-cream complexion is now hard and pale as chalk. "That bastard was willing to let his thugs kill me if you didn't do what he wanted, remember, Cantor? I'll never understand why you still do business with that louse."

"Because he's a louse with the power to cut through a lot of crap, and tonight he's the louse with the power to save my life."

Her hard look rearranges itself into a tight expression of worry, but the kind that's no longer shocked. "Who's after you this time?"

"I don't know. There's already been two killings. Someone's sticking me in the middle of them and I don't know why."

Rosie turns back around, puts the car in gear, pulls away from the curb. "So who are the stiffs?" she says. She sounds as if she's not entirely sure she wants to know.

"Dominic Angeli and his daughter, Edie."

"The Dominic Angeli I read about in the paper? The guy found last night in a warehouse? That old gangster?"

"That's the guy."

"But the paper didn't say anything about a daughter. Hell, I didn't even know he had a daughter."

"She was killed tonight. It'll probably make the papers tomorrow. Maybe even the late news on television tonight. Listen, Rosie, work your magic and make sure we're not followed on the way to Sig's."

"Leave it to me."

Chapter Ten

After Rosie's curlicue trip through Manhattan, taking us along dark streets where no one comes out at night, through fancy neighborhoods where taxi cabs are a sight too common to attract attention, through the fringes of the Theater District where the showbiz neon colors peter out through the windows of second-rate saloons, Rosie finally pulls up in front of Sig's building.

"You want me to wait?" she says.

"No, go earn a night's money."

"Be careful, Cantor. I don't trust that guy."

"Don't worry; neither do I."

Sig's den is a dark and shadowy place, just right for doing his dark and shadowy business. When I walk in, he's seated at his desk, a sleek but imposing mass of burled maple. A desk lamp provides the only light in the room, except for the tip of his burning cigar. The cigar sends a red glow around his eyes, colors his fleshy jowls, and stains red the collar of his crisp white shirt. Even spiffed up in his well-tailored dark, conservative suit, the knot of his tie in perfect alignment, Sig Loreale, seated calmly at his desk, is terrifying.

He nods for me to take a seat in one of the gray leather club chairs facing the desk. He takes the cigar from his lips.

"I assume you were not followed," he says, every word moving slowly through his rough voice.

"Your plan went without a hitch," I say. "I'm here free and clear."

Sig puffs on his cigar. The tip glows red again, burning through the billow of smoke that briefly veils his face. "This Angeli situation must not be allowed to continue," he says. "The killings of father and daughter, one right after the other, it's the sort of thing which attracts the wrong kind of attention. Do you understand, Cantor?" He doesn't expect me to answer. He expects me to understand the implications of that wrong kind of attention. Satisfied that I do, he keeps talking. "And I am not happy that whoever is behind this is involving you in a way that is involving me. You were right to assume he knows of our meeting with Miss Angeli this morning. The question is, what's to be done about it."

"First we have to find the guy," I say.

"And you are taking steps to that end?"

"I'm poking around, yeah."

"Have you turned up anything useful?"

"Possibly," I say. I take a smoke from my pack of Chesterfields, light one up, let the tobacco do its soothing number while I settle into a conversation with the most dangerous guy in town. "It seems Miss Edie Angeli had a fling with Handy Dave Handy, who was handy enough to get her pregnant. I couldn't find anything definite about what happened to the baby, but it looks like she probably terminated the pregnancy."

Sig's only response to this news is to take a draw on his cigar. After an exhale of smoke and a silence so thick I could choke on it, he finally says, "And how would this connect to you? I don't see you as someone involved with babies." His head tilts back, his mouth opens, and he gives me his soundless laugh. That laugh's been giving me the creeps since I was a Coney Island kid and he'd have his thugs scoop me up from the shoot-'em-ups and bumper cars, then brought to him so he could either scold me or laugh about my beachfront pillaging.

When the laugh stops and he resumes his usual menacing self, I say, "Good question. I don't know how it connects to me. I'm still looking into it."

"You see, that is your problem, Cantor. You can't get the answers quickly enough because you insist on working alone. Oh, I know you have that young genius on your payroll. The kid's rather good at digging up information, I understand. But you do the legwork on your own, Cantor."

"What would you have me do, Sig? Join a street gang?" I say. "Even back in my juvenile delinquent days I was never much of a joiner."

"You don't need to join a gang to make use of it, Cantor. Why not make use of the biggest gang in town?"

"Are you offering me your services, Sig?"

His smile could curdle milk. "You are not thinking big enough, Cantor. The handful of people in my immediate organization hardly constitute a gang."

"Tell that to the poor suckers whose heads your guys knock around."

He's not happy with my pushback. I can tell by the way he takes another pull on his cigar, a long draw, his face expressionless behind the glow of the cigar's burning tip. After his exhale, he says, "Never mind the heads whose owners have gotten in my way, Cantor. Use your own head. What is the biggest gang in town, the gang which has been after you for years, but which I can—and often do—steer in another direction."

I stub out my smoke in the ashtray on the small glass table beside my chair. I could really use a drink, a hefty shot of booze to smooth the way for the least favorite words in my vocabulary to come through my throat. "The police. You're talking about the police."

"I am talking about the police."

"What makes you think they'd be cooperative?" I regret saying it before it's even out of my mouth. Sig owns a big chunk of the police department, and even though he doesn't have every single cop in his pocket, he owns enough of the brass who matter.

"They will cooperate," is all he says because it's all he needs to say. "It is possible that they are not yet aware of Miss Angeli's death or that her corpse is at the pier." He picks up the phone. "It is time they knew."

"Wait a minute, Sig," I say before he dials. "If you're going to bring the cops in on this, at least make sure I'm dealing with one who's not itching to collar me for everything from parking tickets I never got to murders I didn't commit."

"Once again, Cantor, the wages of acting alone deprives you of valuable assistance. You really should try to cultivate people in useful positions. Politicians, for instance. Police too."

"Uh-huh," I say with a shrug and a humorless smile. "Unfortunately, politicians like to make laws that throw me in jail just because of who I dance with. And the cops like to make sport of enforcing those laws, among others designed to penalize me for breathing. But I see what you mean about the cops being the biggest gang in town. So if you're going bring them in on this, there's one cop who might give me a fair shake, and he's already involved. He caught the Dominic Angeli case last night, and he knows I didn't kill old man Angeli."

"His name?"

"Adair. Sergeant Liam Adair."

Sig picks up the phone, dials two digits, says, "Have my car brought to the front entrance."

Sig's black '55 Cadillac sedan is tricked out with all the doodads necessary for the comfort and safety of the city's most powerful crime lord. Here in the back seat of the finest black leather upholstery, there's a small stow-away bar, a telephone that flips out from the back of the front seat, a sliding panel on the door on Sig's side that I'm guessing opens into a compartment containing a gun, should Sig need it. A glass panel separates the driver from the passenger seat in the back, and of course the whole heavy rig is bulletproof. In the front seat, the car's driven by Max Novik, the thug with the crew cut and big hands who guarded Sig's private elevator when I visited this morning. No doubt there's a gun under Max's jacket, probably another in his coat pocket, and likely a third in the glove compartment.

I enjoy a badly needed scotch while Sig dials the phone. He says to whoever answers, "Good evening, Captain Sloan. Would you be good enough to have your Sergeant Liam Adair meet me at Pier 32 on the East River. . . . That's right, the pier under the Manhattan Bridge. Have Adair come into the pier shed. . . . Yes, I will meet him inside. Contact Adair directly; do not contact him through police radio, do you understand? The ladies and gentlemen of the press monitor their police scanners, and we do not want the press involved at this time. And tell Adair not to contact the coroner's office either. I will make those arrangements. . . . Yes, a body is involved, and we do not want the press aware of that, at least not yet. . . . I'm glad you understand, Captain Sloan. Thank you and good night." He hangs up.

There was no *Hello, how are you?*, no *How's the family?*, no need to even identify himself. Sig Loreale needs no introduction. He needs only obedience.

It's almost ten when we drive onto the pier. A police green-and-black cruiser is already parked, its twirling roof light smearing the pier and the river red. A dark, unmarked Plymouth, probably Adair's vehicle, is next to the cruiser, getting the red smear treatment too.

Those are the only cars on the pier. There's no horde of press vehicles, no television or radio crowd, meaning that Captain Sloan obeyed Sig's orders. Of course he did. His career would be over or his life would be snuffed if he didn't.

Novik pulls up in front of the cop cars, gets out of the driver's seat, and opens the back door for his boss. I do my own exiting on the other side.

The twirling red light smears the three of us.

Sig and I walk into the pier shed. Novik stays with the car. Adair and two uniformed cops are silhouetted near the sack containing Edie's corpse. The beams of their flashlights hover and dart through the dark shed. The light finds me and Sig as we approach.

Seeing me, Adair says, "Another one, Cantor?"

"I guess somebody wants to keep you employed," I say.

"And I guess you know who the dead woman in the sack happens to be. Isn't that why you're here?"

"Yeah, I know who it is. It's Edie Angeli. Dominic Angeli's daughter."

It's hard to see the expression on Adair's street-tough face in the half light of the flashlights, but the whites of his eyes snap through the darkness. He shakes his head slowly while a long breath hisses between his teeth.

Adair turns his attention to me, then to Sig. He uses his flashlight to give Sig the once-over, starting with his black homburg, then along his black overcoat, and down to his polished oxfords.

Sig doesn't move a muscle.

Finished with Sig, Adair slides the light up to me, nearly blinds me with it. "Nice company you keep, Gold." He slides the light back to Sig. "Look, Mr. Loreale, I know who you are and I know what you are. Captain Sloan says I have to cooperate with you, so I cooperate with you, but I don't have to like it." He pulls the brim of his fedora lower to make his point.

Sig says, "Your affection or lack of it does not interest me, Sergeant Adair. What interests me is making sure the full resources of the New York City police department are brought to bear in the matter of the Angeli killings."

"What makes you think they won't?"

Sig takes a cigar from the leather case in his coat pocket, lights it, lets the flame hover in front of his face, illuminating the hard look he gives Adair. He finally tosses the match, puffs on the cigar, the red glow of its burning tip catching the glare of Adair's flashlight. "I am certain the police will cooperate," he says.

Adair does his best not to be cowed by Sig's intimidating

calm. The cop's more or less holding his own, but if I could peek under his shirt collar, I bet I'd find a film of cold sweat.

I've got to give Adair credit, though. He doesn't shrink from Sig. "And what's your interest in the Angeli business, if I might ask?"

Sig says, "That is not your concern. Be assured that though our interests may not be mutual, our cooperation will be. I have methods and resources to assist you should you need it, Sergeant Adair, and I expect your assistance in return. The sooner this matter is cleared up, the sooner you can go back to your preferred relationship to me. And to Cantor." Sig's actually smiling now, though there's not a shred of humor in it.

"Speaking of Cantor," Adair says to me, "what's your part in this?" He nods toward the sack.

"Someone is stalking me, Adair," I say. "They found me at dinner at a friend's place tonight. They delivered a note telling me there'd be a surprise for me here, and if I didn't show, the surprise would be worse."

"Any chance that whoever wrote the note had the decency to sign their name?" Adair jokes.

"There's nothing decent about whoever stuffed Miss Angeli into a burlap sack," I say.

"No, I . . . I guess not." The guy's gone from wiseacre to sheepish.

His cop's soul takes over, though, that part of him that won't stand for being bested by the likes of me, and he recovers fast. He says, "So, last night someone set you up for the Dominic Angeli killing, and tonight they've thrown his daughter's death around your neck."

"That's the gist of it," I say.

"Someone must really hate you, Gold. Any idea who or why?"

"Why?" I repeat, and take my pack of Chesterfields from my jacket pocket. "I don't know why. Who? Maybe." I light a smoke, take a deep pull, then say, "You remember a fixer named Dave Handy?"

Adair says, "Sure. Used to mingle with all kinds. A real elbow pumper."

"Among other things," I say.

Adair says, "Haven't heard anything on him in a while. His name seems to have faded from the police blotter."

"He fell from the hoodlum heights into a Ninth Avenue dive bar," I say. "He's the bartender."

"What caused his fall?"

"I don't know yet."

Adair looks at Sig. "Maybe now's the time for you to start your cooperation with the police department, Mr. Loreale. Any chance you know Dave Handy's sad story?"

Sig doesn't answer, just takes a draw on his cigar. After several puffs, he finally says, "If that information is relevant to you, you will be provided with it, sergeant. In the meantime, please allow Cantor to continue. Cantor?"

I mumble an "Uh, yeah." It may be my story, but it's Sig's show. It's always Sig's show. I'm just the one in the spotlight at the moment, so I go on talking. "Okay, well, whatever caused Dave to lose his high spot with the rackets and the other power players may or may not have anything to do with the Angeli killings or have anything to do with me. It may not even be very interesting. But here's something that *is* interesting, sergeant: Edie Angeli and Dave Handy had a fling, the sort that results in making a baby, but the baby—well, I don't know what happened to the baby. Probably an abortion, likely arranged by her father."

"Are you telling me you knew Miss Angeli?" Adair's tone has shifted from mere questioning to downright interrogation. "What else have you been holding out on me, Gold?"

"I'd only just met her today."

"And she admitted to the baby thing? Are you kidding me?"

"You oughta know by now, sergeant, that I don't kid around with cops. But no, Edie didn't share that bit of stuff with me."

"Then how did you—?"

Sig cuts him off, "How Cantor learned about it is not important, Sergeant Adair. We are sharing this information with you now. That is all that matters."

Nothing annoys a cop more than being pushed around by a civilian, especially a powerful criminal civilian Adair would sell his mother to put behind bars. But there's nothing he can do about it, not if he wants to make sure the police brass lets him keep his detective's shield. His annoyance is clear, though, in the tightness of his shoulders, and the way he adjusts his hat, as if trying to find a spot on his head that doesn't itch. He says to me, "Is that your only lead?" his voice edgy.

"There's someone else in the picture," I say. "Another of Miss Angeli's boyfriends is a guy named Mel Birnbaum, an actor who goes by the name of Mel Burns. He failed on Broadway but he's doing all right in TV commercials."

"You have a history with this guy?"

"He plays cards in some of the same card rooms I frequent from time to time."

"Good player?"

"Yeah, he's good."

"How does he feel about you?"

"Well, he likes to take my money," I joke.

Our little chitchat is interrupted by the arrival of two guys in white uniforms. They're carrying a stretcher. One of them says, "Somebody called for an ambulance?"

It was a call Sig made in his car on the way here. He says, "You are to transport a body to the coroner's office."

Adair cocks his head toward the burlap sack. The ambulance boys, having seen stiffs of every kind and in every position, give no sign of shock or surprise at finding a woman stuffed into a sack. With the help of Adair's two uniformed cops—one shines a flashlight over the sack, the other holds the sack open—the ambulance fellas carefully pull Edie out.

It's a tough scene for me to take, puts a knot in my gut the size of a boulder, especially since Edie's in rigor mortis, crumpled up in the position her killer had her stuffed into the sack. She's still in her pink sweater and black toreador pants. Her face is battered, her face and hair covered in blood. Blood's soaked into her sweater. "What killed her?" I say. The words scratch like jagged rocks in my throat.

The ambulance guys put her on the stretcher, a lump of a human being who can't lie down, even in death. One of guys says, "The coroner's docs will have to confirm it, but it looks like she was batted around pretty bad, probably with something heavy."

Before they carry her out, Sig says, "I trust you've been given instructions about transporting her to the coroner's office."

"Yeah," ambulance guys says. "No siren, no twirling light." They lift the stretcher and carry Edie through the pier shed and out the door. The sight makes part of me want to cry, but the rest of me is too angry to cry, keeping my tears stuck and my sadness strangled.

When Edie's gone, Sig, calm as an undertaker, says, "I believe that's all we can do this evening. Cantor, starting tomorrow, you will work with Sergeant Adair. Sergeant, I have your assurance that the police department's resources will be available to Cantor?" It's not a question, it's not even a request. Sig never mentions Adair's captain. He doesn't have to.

"I know my job," Adair says, his resentment so sharp it could eat through his teeth.

I say, "Meet me on Charles Street between Bleecker and West Fourth at ten tomorrow morning, sergeant."

"Why? What's there?"

"The other life of Edie Angeli," I say.

There's nothing cops hate more than civilians knowing more than they do. Right now, Adair's annoyance at my intimacy with Edie's other life is all over his bulldog face. "Make it nine in the morning," he says. "The police department doesn't keep your luxury hours, Gold."

Peg Monroe has done a swell job of getting the Green Door Club up and running after last night's raid.

The crowd is sparse when I walk in a little before midnight.

It's always sparse for a few days after a raid. People are jittery. They wrap up for a while, play it safe.

But for those who do drop by, the Green Door Club is a welcoming haven. It's a place to be ourselves, defiantly if we have to, and we usually have to.

Peg pours me a scotch when I take a seat at the bar. I down it fast, ask for another.

"Bad day, Slick?" she asks in her warm Georgia drawl. She pours me another Chivas.

"Bad enough," I say. "I'm glad the joint's open, Peg. I need this." I nod to indicate the scene around the room, the couples dancing, swaying to a mellow tune played by the all female three-piece combo. Last night's raid gives tonight's gathering a sweet spark, the romance pumped up. The crowd's dressed for it. Colorful dresses of satin and lace and taffeta glide against trousers and suit jackets. Here and there, there's even a tuxedo or dinner jacket. Peg's turned the lights down low, letting the amber-shaded lamps on the white cloth'd tables and in the booths send a soft glow through the room. The glow embraces the dancing couples.

So yeah, after my lousy day of death and cops and Sig Loreale, after my interrupted evening with Vivienne, I need this. I need the whiskey, the music, the pleasure of women.

I spot a lovely number nursing a drink all alone at the end of the bar. Her black cocktail dress is the swirly type popular these days, with plenty of skirt below and pleasantly skimpy above. I take my scotch along as I move toward her end of the bar, ask if I could buy her a drink or maybe she'd like to dance.

She gives me a smile. "I'll take the dance," she says. "Don't you even want to know my name?"

"Only if you want me to know it."

"Ah, so it's like that."

"Uh-huh, it's like that tonight. For both of us."

She slides off the bar stool. I escort her to the dance floor.

The band's playing a bluesy rendition of a Broadway tune, "Hey There." My nameless partner and I move against each other slow and easy, getting to know each other's rhythm.

This is exactly what I need. I need this to blot out the sight of Dominic Angeli dead on a warehouse floor, blot out the horror of Edie Angeli battered and stuffed into a sack. I need this to set myself free, even if only for tonight, from whoever it is that's hunting me.

The woman feels good against me. She moves with me, fits herself along my body. I'm lost in her, so lost it takes me a minute to realize Peg is tapping me on my shoulder.

"There's a phone call for you," she says.

I break from the dance, apologize to my lovely partner, and feel a knot in my belly as I make my way from the dance floor. Peg's put the phone on the bar.

I pick it up, say, "Who is this?"

I hear a laugh that sounds like it's wadded in cotton, then a strangely disguised voice says, "You shouldn't leave your loved ones alone, Cantor."

Chapter Eleven

Fifteen minutes later I'm ringing Vivienne's doorbell and banging on the door.

George finally opens up. He's in his pajamas and robe. His eyes are watery and his gray hair sticks up every which way. I must have roused him from bed.

He looks like he's about to have serious words with me, but I don't give him the chance. I'm fast inside the door, say, "Has Vivienne already gone to bed? Come with me, George. We need to check her bedroom."

"But Miss Vivienne's not here."

"What do you mean, not here? Where'd she go? Who'd she go with?"

"After you left, she made a telephone call," George says. "She didn't tell me who she spoke to, and I certainly didn't ask. After the call, she changed from her dinner dress into more casual attire. She told me she was going out and that I was free to retire for the night because she expected to be out late."

"Well, it's getting late now," I say. I glance at my watch, realize it's not actually all that late, only a little past twelve-thirty. But the more reasonable hour doesn't put a dent in my concern for Vivienne.

The old guy looks like he's about to have those serious words with me again, only with less patience this time. "Miss Vivienne is free to enjoy an evening out until she decides it's time to return home. She has an active social life, which is not my place to question. Or yours."

"I'm not questioning her social life, George. I'm questioning her safety."

His sniffy expression stiffens into a face tight with tension and fear.

I say, "You have no way of getting in touch with her?"

"No ... no, I'm sorry. She didn't tell me where she was going, and it would not be my place to ask."

"Well, I'm sorry too, George," I say. "I'm sorry I pushed you around. You look like you could use a drink. I know I could use one. Come on." I place my hand gently on his elbow, lead him to the living room.

Inside, I turn on a lamp on a side table. The mellow light from the single lamp is all George and I need. More light would just get on our already frazzled nerves.

The guy's butler's instincts take over when we're at the bar behind the living room sofa. "What may I offer you?" he says.

"Don't worry about me, George," I say. "Take care of yourself."

His "Thank you," is barely a whisper. He pours himself a stiff brandy. I pour myself a scotch.

We both down our drinks, pour ourselves another.

George says, "What do we do now? Shall we call the police? I'd hate to—"

"We wait," I say. "You say Vivienne went out of her own accord?"

"Yes."

"Then we have to give her a chance to come home of her own accord."

"How long should we wait?"

"You'd know that better than I would," I say. "You've known her a long time, George. You know her habits. You tell me how long we should wait."

"Well, I don't—" The guy looks like he's about to fold up.

"Do you mind if I sit down?"

I'm tempted to tell him he doesn't need my permission, but his sense of himself as a servant is so deep in his marrow my words would likely mean nothing. So I don't address the issue at all, just help the old guy onto the sofa. The light from the lamp on the side table finds every tired and sagging line on his face.

I take the chair opposite.

We quietly sip our drinks, and we wait.

And I think. I try to figure who to call first if Vivienne doesn't come home: Sig? Adair? I tumble the question back and forth, then snap it shut. I can't admit the possibility of Vivienne not coming home.

So I move on to other things. I think about Handy Dave Handy, think about Mel Burns, try to figure which of them has a reason to come after me, wonder which of them is smart enough to set in motion this wild ride of stalking and murder. I think about which one of them might have the skill to break into Vivienne's house quietly, twice: once to steal paintings, and again to leave tonight's note. Neither guy has ever come across as a genius.

But Dave must've known some tricks in his time as a first-rate fixer, and the way he was flipping those shot glasses, he's got good hands. As for Mel, he's a crafty card player, slick with his hands, alert to the run of the cards. Could be both Dave and Mel have more brains than I give them credit for.

I get up, walk around, light a cigarette, pour another scotch, loosen my tie, look at my watch. A half hour passes, then another. Vivienne's still not home.

George is asleep on the sofa, his head lolling to the side. I take his brandy glass from his hand, put it on the coffee table.

I don't know what's worse: my nerves twisted so tight my skin hurts, or the lousy sensation of being helpless to keep Vivienne safe.

Another scotch calms me a bit. I sit down again, and realize I'm exhausted, exhausted from too little sleep before Adair showed up this morning, exhausted from running around without a stop all day and night, exhausted from all the death at my feet. The exhaustion takes over. My body's had enough. I can't stop myself from falling asleep.

It's not an easy sleep, just a fitful doze full of quick dreams of unseen things clinging to me, riding on my back, grabbing at my throat, clawing at my face, until the clawing smooths into something silkier, bringing me slowly into wakefulness. I open my eyes. I see Vivienne's shadowed face hovering above mine. Her gloved fingers stroke my cheek.

She stands up, looks across to George asleep on the sofa. "Well, aren't you two a pretty pair," she says with a laugh.

I mumble, "What time is it?" still unfolding from sleep.

"Two-thirty," Vivienne says. "I'll just wake George and help the poor dear go back to bed, and then you can tell me why the two of you were asleep in my living room."

I give the idea a nod. The last of me pulls out from my stupor of sleep.

Vivienne, an elegant angel of mercy in a swirling black silk coat, gently wakes George and helps him off the sofa. Through his waking haze, he's clearly relieved to see her. "I'm fine," he says when they're at the living room door. "Please see to your guest, Miss Vivienne. Good night." He shuffles out the door.

Vivienne removes her coat with a movement so smooth the garment seems to slide off her body and onto a chair. She's wearing a light blue linen sheath, the sleeves ending just below the elbow, her black silk gloves taking over from there. This is the outfit George described as more casual attire than the dress Vivienne wore for our dinner. I've seen less elegant getups gliding into opera boxes. Or maybe it's the woman wearing it that gives the simple dress so much class.

"Well," she says, sitting down on the sofa and removing her gloves, "why the sleepover party in my living room?" The soft light of the lamp glides along her face and body as if it's enjoying the ride.

I light a smoke, say, "I needed to make sure you're okay."

"I told you not to worry about me, Cantor. I can handle myself. After last night's break-in, I decided it's wise to be prepared." To prove her point, she opens her handbag and takes out a sweet, nickel-plated .22 snub nose revolver. "Marksmanship with sporting firearms isn't my only talent, you know. I enjoy target practice with small arms too. There's an excellent shooting range at my club. I can get you in for a little target practice, if you like."

"No thanks," I say. "I can't quite get used to shooting as sport."

"Your life is risky, Cantor. That's why you carry a gun. Don't you want to keep your skill sharp?"

"My skill is sharp enough to survive, and I try to survive without killing anyone."

"Do you succeed?"

"Well, I'm still alive."

"No, I meant—"

"I know what you meant, Vivienne."

She leans back into the sofa, resigned if not satisfied to leave that subject alone. I get the feeling she might bring the question up again some day, maybe try to slip the answer out of me on the sly. Right now, though, Vivienne just gives it a leisurely shrug. She takes her cigarette case from her bag, lights a smoke with the fancy silver lighter on the coffee table, then says, "Why are you here, Cantor? You said you wanted to make sure I'm all right. Does it have anything to do with what you found at the pier?"

"Listen, Vivienne, someone is playing very nasty games with me."

"And me," she says, nodding toward the paintings restored to her living room wall.

"True enough," I say. "So it's a good idea to keep that gun close. You don't want to end up like Edie Angeli. She's dead."

The color drains from Vivienne's face fast. She barely manages to say, "Murdered? Like her father?"

"Probably beaten with something heavy. Then she was

101

stuffed into a burlap sack. That's how I found her." Just saying it is tough.

Even through the soft light of the single lamp, Vivienne's face is so pale even the red of her lipstick seems to dull on lips that no doubt have gone pale as chalk. When she's able, she says, "And the person who wrote that note wanted you to see that. But why?"

"I'm not sure. I wish I knew what the hell is going on, and what this guy's got in store for me."

"Are you so sure it's a guy?"

The question sneaks up on me sidewise. I think fast about the phone call at the Green Door Club, remember the weirdly disguised voice on the phone. Yeah, sure, it sort of sounded like a guy, but maybe the caller played vocal tricks on me.

Still, I say, "Well, two guys who were involved with Edie Angeli also know me."

"The two you asked me about, Handy and that other one, Burns."

"Yeah. So I assumed . . ." But my voice trails off, the thought fading. My money's still riding on Mel Burns or Handy Dave Handy, but the size of the bet just got a lot smaller.

While I try to digest this new angle, I hear Vivienne say, "You of all people should know that a woman can be just as dangerous as a man." There's a hefty dollop of humor in her voice. "The wife of the gentleman I had drinks with tonight has wanted to kill me for years. She could do it too. She's as good a shot as I am."

"Then you shouldn't try to steal husbands," I say, but shouldn't have.

"Really, Cantor. Your umbrage is showing. I wasn't trying to steal her husband, just his money, which annoys his wife as much as if I really did try to steal him away from her. Believe me, she can have him. Look, after you tossed cold water on my request to go dancing, I decided to do a little business with someone whose money could strengthen my position at the museum. I guess I needed a bit of . . . I don't know . . . maybe affirmation, after you threw me over."

"I didn't throw you over. I said I—"

"Save it, Cantor. You opened this can; you're going to eat the worms inside. All right, here they are." She takes a slow drag of her smoke, exhales it and doesn't take her eyes off me. "I've been after this man for months to fund a major exhibition I'm organizing about the use of images of classical Greek and Roman gods in Renaissance art. I've secured loans from museums and collectors all over the world, but in order to mount the show the way I want, I'll still need more funding. The guy I had a drink with made his millions in manufacturing mass-produced furniture for the new suburban set. His money is so new it's still wet from the printing press. He wants to age it up a little, at least in appearance. Give it some class. That's what I can offer him, and I've been getting close to an agreement. I thought an evening of drinks and flattery would bring him over the fence. So that's where I was tonight, Cantor, at the bar the 21 Club, talking a rich man's ear off, telling him he'll take his place in cultural history if he hands me a suitcase full of money." Vivienne finishes up with a look that tells me to take my umbrage elsewhere, but stops short of telling me to drop dead. The aggressive way she stubs her cigarette out in the ashtray on the coffee table, I worry for the strength of the table's legs.

But Vivienne is safe, at least for the moment, and that matters more than my shredded chivalry.

So who was the caller who found me at the Green Door Club talking about? Who was the caller warning me not to leave alone?

My mind flashes with the faces of Mom Sheinbaum and Rosie. If either of them is in danger I can't hang around here playing flirt games with Vivienne.

"I need to make a call," I say on my way to the phone at the bar.

"At this hour? It's nearly three o'clock in the morning."

I don't answer her, just dial the phone, hoping that my call is picked up no matter how bad an argument I'll get about calling in at this late hour.

I let the phone ring over and over, must be half a dozen times, and still no answer. My jaw's so tight I can barely swallow. After a few more rings, I lower the receiver, ready to run out the door, but then I hear a sleepy "'Lo?" before the receiver's back in its cradle.

Rosie is safe.

I hang up, dial Mom's number. It rings, ten times, twelve, more. There's no answer.

Chapter Twelve

I park the Buick in front of Mom's place.

There's nothing unusual happening on the street: no cop cars in front of the house, no coroner's meat wagon waiting for a body, no rubberneckers looking for a thrill. I don't know whether to be relieved that Mom is just asleep in her bed and didn't wake to answer her phone, or whether I should be scared stiff that I'm too late, that the cops and coroner's boys have already come and gone.

There's only one way to find out.

I run up the front stairs, bang on her door, press the door buzzer.

Too much time passes without an answer.

I take out my lockpicks. In seconds, I'm inside.

The house is quiet and dark. After I stumble on a foot of a living room chair, I turn on a lamp. The old-fashioned room comes into view, full of antique shadows and bygone secrets but no answers.

I call out, "Mom! Mom Sheinbaum!" as I run upstairs to her bedroom. With any luck, the old woman will give me a piece of her mind for barging in on her in the middle of the night.

Her bedroom's empty.

I turn on a bedside lamp. The bedcovers haven't been touched. The bed's not been slept in.

But there's no blood. No body.

And there's no note.

I go back downstairs to the living room, dial Sig's number. I don't give a damn how late it is.

A flunkie answers the phone after a few rings.

"Get Sig to the phone," I say.

"He's sleepin'. Who the hell is this?"

"It's Cantor Gold. Wake him."

"This better be good, Gold."

I recognize the voice now. It's Max Novick. "No, it's not good, Max. It might be the worst thing Sig's ever heard. Wake him up."

There's heavy breathing at the other end of the line, then, "Gimme me a minute."

I light a cigarette, start to sit down in the overstuffed chair next to the phone table while I wait for Sig, but decide I'm too jittery to sit.

My jitters aren't soothed any when I finally hear Sig's slow, gravelly, sleep-heavy voice say, "What do you want, Cantor?"

"I'm at Mom's. She's not here. I thought you—"

"Mrs. Sheinbaum is here, Cantor. After the murder of Miss Angeli, I thought it safer to bring her here. She is sleeping in my guest room, well guarded. Go home, Cantor. Good night."

I finally sit down, and let out the longest breath I've ever breathed in my life.

The elevator ride up to the tenth floor of my apartment building feels like it's crawling up the shaft. By the time I get to my door, all I want is a quick shot of whiskey and an even faster fall into my bed.

Inside, I switch on the light. My foot slides on something on the carpet, something that makes my nerves twitch. It's an envelope.

I pick it up and pull out the note. The strange handwriting hits harder than a punch to the guts:

WE'RE NOT DONE, CANTOR. I'M
GOING TO GRIND YOU DOWN
AND THEN I'M GOING TO TAKE
EVERYTHING AWAY FROM YOU.

After a long shower and slipping into a gray shirt and black pinstripe suit, it takes three cups of Doris's strong coffee at Pete's Luncheonette to take enough sleep out of me to drive down to Greenwich Village. I make it in time to meet Adair in front of Edie's place at nine on this Wednesday morning.

When I see his Plymouth turn the corner onto Charles Street I wave him to the curb.

He gets out of the car, says, "What's this about Edie Angeli's other life?"

"Good morning to you too, sergeant." I give my smile a touch of sincerity.

But Adair's not buying it. I don't blame him. "Our arrangement will work much better, Gold, if we dispense with the chitchat. I am not your partner, and I'm damn sure not your pal."

"Then I'll cross you off my guest list for my next birthday party. C'mon, let's go upstairs."

At the door to Edie's brownstone, Adair looks at the registry for the super's bell.

"Don't waste your time," I say, taking my lockpicks from my inside pocket.

He gives me a look born of a cop's automatic instinct to arrest me for breaking and entering, but I get the door open before that instinct has a chance to ripen.

Inside the first-floor hall, the jazz trumpeter gets no competition today from yesterday's crying baby, so the horn's melody winds around the hall on its own sweet self. As Adair and I climb the stairs, the life of the building filters through the halls: television jingles, a couple arguing, someone laughing.

When we get to Edie's door on the third floor, I pick that lock too. Adair pretends not to notice.

We step inside. The smell of oil paint and turpentine drifts toward us.

Adair looks around, eyes wide at the roomful of paintings, easels, cans of brushes and tubes of paint on spattered tables.

"Say hello to Edie Dumont, artist," I say.

The expression on Adair's face tells me he doesn't know a thing about art but he knows what he likes, and modern abstract art ain't it. I guess he's more of a landscape guy.

Once he's finished being surprised at where we are and what he sees here, he says, "Edie Dumont. Edie Angeli. Why the phony name?"

"Because she wanted her art to stand on its own. She was afraid the Angeli name would either scare people off, or that gallery owners would only give her a show if they were afraid they'd suffer her father's deadly wrath."

Adair says, "So this is all legit?" sweeping his arm around the room.

"This part of her life was legit, yeah."

"And the rest? The Angeli part?"

"Well, she certainly inherited her father's money, and she grew up in a crime family with lots of connections. Look, Adair, I hardly knew the woman. I met her just yesterday. So I'm not sure how involved she was in the Angeli family business, or rather what there was left of it."

He gives that a thoughtful nod, then walks around the room, looks at a painting here and there. "Sure, I remember the reports about the old Don calling it quits after his wife died. Listen, Gold," he says, coming back to me, "you didn't bring me here to show me a bunch of pictures I don't like. So why are we here?"

"Just because Edie used the name Dumont as an artist doesn't mean the art world wasn't wise to who she really was. Maybe they were, maybe they weren't. We need to find out where she exhibited her paintings, talk to the people at any of the galleries that showed her work, see if anyone knew the real Edie, or who might have had it in for her. I figured we'd look around for any paperwork or news clippings about any exhibitions of the work of Edie Dumont."

"Is that the tie-in with you, Gold? The art game?"

I toss off a shrug, say, "Maybe," but I don't give him any more.

"Okay, but how does the art angle tie up with Dave Handy, or that actor guy, Burns?"

"Well, they both ran around with Edie. Maybe someone at an art gallery remembers seeing either of them at one of Edie's shows. Anyway, it's a place to start. I brought us here so we could look around, see if we find any gallery paper." That's all Adair's gonna get from me right now, not until I get a better handle of what Adair plans to do about what we find out, and what he has in mind about me. Sig Loreale or no Sig Loreale, Adair is still a cop. Worse, he's not one of Sig's cops. He couldn't care less if Sig wants me alive today or dead tomorrow.

So I don't tell him about the phone call I got at the Green Door Club, or the note I found under my door. The note stays in my pocket.

We start sifting through the stuff in Edie's studio. Adair looks through Edie's desk. I look through her file cabinet.

Most of the files contain quick drawings or images cut out from books or magazines, images for reference arranged by subject matter or ideas. There are files labeled *Street Scenes, Color Studies, Faces, Country Scenes, Shapes & Lines.* I take a quick look through each file, looking for any gallery paper. No paper, but the files have interesting images, the inner workings of Edie's talent. A few sketches and snapshots in the *Country Scenes* file catch my attention; images of a grand estate with a palatial house, carefully tended gardens, and here and there a few people wandering through. No doubt these are scenes of Dominic Angeli's rural retreat, the place where Edie spent her youth when she was home from her fancy Swiss school. I take a good look at these, especially the photos, try to make out the faces of the people scattered through the estate, see if there's anyone familiar, maybe Dave Handy or Mel Burns or anyone else I might know. Hard to tell, though. The distance is too great, the faces too small or blurry.

Adair says, "Gold? I might've found something. There's a file on the desk labeled *Perkins Show*. Inside there's some sort of list. Does *Study Of A Heartbeat #12*, or *Deep Red Swing* mean anything to you? There's a whole bunch of stuff like that."

Bingo. "They're likely titles of paintings," I say.

"And Perkins?"

"That would be Adele Perkins."

"Who's she?"

"Maybe the key to the life and death of Edie Angeli."

West Eighth Street is one of Greenwich Village's main arteries. Though not as wide as the avenues, West Eighth has plenty of Village spirit. Tucked into the first and second floors of the old brick tenements are music stores, coffee joints, small grocery shops whose streetside bins of fruits and vegetables teem with color, and cheap Chinese and Italian restaurants catering to the Beat crowd of writers, musicians and artists who give the Village its zing.

A few art galleries dot the street. The Perkins Gallery is in the middle of the block, above a music shop selling jazz records and up the steep cast-iron front stairs of a brick tenement painted white, its paint peeling and worn away.

It's nearly ten-thirty when I park my Buick in front of the gallery. Adair parks his Plymouth police cruiser behind me. When he gets out of the car, he gives the street the "cop eye," that suspicious glance at whoever's walking by. The denim-and-beret crowd of every race and romantic preference mixing it up on the street aren't Adair's kind of people. Then again, they wouldn't like him either.

He shakes his head, utters a *tsk* when he looks up and sees the artwork in the Perkins Gallery's second-story window, a large painting of a colorful tangle of lines sizzling with energy.

"It looks like something my six-year-old nephew did during a temper tantrum," he says. "People actually buy this stuff?"

"Sure, people buy it," I say, then can't resist ribbing him. "Don't you know temper tantrums are all the rage?"

He gives that another *tsk*, says, "I guess it takes all kinds," and starts up the stairs.

"Wait a minute, Adair," I say, and pick up a morning paper from the rack outside the grocery next door. A quick scan through the pages tells me that Sig succeeded in keeping Edie's death out of the news.

Adair gives me a questioning look.

"There's nothing," I say. "Sig's kept the lid on it for now."

In a minute, we're up the stairs. I ring the doorbell. The sign on the glass and cast iron door says the gallery opens at eleven, but I know Adele's inside, getting the place ready for the day. So I keep ringing until the sound annoys Adele enough to emerge from the back office and come to the door.

Adele's good-looking in that unusual way of some women whose features aren't the perfect All American variety. Her oval face and strong bones are enhanced by the wit and intelligence simmering in her dark eyes. There's passion in her eyes, too, passion for life and a passion for art, both of which she indulges with gusto. Her severely pulled-back black hair suits her severely demanding personality. Adele's not unkind; she just demands the best efforts of everyone she meets, especially if they're artists. Adele has no patience for the second rate.

As always, she's carefully dressed in a style that advertises her offbeat, sensual elegance. Today it's a pale blue high-necked sweater, a pencil thin black skirt, and a heavy necklace of polished brown and black irregularly shaped stones. It's the sort of unconventional jewelry one picks up at outdoor bazaars in exotic places or in one of Greenwich Village's arty shops selling stuff handmade by the locals.

Seeing me, Adele gives an eyebrow-raised smile, as if seeing me is a pleasant surprise, though maybe more surprise than pleasant. When she opens the door, she says, "Cantor Gold,

111

well, well." Adele has what you might call a cigarettes-and-wine voice—throaty but smooth, the sort of seductive voice that makes you think it's nighttime even if the sun's shining. "Shopping for a change? Or should I bolt the artwork to the walls?" Her dark eyes twinkle with the joke.

"I guess I'm shopping for information," I say.

"Ah, that explains why you're here with a police officer."

Adair couldn't look more surprised if she'd said his fly was open. I don't bother telling him he's got "cop" written all over his badly fitting suit and lumpy fedora.

Adele escorts us inside. I give a quick glance to the paintings on the pale gray walls of the small gallery. The paintings are variations on the sizzling lines seen in the gallery window. "Nice show," I say. "Who's the artist?"

"A new kid. I'm betting he's going places."

"That's your specialty, Adele, spotting talent. By the way, you're looking well. Business must be good."

"I can't complain. You're looking well too, Cantor. Still a snappy dresser." She accents this with a wink. "You always did look good in black."

Adair takes out his gold detective's shield, says, "If you two don't mind."

I say, "Sorry, sergeant. Adele, this is Sergeant Liam Adair of the New York City Police Department. Sergeant, Adele Perkins."

Adele, her arms crossed, says, "So, what's this all about, sergeant? How can I help you?" Her tone's friendly enough. Her eyes, though, are wary. That's the general attitude around here toward the police. In a neighborhood full of nonconformists who hold society's rules of behavior in low esteem, too much interest by the cops annoys everyone.

Adair, though, is a by-the-book detective. He won't badger Adele; it's not his style, but he gets to the point. "I understand you know an artist named Edie Dumont."

Adele's, "Yes," is direct, honest, and as generous as someone guarding a door.

Adair's clearly no stranger to tight-lipped respondents. He

doesn't get angry, doesn't get tough. He smiles, but it's not the sort of smile that sends out best wishes. "Good, then I hope you can help us. How do you know her?"

Adele uncrosses her arms, seems to run something through her mind, then crosses her arms again. "Evidently you know she's an artist, sergeant, or you wouldn't be here. So, to answer your question, my relationship to Edie Dumont is strictly professional. I'm planning to exhibit her paintings."

Adair's "I see" skirts the edge of patronizing. "Maybe you know some of her friends? Maybe her love interests?"

"Sergeant," Adele says with a laugh, "if you've met Edie, then you know she's a beautiful woman. Her line of suitors could fill a city block."

"I bet," he says, giving nothing away. I have to hand it to Adair. He's as careful in interrogation as a surgeon with a scalpel. "Well, have you ever heard her speak about someone named Dave Handy?"

Adele gives that a shrug.

"What about Mel Birnbaum or Mel Burns?"

"I never heard her mention those names. What is this about, sergeant? Is Edie in some kind of trouble?"

I jump in before Adair handles the question. "Maybe Edie didn't mention Dave Handy or Mel Burns, but do you know either of them, Adele?"

It's the little things that tell you you've hit a nerve, little things like Adele's nearly imperceptible tightening at a corner of her pretty mouth.

This could land in either guy's lap. Maybe Dave did a little fixing for Adele, maybe he took care of a business licensing problem, or maybe he did a favor for one of the buyers of her gallery's art. Maybe Mel got involved with some Beat crowd actors who hang around with Adele's artists.

Adair picks up on Adele's tension with a simple, "Well, Miss Perkins?"

But Adele doesn't look at Adair. She looks at me. Her slowly spreading smile isn't especially warm. It's not cold either. It's sly, and she's enjoying it. "I never thought I'd see the day when you'd be working with the police, Cantor."

"Life's full of surprises, Adele, like the surprise you know Dave Handy or Mel Burns. Which is it?"

"Do either of you have a cigarette?" she says. "I left mine in the back office."

Adair says, "Stop stalling, Miss Perkins."

I take out my pack of Chesterfields, offer one to Adele. She takes it. I light it for her, say, "Any other requests before Sergeant Adair gets tough with you, Adele?"

Her calm cracks. "All right," she snaps. "I know Dave Handy. He used to come around with some of my big-money clients. I, uh, I had an arrangement with him to steer the midtown money to my gallery."

Adair says, "Arrangement, meaning you paid him."

"Call it a consulting fee, sergeant, okay? It's how the world works. Even cops know that."

Adair's face tightens at Adele's inference of cops on the take, but he can't contradict it, so he leaves it alone. But the look he gives her makes it clear she needs to keep talking.

She takes the hint. "Anyway, I haven't seen Dave in quite a while. He seems to have dropped off the face of the earth, so I can't tell you any more about him. Now, you still haven't told me what this is about. If Edie Dumont is in trouble with the police, I have a right to know what it is if I'm to do business with her."

Adair says, "Does the name Edie Angeli mean anything to you, Miss Perkins?"

Adele's short laugh takes me and Adair by surprise. After the laugh subsides, another sly smile lingers. "Well, that took you long enough," she says.

Adair says, "So you knew Edie Dumont and Edie Angeli—"

"Are the same person?" Adele finishes for him. "Sure. But it's Edie's secret to keep, not my secret to betray."

"How did you know?"

"Look, sergeant, I may be in the kind of business that sells an artist's deepest, strangest dreams to people who want to live in those dreams, but it's still a business. I need to know as much as I can about the artists I take into my gallery. Artists can be pretty wild people. A lot of that wildness sells paintings. But I need to be able to keep control. So I dig and I dig and I ask people and I find out who's who and who's what. That's how I learned about Edie. And now that her father is dead—oh, sure, I saw the story on the TV news. Poor guy, dumped in a warehouse."

I say, "Did you know that Dave Handy and Edie Angeli were an item for a while?"

"It doesn't surprise me. Edie always did have an eye for lousy boyfriends."

Adair says, "Thank you, Miss Perkins, that's all for now."

I want to ask him why the hell he's cut things short, but the look on his face—cunning, even a little happy—stops me. Whatever his cop's instincts are up to, I decide it's best to play along.

On our way to the door, Adele calls after us, "You still haven't said what this is all about."

Adair says, "We'll be in touch, Miss Perkins."

Outside, I say, "Why didn't you tell her Edie's dead?"

"Maybe she knows already.

Chapter Thirteen

Adair opens the door of his Plymouth, but doesn't get in. "We need to know more about Dave Handy's setup with the Perkins woman," he says.

"What are you going to do, Adair? Sweat it out of him? He's even less likely to chat up a cop than Adele was."

"Which is why you're going to handle him. While you're getting the story from Handy, I'll go into the police files, see what I can dig up that might be useful. Handy was connected to some pretty nasty articles."

"Nasty enough to let him drown when he fell into hot water."

"Maybe the Perkins woman was one of the people who let him drown."

I don't figure that's Adele's style, same way I can't figure Adele as a killer, but as Vivienne pointed out, you never know. Women can kill just as well as men. Maybe better. "Okay, Adair," I say, "if I get anything from Dave, I'll hand it over. I trust you'll return the favor?"

"I'm the one who's being forced to do the trusting, Gold." He gets into the Plymouth, drives away.

I'm tempted to go back into the gallery and press Adele for more. I suppose Adair has his cop reasons for cutting the interview short, but those reasons are mud to me.

I decide to let the guy make his play, at least for now. And besides, he's right about being forced to trust me, and so far I haven't given him a whole lot of reasons to snuggle up to the idea. But I don't entirely trust him either. He may be a decent cop, but he's still a cop, and my experience with cops has been less than warm and fuzzy. The still raw gash on my head from the raid on the Green Door Club is a reminder to keep my cards close with the Law. Not that I need reminding.

I open the door of my Buick, start to get in, but something catches the corner of my eye, a glint of something, maybe sun flashing off the chrome mouth-like grille of a passing light-green Packard coupe. The car's moving slowly, maybe too slowly, but passes me by before I can get a look at the driver, see if it's a man or a woman.

Maybe the driver's just cruising for a parking spot.

Maybe the driver's my stalker.

I reach into my pocket for my pack of smokes. My fingers touch the note I didn't share with Adair, the note threatening to grind me down and take everything from me.

The Packard's down the block, pulling into a parking space. A guy in a black lumber jacket and porkpie hat gets out of the car, goes into a coffee joint. He doesn't even look my way.

I light up a smoke, force back a shiver.

The cigarette and the drive to Hell's Kitchen finally get rid of the shivers by the time I park on Ninth Avenue.

I walk into the Happy Hour Saloon. The heavy smoke in the air is kind to the noontime crowd drinking their lunch, softening their hard-knocks faces a bit.

Dave's pouring shots at the bar. When he sees me, he's not happy about it. Everything on his pasty face seems to harden. "I thought I got rid of you yesterday," he says.

"I'm like that blob of gum on the sole of your shoe."

"Or something else I shouldn't have stepped in," Dave says. "Get this, Cantor, I said all I'm gonna say about Edie Angeli."

"Then talk to me about Adele Perkins. And while you're at

it, pour me a scotch." I put a buck on the bar. "Keep the change."

He pours my drink, puts my buck into the cash register, takes out the change and puts it in his pocket. He does all this slowly, turns it into busy work, a way to put off dealing with me and my annoying excavation of his earlier life.

A guy walks in, takes a seat at the end of the bar and asks for a shot of rye. Dave takes a bottle from the row behind the bar, flips a shot glass with the flashy skill I saw yesterday, and pours the guy his drink.

By the time Dave gets back to me, he's wearing his trademark sneery smile. "What about Adele Perkins? She get a laugh knowing what I'm doing these days?"

"Why? You worried she'll saunter in here?"

"Very funny," he says, the smile gone but the sneer lingering. "Look, Adele wanted me to bring the city's money boys down to her gallery, and if anybody bought a painting, I'd get a cut. Call it a business arrangement. But why have you been talking to Adele? What's that got to do with Edie?"

"Adele wants to show Edie's paintings at her gallery."

"Paintings? What paintings?"

I give him a hard look, try to figure if he's handing me a bill of goods or not. "You mean you've never been to Edie's studio? I thought you two were a hot item."

"Sure, we were an item, but Edie called the shots about where we'd go and where we'd be seen, or not seen. I can't blame her. When your old man's a gangster, you play your life pretty close and quiet. So you're telling me Edie was an artist?"

"Why *was*?"

"What kind of question is that? I didn't know she was an artist when we were running around because we didn't run around together all that long and the bitch called all the shots. So what are you getting at, Gold? Why are you nosing around in old news about me and Edie and Adele?" The cagey look slowly overtaking Dave's face makes my jaw tighten. I'm not sure if I'm looking at the face of a killer, or the face of a guy who hasn't a clue his old flame is dead, or just the face of a guy who's annoyed at having been taken for a ride by that old flame.

"Well, you know what they say about it being a small world," I say. "Funny thing is, it turns out my world is pretty small. I mean, how do you figure that I'd know you and Adele and Edie?"

"Sure, small world." If the sneer in his smile was any colder everyone's drink would be over ice. "Except your world is still bright and shiny, Cantor, full of cash and flashy clothes. Flashy women, too, I bet." He says this last bit with a nasty grin that makes me want to knock his teeth back. "You know what's in my world, Cantor? Look around. This is it. Boozers and losers."

I give the saloon a glance, have a look at the broken-down drinkers who've replaced Handy Dave Handy's once-upon-a-time crowd of high hats and high stakes. "I bet you'd like to get revenge on who did this to you, Dave." And then I look straight at him. "I bet you'd like to take everything from them," purposely saying the words my stalker wrote in the latest note.

Dave leans in close to me, face to face across the bar. "Wouldn't *you*?" he says.

"Is that what you're doing, Dave?"

"To who?"

"You tell me? Who did this to you? Who'd you screw over who then screwed you back?"

A female voice, scratchy with cigarettes and liquor, says, "Hey, Dave, can't a lady get a little service over here? I need a refill."

Dave's pasty complexion takes on a little color, a slightly fevered pink in his hollow cheeks. It matches the feverish curl of his smile as he backs away from me and grabs a bottle of bourbon from behind the bar.

He takes the bottle to the woman demanding a refill, pours the drink then comes back to me. "You want to know about me and Edie? You'd have to ask Edie. You want to know about me and Adele? Ask Adele. You want to know who brought me down?" He brings his face close to mine. The sneer is back again, this time riding on a snicker so bitter it twists his lips and makes the air stink. "Your world really is small, Cantor, and getting tighter all the time."

When I walk back into Adele's gallery, she's chatting up a customer, a guy whose double-breasted gray suit and conservative blue tie announces bright as a flashing sign that he doesn't live around here. Adele's giving him a spiel about the profound meaning inside every line of one of the paintings on the wall. The guy's eating it up, nodding like a snooty scholar. His nods and "um-hmms" are meant to paper over that he's clearly new to buying art, doesn't get it that the painting is really good on its own and doesn't need a phony philosophical song and dance. But Adele knows what she's doing. A speech spilling plenty of art scene gibberish pumps up the sale price.

Adele gives me a quick glance, a movement with her eyes directing me to get out of sight in her back office. I don't mind. Far be it from me to interfere with Adele's livelihood.

But I leave the office door open, keep an eye on Adele while I sit at her desk. I can see all the way through the gallery to the front door. I'm not about to let her pull a fast one on me and leave the place. Not after the tidbit I got from Dave.

After a little more chitchat, the customer pulls out his wallet and hands Adele some cash. She walks with him to the counter by the front door, puts the cash into a strongbox, locks it, and gives him a receipt. The guy puts his hat on and goes out the door. Adele walks through the gallery and into the office.

"Nice sale?" I say.

Adele leans against her desk, takes a pack of Pall Malls and a book of matches from the desktop. She doesn't wait for me to light her cigarette. Adele's not the type. Ordinarily, I enjoy lighting a woman's smoke, give her a bit of chivalry, but Adele's independence from all that has its own spicy charm. "The guy gave me a down payment to hold the painting," she says through an exhale, which only enhances the seductive charm of her smoky voice. "When the show closes, he'll either buy the painting or he won't, but I think I can talk him into it. I told him I'd throw in framing it, even do it myself so it's done right."

"Yeah, I remember you're an excellent framer," I say.

"Thanks," Adele says. "It'll be a delicate job. The impasto on that thing is pretty brittle, easy to damage. Anyway, my guess is there's someone the guy wants to impress, and he thinks owning a piece of the local bohemian scene will do the trick. So what are you doing here, Cantor? I don't see you for months, and now I have the pleasure of your company twice in one day?"

"I'm glad my company is still a pleasure."

"Well, it's certainly better than when you showed up with the police and all those questions about Edie. By the way, I've been trying to reach Edie all day to talk about her upcoming show, but she doesn't answer her phone."

I study Adele's face hard, look into those dark, seductive eyes for any sign she's giving me the runaround.

Adair might disapprove, but I know Adele and he doesn't, so it's time for me to deal with her my way. It's worth the risk to see if Adele's playing straight with me or treating me like the sucker who just handed her his cash for a speech about a painting. "Edie can't answer her phone," I say. "She's never going to answer her phone again, Adele. Edie's dead."

She takes a long, deep inhale of the cigarette then lets it out slowly. Smoke drifts up to her face, obscuring her eyes. When the haze clears, her eyes are red and teary. "How?" she says, clearing her throat. "When?"

"Last night," I say. "Battered bloody and stuffed into a burlap sack."

Adele takes another drag on her cigarette. Her hand shakes, causing the smoke to rise in zigzag lines in front of her face. She wipes her teary eyes with the back of her hand. "So that's why you showed up with a cop today. You and that cop already knew Edie was dead, but you didn't say so. What were you doing? Waiting for me to confess?"

"Do you have something to confess, Adele?"

She stubs out her half-finished cigarette, looks at me like she's getting ready to slap me. "You've got your nerve, Cantor.

Do you really think I'm capable of murder?"

"I think anyone's capable of murder if they think they have a good reason. But whoever killed Edie—and her father, by the way. You must've seen it in the papers."

Adele answers with a nod and another exhale.

I say, "Well, whoever killed Edie and Dominic Angeli wasn't really out to get either of them. The killer used the murders to get to me. It didn't matter that I'd never met Edie until yesterday and never met her father at all. The killer traced some vague connection between us and is using it to set me up and grind me down. Someone has a helluva grudge against me. So I have to ask, are you harboring any grudges against me, Adele?"

The question's meant to provoke indignation at what it implies, or else some slick story to hide behind. But Adele doesn't come across with either. She just unpins the knot of hair behind her neck, shakes it loose, lets her dark hair fall in soft waves along her shoulders and down her back. "Do I hold a grudge against you, Cantor? I should," she says. "You were a louse, you know. Cheated on me with anything in a skirt. And it hurt twice as bad because I was struggling to get this gallery open, so I didn't have much energy left over to handle heartbreak. I knew you couldn't give me love. Something or someone ripped that part out of you. But all I got was your two-timing."

She's got me there. My "Okay," rides on a guilty shrug. "So I was a cad. Sometimes I'm still a cad. But our affair was delicious, Adele, full of great nights, great talk, and truly memorable hours rolling around under the sheets. I was sorry when it all ended, but it was a long time ago. We've stayed friends, even shared a drink from time to time."

"So what? Now you show up and maybe accuse me of murder. Hurting me seems to be a specialty with you, Cantor."

"I'm sorry I hurt you, Adele," I say with as much tenderness as I can muster for a woman who might be involved in a couple of killings. "And I don't mean to hurt you now. But someone has it in for me. Someone's hunting me, and using murder to rattle me. So you'll excuse me if I'm a little rough with my questions.

I'm trying to outrun a predator, someone who wants to reduce me to a pebble the world can crush, and I have no idea why."

Adele says, "What makes you think I can help you?"

"You can start by telling me who ruined Dave Handy."

There's a flicker of surprise in her eyes before she gets the emotion under control. "Why would I know that? Like I told you and that cop this morning, I haven't seen Dave in quite a while."

"But Dave hinted that you *do* know," I say. "Was it you, Adele? Did you do something, maybe pull some strings with certain people to knock Dave down because he hurt you too? Hurt you like I hurt you?"

A change comes over Adele. The stiff defensiveness gives way to something looser. Her body relaxes against her desk. A small smile creeps from the corner of her mouth, parting her lips just enough to show a trace of teeth. She bends a little toward me, runs a finger along my lapel. "You know, Cantor, in this black pinstripe suit and that gray shirt you look every inch the criminal you are. And you know what? I like it. I like the idea that you think I could commit murder. It's actually rather exciting. Sort of lets me share your criminal world."

"But I'm not a murderer, Adele."

"Maybe not, but you probably know a few. What are murderers like, Cantor?"

"Heartless," I say. "Ice cold."

"Well, I'm not heartless," she says, bending down to me, "and you know I'm anything but cold. Don't you remember, Cantor?" And then she kisses me, slides herself onto my lap.

Adele's kiss makes me remember: remember the nights in her tiny Greenwich Village apartment, the place lit only by candles because she couldn't afford to pay her electric bill; remember the narrow bed that creaked under us; remember Adele's long legs around my waist, her fingers sliding along my chest . . .

Just like they're doing now.

I push Adele away because if I don't we'll wind up on the floor, rutting like feral animals. I can't afford to get lost in all that lust, set my body on fire while my mind dulls. I have to stay sharp if I want to outsmart the woman who might be my hunter.

If looks could kill, well, the way Adele's looking at me I'd be dead.

But the look cracks as she gets up from my lap. She turns her back to me. Her shoulders droop as she leans against her desk. "Get out of here, Cantor. Just get out. I don't want to see you. I don't want to talk to you."

I get up from the chair, take her arm and turn her around to me. "But I want to talk to you, Adele. Listen, I didn't push you away just now because I didn't want you. I pushed you away because I wanted you so hard we'd have been all over each other and I'd forget what I came for. I can't afford to forget that, Adele. I'm being hunted and I can't let my defenses down. I have to know what's going on. I have to know what happened to Dave Handy." She tries to turn away. I keep a tight hold on her arm.

The expression on her face is so sour I swear I can feel the air around us curdle. "I don't owe you any explanations about Dave or anyone else, Cantor. Now just get out of here."

My grip gets tighter. I feel my face tighten too. I'm sure I don't look friendly.

Adele says, "What are you going to do? Try to squeeze something out of me? Go ahead and try. Sure, go ahead and try."

What was the heat of my passion five minutes ago is the heat of my anger now. An anger that roars through me down to my fingers, threatens to tighten my grip even more on Adele's arm, and maybe worse.

But I can't let it get any worse. I don't beat up on women, and loathe the creeps who do. I let go of Adele's arm.

Whatever secret Adele has about Dave Handy is going to stay inside Adele.

I'll have to find another way.

Outside, I take a last look through the gallery's glass-and-iron front door, see Adele close the door to her office.

I light a smoke on my way down the stairs, let the tobacco settle my spiking nerves. What I could really use is a drink. I look up and down Eighth Street for a bar, spot one at the corner of Sixth Avenue, start walking.

I'm halfway up the block when there's a tug on my sleeve, and a kid's "Hey!" shouting up at me. I look down to see a street kid, maybe ten years old, his brown hair falling over his forehead. "I'm supposed to give you this," he says, hands me an envelope, then runs away. He ducks into an alley before I get the chance to ask him who gave him the envelope.

If my nerves were raw when I left Adele's gallery, they're jumping up and down on their hind legs now.

I open the envelope and take out the note. What it says nearly brings me to my knees:

> WAS THAT FUN, CANTOR? YOU
> SURE KNOW HOW TO TREAT
> A GIRL. YOU'LL PAY FOR YOUR
> CRIMES. YOU WILL BE NOTHING.

Chapter Fourteen

My mouth is dry. My skin's gone cold. I even have the shivers again. If I was standing naked in the middle of rush hour traffic, I couldn't feel any more helpless than I do right now.

Whoever's hunting me has gotten close enough to crawl up my back, look over my shoulder and watch every move I make, be part of every move I make and see who I make my moves with.

This last bit knocks me back into my senses, gets me running back along Eighth Street, back to Adele's gallery. I'm scared to death she'll wind up like Edie, dead because she spent time with me.

I look up to the window when I reach the gallery, relieved to see Adele greet a young woman in brown toreador pants and a red sweater, her black hair cut short. A Village denizen, no doubt, maybe an artist Adele does business with.

So, sure, it's a relief to see Adele alive and well. But the relief has a dark side, the side that wonders if it was Adele who wrote the note that shook me to my core.

Police stations don't normally give me a warm welcome unless I'm in handcuffs, a situation I do my best to avoid. But here I am in a midtown police station whose walls are pocked with peeling green paint, the air choked with tobacco smoke, and the whole place clogged with cops who've taken bets on which one of them will eventually have the honor of sending me to prison. I'm here because it's time to make better use of the New York City Police Department and Sergeant Liam Adair, and not just because Sig Loreale says so, but because I need Adair's gang of blue.

Adair's office is on the second floor, which means I have to navigate two floors of cops giving me everything from the stink-eye to insults to lewd jokes. But I give as good as I get, even call out to one of the cops, a curly haired detective who fancies himself a Don Juan, "She told me all about you, Callahan. She says your equipment needs tuning."

I enter Adair's office, leaving the squad room to its laughter.

Adair's in his shirtsleeves at his desk, a battered dark wood relic with the history of all the frustrations of the previous cops who've sat there etched into its surface: cigarette and cigar burns, deep scratches, gashes, coffee and booze stains. Adair's clean white shirt almost glows in contrast to the dirty window behind him, the glass smeared with years of grime in horror movie colors.

He looks up from a pile of police files when I walk in, doesn't seem surprised to see me. "I've been digging into what we've got on Dave Handy. He was a pretty slick character. His name comes up in connection with some big-time big shots, everyone from powerful politicians to Broadway types, a bunch of gangsters, and even—would you believe it—teenage street gangs. The guy got around."

"Anyone you pick out as his tormentor?"

"Hard to say."

"Any of them connected to me?"

Adair greets that with an annoying smirk across his thick face. "You tell me," he says.

I sit down in the chair opposite Adair's desk, give him a smirk that sends his own back to him. "Run some names by me, sergeant. Maybe one of them holds Dave and me in equal contempt."

"The list would be too long," he says with a snort. "But something interesting did show up, something connected to what the Perkins woman said this morning about her arrangement with Handy to bring deep pockets to her gallery. It seems Handy was seen in the company of that Broadway gossip columnist, goes by the moniker Stage Door Johnny. They were seen together on more than one occasion, some of them shady, but a few times at Miss Perkins' gallery. You ever have any dealings with him?"

Stage Door Johnny Delmore. He spills Broadway's secrets in his daily column and his radio feature. I see him sometimes around my neighborhood on his way in and out of the theaters and nightspots, stalking the Broadway crowd's eateries and watering holes for titillating show biz tidbits. Big-time Broadway producers love him when he throws in a kind word in his column for some matinee idol or the show the idol's starring in. The same producers want to strangle him when he reveals the kind of dirt that can kill a star's career or sink a show.

"I've met the guy," I say, "see him around my neighborhood. We say hello now and then."

"No connection stronger than that?"

"Not that I know of. But something Dave told me today might open things up. When I asked him who brought him low, he sidestepped it but hinted I might ask Adele."

"And did you?"

"Yeah, I went back to her gallery after I left Dave. She gave me the runaround." I'm not about to tell Adair the sordid details. "Didn't own up about it one way or the other," is all I give him.

Adair says, "The lady plays it pretty slick if you ask me. I, uh, assume you tried your best to worm it out of her?" The smirk's back.

"You have your ways, Adair. I have mine. Let's leave it at that. Listen, how about if I give you the opportunity to convince me just how efficient the New York City Police can be," I say and take the latest note out of my suit pocket. "After I left Adele's gallery, some kid on the street gave me this. Maybe the department's fingerprint guys can lift some prints, though something tells me they won't find any except mine and the kid's. Worth a try, though." I give Adair the note.

He reads it. This is the third time he's smirked in the last five minutes. He doesn't know how close he's coming to having me rip his lips off. "Was what fun?" he says.

"None of it," I say, shutting the conversation down.

He gets the hint, takes another look at the note. "The handwriting looks disguised. That might tell us something. We got a guy in the lab who examines stuff like that. Handwriting specialist."

"Maybe he can figure if it was written by a man or a woman," I say.

Adair looks up from the note, looks at me. "You thinking the Perkins woman?"

"I don't know what I'm thinking. Meantime, the Johnny Delmore angle is worth a look."

He picks up the phone, says as he dials, "Let me get an address on him."

"Don't bother," I say. "He won't be home. He'll be prowling Broadway for tomorrow morning's edition. But I know someone who might have a line on where he sets up when he's on the prowl."

It's already four o'clock and I haven't had anything to eat since breakfast, so I ask Doris for a chicken on rye. Adair, who Doris figured for a cop the minute he walked in the door, orders a coffee.

The place is quiet at this hour, between the lunch and dinner trade. It's just me and Adair at the counter, and only four people at tables: a couple of out-of-work ingenues scanning the notices in *Variety*, the showbiz newspaper; a bony-faced guy I've seen around the neighborhood and whose fedora looks like it could fall off his head while he studies the racing form; and a doughy faced guy in a porkpie hat who's not paying attention to me or to anyone as he eats his sandwich but he gives me the creeps anyway. I wonder if he's the same guy I saw driving the Packard on Eighth Street. I look at the coat rack near the front door to see if there's a black lumber jacket like I saw on the guy on Eighth Street. There isn't.

Doris comes back with my sandwich and a pot of coffee, eyes Adair while she refills his cuppa. Then she slides her eyes to me with a questioning look, the kind that says she's surprised to see me in the company of a cop. Not that Doris has anything against cops—unlike me, she has no reason to—but seeing me break bread with an officer of the Law turns her sense of the world upside down.

I'm happy to come to her rescue. "Sergeant Adair and I need some information, Doris. Maybe you can help. We're looking for Johnny Delmore. You happen to know where he hangs around in the afternoons?"

"Stage Door Johnny? He in trouble?" she says with a nod toward Adair.

Adair, like all cops, hates to be second-guessed, and his attitude hardens. "If you know where we can find him, just say so," he says.

If Doris didn't have anything against cops before, she's having a change of heart now, at least about this cop. Still holding the coffeepot, she puts her other hand on her hip, and looks at Adair like she's getting ready to scold a bratty kid. "What? You think I'm Stage Door Johnny's personal secretary?" she says. "I just pour his coffee, just like I did for you, sergeant."

I get back into the conversation before Adair makes more of a mess of it. "I need to talk to the guy, Doris. It's important. Real important. You pour coffee for everyone on Broadway. Johnny ever mention where he digs around for stuff for his column?"

A frown tightens over Doris's street-savvy eyes. I've put her in a bind and I know it. I'm asking her to do what she prides herself on not doing: talking behind her customers' backs. In an anything-goes neighborhood like ours, where colorful people are known to lead off-color lives, Doris overhears a lot but keeps it all to herself. She's certainly earned my trust over the years. Now I'm asking her to spill some beans, and to a cop too.

With a *tsk* and a shake of her head, she says, "So how important is real important?"

I take her hand, hold it gently. "Life and death important," I say.

Doris looks at me, then at Adair, then up at the clock on the wall and back to me. Finally, she says, "At this hour? Try Goody's. Y'know, the saloon next door to the Broadhurst theater."

Goody's Bar is a Broadway watering hole that caters to the backstage crowd: stagehands, makeup and wardrobe people, props people, set dressers, lighting crew, the workhorse geniuses who keep a show on its feet and looking sharp.

The joint's smoky and loud when Adair and I walk in, the chatter and laughter nearly drowning out the tune on the jukebox, an Ames Brothers hit I get a kick out of, "The Naughty Lady of Shady Lane."

Some of the crowd chatter over cocktail-hour drinks. Others are having coffee or a quick bite at the bar or in the booths before they get ready to set up the stages for tonight's shows; at least those lucky enough to have a show to work on. Show biz is a dicey game. One day you're making good money in a hit show, or you're stuck with a turkey that closes the next day and you're scraping the sidewalk and drinking Goody's whiskey on a pal's wallet.

I spot Johnny Delmore at the bar. He's wedged between a woman in a yellow dress and a hefty guy in a black lumber jacket and a fedora. At least the guy's not wearing a porkpie hat. Still, I give the place a look-around. I can't shake the feeling of being watched, hunted.

"There's Stage Door Johnny Delmore," I say to Adair. "The guy with the blond crew cut and brown suit." Adair starts to walk over. I hold him back. "Listen sergeant, I wouldn't flash your badge too fast. Show business types have messy lives, the

131

kind of lives they're not crazy about sharing with cops."

"I'll keep that in mind," he says, not meaning a word of it.

We walk over to the bar, cutting our way through the knots of people moving between the bar and the booths. Adair raises his hand to tap Johnny on the shoulder, but I get in a "Hello, Johnny," before Adair can connect.

Johnny turns around at the sound of his name. "Well," he says, drawing out the word as he flashes me a smile, "Cantor Gold, right? Didn't know you hang around this saloon."

"Now and then," I say. "Actually, we're here looking for you."

"Yeah? You have a nugget I can use for my column or my radio gig? From what I've heard, you lead an interesting life, Gold." His blue eyes twinkle with a lust for dirt.

"It pays the bills," I say. "Listen—"

But Adair cuts me off. "Before you two start trading life stories, let's get something straight, okay, Mr. Delmore? We're not here to give you nuggets. We're here to get information, information you're going to open up about, so don't bother throwing me that business about the sanctity of the press and protecting your sources."

Stage Door Johnny may be a gossip monger, but like most newshounds he's a smart gossip monger. He gives Adair the once-over, says, "With that spiel, you're either a thug or a cop. And since I know most of the thugs around here, that leaves cop." Looking at me now, he says, "Didn't peg you as the type to hang around with a cop, Gold."

"Not my usual choice of chum," I say, "but Sergeant Adair and I have a once-in-a-lifetime mutual interest."

"And you figure I know something about that mutual interest." He gives that his flashiest Broadway smile. "Well, maybe if you tell me what this mutual interest is all about, I might be able to help. Always happy to lend a hand to our fine New York City Police Department."

Adair says, "What's your connection to Dave Handy and Adele Perkins?"

Johnny gives that a chuckle. "Now there's a couple of names

I haven't heard in some time."

I say, "And when you heard about them, what did you hear?"

Johnny gives a glad-hand hello to a red-shirted guy passing by, then says, "I can tell you that Dave and the Perkins woman didn't like each other much. Probably still don't."

Adair says, "And why is that?"

"Frankly, I'm not sure," Johnny says, "but it could be that Perkins thought Dave held out on her."

Adair says, "Held out on her how? Money?"

"Or another woman?" I say.

Johnny gives that shrug, says, "Could be either, for all I know. But on the few occasions when I went with Dave to Perkins' art gallery, there were times when the chill between them could've froze my skin off."

Adair says, "And you never knew why? A reporter like you who makes his living digging for dirt? I have a hard time believing you, Mr. Delmore. It's time you come across with the truth."

"The truth? What the hell is that, sergeant?"

"The truth is what I see in front of me, Mr. Delmore, and right now I see a guy too slippery for his own good."

"Maybe your eyes are playing tricks on you, Sergeant Adair. I mean, look around." Johnny waves his arm around the room, nearly bumps the back of his hand against a beefy guy carrying his drink from the bar to a booth. "You see that woman over there in blue jeans and a purple sweater? The one with the red hair who's talking to the guy with the curly black beard? She's a makeup artist. She *made* that beard, Adair. The guy wearing it is her assistant. She set him up with the beard so she could see how it moves when the guy talks or drinks or laughs, how it shapes a face, how it would shape a character in a show she's working on that's set to open at the Shubert next month."

Adair just shrugs, unimpressed.

Johnny doesn't give up. He turns Adair to face another part of the room. "Or how about that guy over there, sergeant," he says, "the bald guy in the checkerboard jacket. He's a set decorator. He's one of the people who makes something made of canvas and glue look like a craggy mountain in the Rockies. Even people way up in the cheap seats would swear it was Pike's Peak, complete with snow on top."

Adair tries to get a word in but Johnny's really on a roll now, spinning Adair in yet another direction. "Look over there, sergeant, at that guy leaning against the bar, the guy with the thick eyeglasses. Looks like a real nebbish, right? Well, he's a stage manager. Once the show opens, the big-name director is yesterday's news. When the curtain goes up, the show belongs to the stage manager. He's the guy who keeps the illusion going, keeps the actors on track, the light cues on time and the scene changes smooth. He keeps the magic going night after night. So, sergeant, truth? What is that? Things and people are not always what they seem." I wonder if Johnny's talking only to Adair or performing for the barflies walking by us, bumping into us. "After all," he says with a flourish, "Shakespeare said all the world's a stage, and all the men and women merely players. For all I know, Dave Handy and Adele Perkins were playing each other, or me."

Or me. "Did either of them ever mention me?" I say.

Johnny's eyes light up again with his lust for dirt. "Listen, Cantor, whatever angle you and the sergeant are working, something tells me there's a great story there, something that could get me space on the front page, maybe even a spot on the television news. I've been looking to spread out from radio, and television is taking over. Every columnist in town is trying to grab a spot. So how about a little quid pro quo, Cantor? You know the game. You give, you get."

"Turn that around," I say. "There may be something in it for Stage Door Johnny, but Johnny Delmore's got to come across first. So I ask you again, did Dave or Adele ever mention me?"

The blue in Johnny's eyes darkens, giving him a hungry look, like a vulture sensing a meal. "As a matter of fact," he says slowly, stretching out the drama, "yeah, your name came up once, the night I brought a Broadway producer's secretary to the Perkins gallery for the opening of a show of some crazy paintings I couldn't make head or tail of. Lotta blobs, if you ask me. Anyway, Dave wanted me to introduce the secretary to Adele, maybe see if Adele could convince the kid to bring the producer down to the Village and throw a little money around, buy some of the art Adele was peddling."

"What's that got to do with me?" I say.

"Nothing. I just remember it as the night that your name came up. It was one of those nights when Dave and Adele could've frozen the air in the room. Y'see, Dave gave Adele a hard time that night about a small clay jar in Adele's office, some antique or other." Johnny gives me a smarmy Cheshire cat grin, and says, "He asked if she bought it or of it was a present from you." Still grinning, he takes a pad and pen from his pocket. "Now, your turn, Gold. What gives? Why are you here with the police asking about an old Punch and Judy story?"

I don't remember seeing a clay jar in Adele's office today, but I do remember giving her one when we still played house. It was an aryballos, a small, round ancient Greek jar with a pinched neck and a broad lip. I picked it up during a heist at an archeological dig outside Athens. Someone two thousand years ago with cash to spare used the aryballos for perfumes or fragrant oils. The little jar was beautifully decorated with an image of Athena, goddess of wisdom. That's how I thought about Adele at the time, a wise woman with a wise eye for talented undiscovered artists. She kept the aryballos on her dresser in that seedy little apartment in Greenwich Village. I guess she didn't want it in her fancier new digs once she made some money, but evidently she didn't want to toss it, either, so it went to a less intimate spot: her office.

"Put your pad away, Johnny," I say. "We're still off the record. How did the argument end? What happened to the jar?"

"She threw it at him. The guy ducked just in time," he says with a laugh. "It smashed against the wall behind him. Everyone in the gallery heard it, everyone in the gallery got spooked, and everyone left. Even the artist, whose big night just laid an egg."

The aryballos survived two thousand years through wars, the fall of civilizations, millennia of burial, a tricky trip out of Greece and across the ocean with me, only to be done in by an irate woman. Poor Athena. Her wisdom did her no good.

Adair jumps back in. "Okay, so Handy and the Perkins woman hated each other, and maybe Gold was part of the reason. But what came of it? Dave Handy used to be a hotshot, but now he's cold coffee. Any idea who brought him down, Delmore? Was it Adele Perkins?"

Johnny gives it a thought, his eyes narrowing and his head tilting to one side and then the other. "Could be," he says while waving to the woman in the yellow dress as she crosses the room, and I step out of the way of a guy carrying a beer. Coming back into the conversation, Johnny says, "I mean, I never knew Adele Perkins all that well, but she didn't strike me as a weak sister. I wouldn't want to get on her bad side. The dame's got claws. A real killer instinct. Okay, Gold. Now it really is your turn. Or maybe it's yours, Sergeant Adair. I told you all I know about the Dave and Adele drama. It's time you two fork over with what's behind all this."

A cop's natural loathing for the press is all over Adair. He pulls his fedora down low with a sharp tug, says, "Nothing you need to know, Mr. Delmore. C'mon, Gold. Let's go."

"Just a minute, Adair," I say. An idea runs around in my head, a dicey idea, one that Adair will hate, an idea that risks Sig Loreale's wrath, but maybe an idea whose time has come. Maybe it's time to shine a light into the woodwork and see what vermin crawl out. "Okay, Johnny, get your pen and pad ready, here's your chance to make it to the front page. But you're going to leave my name out of the story, and you're gonna owe me. You'll owe me big if I ever call in the favor. Deal?"

"That's always the game, isn't it?" he says, the Broadway wiseacre at his slickest.

I light a smoke, make the guy sweat a little. Hell, I've lived in the Theater District long enough to know how to milk a performance. After a showy exhale, I say, "I'm sure you know about the killing of Dominic Angeli."

Johnny says, "So who doesn't? Been all over the papers. Television and radio too. Old-time mobster gets whacked. Now that's a story."

"Did you know he had a daughter?"

"Mmm . . . yeah. The guy was secretive, kept his family out of the picture, but yeah, I seem to remember something or other about a daughter. Why?" He's got that vulture's glint again. "She do in Daddy?"

"Her name was Edie, and she's dead. Murdered last night, stuffed into a burlap sack and dumped into the shed on an East River pier."

The look on his face is something between shocked and giddy. It's the shocked part that says, "How the hell did this stay off the police scanners? Nobody at the paper—" He stops short, looks at me like he doesn't know whether to be afraid of me or shake my hand. "Someone's got the cops by the balls. Someone you know, Gold, right? Oh boy, don't hold out on me now."

"That's all you get," I say. "You know how to dig for dirt, well, go dig. Go be an ace reporter, be something more than just Stage Door Johnny. And then pay up on the deal and tell me everything you dig up."

Outside, Adair grabs my arm, says, "You've got more nerve than brain, Gold. That was a helluva play." But he's smiling when he says it. "Well, maybe it'll work out. Maybe breaking the story will shake things up."

"That's the general idea," I say.

"And if it doesn't work, you'll be dead. Mr. Loreale will see to that."

"Or whoever's hunting me. Either way, Adair, the New York City police department will finally be rid of me, which should make every cop in town very happy."

"We'll bring flowers to your funeral."

He's chuckling and I'm barely smiling when we hear a

scream from inside Goody's.

A mob's suddenly running out of the place, beer mugs and cocktails dropped on the sidewalk, coats and jackets flung hastily around shoulders. People yelling, faces contorted in shock and fear. Adair and I have to push our way through the mob to get back inside the saloon.

When we're finally inside, the room's silent except for what's playing on the juke, Fats Domino rocking "Ain't That A Shame." The saloon's empty except for Stage Door Johnny face up on the floor, his eyes open with the shock of sudden and painful death, his blood spreading around him.

There's a square of white on his chest. Seeing it makes my every nerve stand up and sting like hot wires under my flesh.

It's another note. This one's written on a bar napkin. I can't stop my fingers from shaking when I reach to pick it up, but Adair holds me back. "Don't touch it, Gold. Maybe we'll get lucky this time and the killer left prints."

"I doubt it," I say.

"So do I, but you never know. Maybe he got sloppy in the crowded bar."

Adair takes his handkerchief from his pocket, picks up the note, opens it. We both read it:

> IT DOESN'T MATTER WHO YOU
> TALK TO, CANTOR. YOU CAN'T
> WIN. FEELING PAIN YET?

Chapter Fifteen

Pain? I've gone from stinging nerves to feeling numb, the kind of numb that crawls up my bones and eats my marrow. The kind of numb that feels no pain and every pain, but I can't do anything about it because it paralyzes me. I can barely breathe. I can barely hear that Fats Domino song on the juke, still singing his bit about shame and blame.

The song's abruptly gone. Fats quits singing in the middle of a note. The room goes deadly quiet. Adair's by the jukebox, the plug in his hand. He drops it to the floor and mumbles something I can't make out as he walks back to me.

Adair takes my arm, says, "Maybe you oughta sit down."

He means well, but the touch of a cop's hand on me shakes me back to myself. "I'm okay," I say, and loose my arm from Adair's grip. My ability to speak still feels choked in my throat, but I manage to force out, "Someone must've got Johnny in the back."

"Yeah, looks like it," Adair says.

"The place was pretty loud," I say, my head and throat starting to clear. "The noise must've muffled the shot, or maybe the killer had a silencer."

Adair says, "Or the guy was knifed."

I nod, think, yeah, that's probably it. The saloon was packed. People walked around, talked in groups, walked back and forth across the room from the bar to the booths. People bumped into other people, bumped into Johnny. It was the perfect setup for a fast, quiet knife in the back.

I get the shivers again; my hunter was here, followed me here. Maybe he was the guy who walked by me with a beer. But I can't forget what Vivienne said, about a woman being as deadly as a man. So maybe the hunter was the woman in the yellow dress, the woman who stood next to Johnny at the bar, and walked by him later as she crossed the room.

The hunter took a risk showing up here, risked my recognition. But I remember Johnny's spiel about things and people not being what they seem. In a room full of magic makers, a room full of people whose job it is to fool your eyes, my hunter could be one of the people who know how to hide inside the make-believe of greasepaint and fake hair.

Adair says, "I need a phone."

"There's probably one behind the bar," I say.

We cross the room to the bar, which a few minutes ago was loud with people living colorful lives. It's now quiet as a tomb. Stage Door Johnny's tomb. I barely knew the guy, a guy who never did me any harm, a guy who's dead just because he spoke to me. I get the shakes again.

We find the phone behind the bar, but we also find a guy quivering like a mound of gelatin on the floor. I recognize him. He owns the place. Hank Goodman, known to all as Goody.

I help him up while Adair phones his precinct, asks for a police doc, a homicide photographer, and the coroner's boys to take the body.

"C'mon, Goody," I say, "it's all over. The killer wouldn't hang around. There's no one here but you, me, and Sergeant Adair."

I help him up, his bar towel slipping from his shoulder onto the floor, his white apron stretched across his bulk. He gives me a look of thanks through worried eyes, then says, "I . . . I know you, don't I? Y'been in here before, yeah?"

"Sure, now and then," I say. "My name's Cantor Gold. I live in the neighborhood. Listen, I think we could both use a drink.

Mind if I pour ourselves a couple?"

"Be my guest," he says, leaning heavily against the bar. "Make mine a double of whatever y'drinkin'."

I pour us two hefty dollops of Chivas.

Adair, off the phone, says to Goody, "You the bartender?"

"I own the place," he says. "Name's Hank Goodman, but everyone calls me Goody." He takes the glass of scotch from me, his hand shaking, then downs the double whiskey in one long swallow. It seems to give him his spine back, at least enough of it to keep him standing.

Adair says, "Did you see what happened? Maybe see whoever killed Delmore?"

Goody shakes his head, says, "Nah, I just heard someone scream, heard 'em holler somethin' like *Oh my god*, and then everyone started runnin' outta the place. I couldn't get out from behind the bar fast enough, and I didn't know if maybe the killer was still around, so I hid here behind the bar."

I say, "Look, I know the place was jammed, but you've been around for a long time, Goody. You know everyone who comes in here, right?"

"Oh yeah," he says, his pride in his popular bar getting the better of his fear. "I know 'em all. Even the new kids just off the bus from the sticks with big dreams about Broadway. They all come here, they all become regulars."

"So, besides me and Sergeant Adair, did you see anyone here you didn't recognize? Someone who didn't belong?"

Goody scratches at his graying stubble, says, "Hard to say. There's always new people, y'know. New today, regulars tomorra."

It's time to widen the crowd. "I know this is a backstage joint, Goody, but any actors ever come in here?"

"Sure, from time to time."

"You know an actor named Mel Burns?"

"The guy with the pretty face? Hell yeah."

"Was he in here today?"

"Not that I seen him," he says with a shrug.

"What if he changed his face?" I say. "You know, fooled

around with stage makeup to disguise himself. Would you recognize him?"

Goody pours himself another drink, downs it, says, "Huh, can't say that I would. These actor types can really fool ya, y'know. I wouldn't know my own mother if they went to work on her with their makeup and fake hair."

Our chitchat's interrupted by the arrival of the photographer, the police doc, two guys in white from the coroner's office, and a couple of uniformed cops. Adair greets them, fills them in on the situation, tells the doc that Johnny's been dead maybe fifteen minutes, "At least, that's when we heard someone scream. We got back in here and saw Delmore lying here, dead."

We all stand around while the photographer snaps detailed photos of Stage Door Johnny on the barroom floor. The flashbulbs light Johnny up in their gruesome glare, the whites of his eyes glossy and bright as wet paint.

When the photographer's done, one of the uniformed cops draws the chalk line around the body, and then the doc takes over. He takes his time checking Johnny's eyes, his skin, his temperature, giving the corpse a thorough going over. The doc then asks the coroner's crew to help turn the body over, bring the guy's back into view.

We all see the blood oozing from Johnny's back, staining his brown suit jacket with death's dark blotch. The smell of death rises from him, too, the sour perfume of a body surrendering all dignity to that grimmest of grim reapers, murder.

Adair says, "Knifed, doc?"

"Looks like it," the doc says. "I'll know more about the weapon after the autopsy, but yeah, looks like the guy was knifed once, hard, and then the weapon pulled out. Based on how fast he died, I'd say the knife went in pretty deep." The doc circles the stabbed area with his finger. "Got him in the lung, maybe more. The poor guy never stood a chance."

Johnny's been on the floor at least a half hour by the time the doc packs up his bag and gets out of the way to let the coroner's boys load the corpse onto a stretcher and carry him out. The two uniformed cops leave too.

Adair and the doc are exchanging a few last words when another guy walks in, a handsome, sandy haired guy of about thirty whose narrow brown eyes, rat's eyes, always seem to be on the lookout for the main chance. His getup of a belted black-and-white houndstooth sports jacket over a bright yellow shirt and black trousers is a little too flashy for my taste. When he takes off his hat, a snap-brim black trilby, his hair's combed so neat it's still damp, like he just got out of the shower.

I know the guy. His name's Danny Bell. The guy's a lightfinger, a good one. He pulled off some nice lifts until his brains got a little too smart for his own good and he tripped himself up, got caught with jewelry that was too hot to move. The bust earned him a stretch in Sing Sing.

I'm surprised to see him here, but when he waves to Goody and says, "Hi, Pop," I think my head might snap off my neck. "What's going on?" he says. "What's the story with the cops outside loading a stiff? Somebody drop dead? And where is everybody?" Before I can even digest that he's called Goody *Pop*, he spots me, says, "Cantor? Hey, you look like you just swallowed a rock. Surprised to see me?"

"You might say that. But if I had to choose, I guess the idea that Goody's your father wins the surprise prize. You don't even have his last name."

"Bell's my middle name," he says. "It's was my mom's maiden name, may she rest in peace. Anyway, I like the sound of Danny Bell. Has a ring to it, yeah?" He smirks at his own joke.

I try not to gag. "By the way," I say, "when did you get out?"

"A month ago," he says. "Feels good to be free, y'know?" He looks at Adair, says, "And who the hell are you?"

Adair takes his badge from his pants pocket, shows it to Danny, and introduces himself. "Sergeant Liam Adair. Just what were you in for, Mr. Bell?"

Danny gives that a snicker, says, "Ask Cantor."

"Some jewelry burned his hands," I say.

Adair says, "It figures you two would know each other." He

couldn't sound any more disgusted if he drank sour milk.

Danny says, "Sure, Cantor and I go back a ways, sergeant." He says it with a wink at me, then leaves us and goes to the bar where Goody's downing another drink. "You okay, Pop?"

"Yeah, sure, I'm fine. I'm getting too old for so much excitement, I guess. I never had a murder in my place before and never want to again."

"A murder? Here? No kidding," Danny says and puts his arm around Goody. "So sorry, Pop. I'm just glad you're okay. So who bought it?"

"That newspaper fella," Goody says. "Stage Door Johnny. Took a knife in the back, the cops say."

Danny says, "Anyone see who got him?"

Goody shakes his head as if the weight of it is almost too heavy to carry. "Nope. Scary to think the killer's still out there. I don't want no killer to come back here."

"Maybe you should hire some help here, Pop. Like you say, you're not getting any younger, and if there's ever any trouble again it couldn't hurt to have someone else around. I'd love to help you out, but . . ." He finishes with a shrug.

"Yeah, I know," Goody says. "You ain't allowed, not with that felony rap. Seems a pity. A guy pays his debt but can't even work in his family's saloon."

Danny says, "Tell it to the New York State Liquor Authority."

"I did," Goody says. "They gave me the bum's rush."

Adair looks like he's heard all he can stand of this family melodrama. "Let's get outta here, Gold."

For once in my life, I agree with a cop.

Chapter Sixteen

Adair goes his way, I go mine, glad to be rid of each other for a while.

So I head home, walk the few blocks through the Theater District back to my place. It's a little after six-thirty, daylight darkening into the neighborhood's neon dusk. The streets are crowded with people heading home or on their way to grab a drink and dinner before an eight o'clock show.

People walk by me, brush by me, even bump into me, events so common on New York's crowded streets I usually pay no attention. But tonight I'm all attention. The face of every passerby, every brush of a sleeve, every bump against my elbow, feels like a threat. Here in my city, in my own neighborhood, where I always stride the streets with the comfortable swagger of someone who has every right to be here despite what the Law and the straight-backs think, I swagger less tonight, cringe more. I can live with threats to my life and limb; hell, I live with that in my racket every day. But someone wants to grind me down, take away what I've fought for all my life—my place in the human crowd—and that cuts deeper than any bullet or knife that might find me.

By the time I get off the elevator in my building I'm tense as a stretched rubber band, dreading the possibility of finding another note tucked under my door.

There isn't one.

A shower, a quick sandwich, and a change of clothes into a light gray suit, dark brown shirt, and a gray and red-flecked tie, restores me enough for another attempt to pick at the knot in the rope tightening around me. Tonight's tool to pick that knot is money, lots of it, taken from the safe behind an early Picasso on my bedroom wall. I stash the cash in my billfold in the inside pocket of my suit jacket.

An hour later, I knock on the door of a fourth-floor apartment on East Thirty-Second Street, way over by the East River. The door's opened only halfway by a woman who wears her extra few pounds well in a classy black satin dress and whose wise blue eyes seem mildly surprised to see me. Not unhappy, just surprised. Her name's Miriam Fine, and she's the hostess of the card room inside. In addition to monitoring the door, she serves the drinks, empties the ashtrays of the players, handles the buy-in cash, pays out the wins, and collects the losses. Her brothers Sam and Harry run the game. It's Sam's apartment.

Smiling, Miriam says, "Cantor Gold," and opens the door more fully to let me in. "Good to have you back."

"Miss me?"

"Missed your money," she says with a laugh so charming it could probably coax the silver fillings from my teeth.

She takes my cap and coat. I walk into the large living room. The room's smoky from the cigarettes and cigars of the dozen players at two round tables. Low-hanging ceiling lamps illuminate each table, leaving the rest of the living room in shadow, the darkness broken up by streetlight coming through the Venetian blinds.

I don't know all the players at the tables, but I know a few. I get a wave from Charlie Shaw, a poker maven who winters in Vegas; get a nod from Loretta Rossi, who doesn't mind losing thousands because she's got millions more to throw away; and get a slick grin from Mel Burns.

Miriam says, "It's still a two hundred dollar buy-in, Cantor."

"As long as I can sit at Mel's table."

"Think you can take him? He's really sharp tonight."

"Maybe I can beat him at his own game."

Miriam's no fool. Her smile might be friendly, but her eyes drill deep into me. "What are you after tonight, Cantor? It's not Mel's money."

"I'll take what I can get. Here's your two hundred for the buy-in, Miriam, and five hundred to keep me in chips. Now how about a chair."

She waits for the current hand to finish up, then gets a chair from the extras lined up against a wall. I nod for her to place it opposite Mel. I want to watch his eyes. I'm not interested in catching his tell—when he blinks or squints or looks at his watch—to beat his hand and take his money. He's a sharp enough player to stifle those. I want to catch his moods.

I sit down. Loretta Rossi is on my left. Her diamond bracelet is an intentionally glittering distraction that's never distracted other players from beating her at cards. On my right is a guy I don't know, a tall thin Negro whose light blue suit is so well-tailored it could probably walk around by itself. Sam Fine's the dealer, seated to Loretta's left.

The harsh overhead light isn't especially kind to everyone's faces, finding every line, every whiskey blotch, every glazed or bloodshot eye. Except for Mel. There isn't a light on this earth that doesn't love his pretty face.

Miriam places the five hundred bucks' worth of chips in front of me and an ashtray at my side. She asks if I'm still drinking Chivas scotch, neat. The woman knows how to keep a customer.

Sam says, "Say hello to Cantor Gold, ladies and gentlemen. Some of you know her, some of you don't. Her cash is always welcome."

Everyone nods. Some mumble their hellos. Mel says, "Quite a coincidence, you showing up tonight, Cantor."

"It's no coincidence," I say. "It's Thursday night. This is where you've always done your card playing on Thursdays."

"Well, like I told you yesterday, I've been working on some new strategies. You're going to have to keep up, Cantor, if you want to take me."

"Play the cards you're dealt, Mel. Just play the cards."

Miriam places a tumbler of scotch next to my ashtray. I take a swallow, light up a smoke, ante up while Sam deals around the table.

My hand's weak, a pair of fives. Even taking three cards doesn't help. I fold.

Mel's still in. So's the Negro, whose name turns out to be James Rolands. Ethel Stein, a doctor's wife from Brooklyn, is still in, but Buck Langstrom, a guy from Wyoming in town for business he's cagey about, folds. So does Eddie "EeeZee" Zhang, a gambler who also runs a Mah-Jongg room in Chinatown.

The play's between Loretta, Rolands, Ethel Stein, and Mel. Unless Loretta's got a good hand, she's on her way to losing the bundle she always loses, staying in after several raises. Rolands eventually folds; so does Ethel. Loretta is Mel's for the taking. He does. He's kept his eyes on her diamond bracelet, watching how it flashes with every move of her wrist. No doubt he's memorized its movements as professionally as he memorizes lines in a script.

I watch Mel through the next couple of hours of play, watch how he handles the cards, how he picks them up, fans them, slips them around in his hand. I watch how he looks at the other players, how he reads them, how he reads me. I watch him when he wins, watch him when he loses. He wins big pots, loses small ones.

It doesn't take me long to figure two things about Mel: he's a strategy player, a good one, the kind of player who gauges the odds of every deal and every player's tossed cards, and he has good hands, handles the cards as if they're extensions of his fingers. He knows the feel of the cards, and the cards know him.

Sam, the dealer, calls for a break in the action. The players at our table stand up. Some stretch. EeeZee Zhang and Buck Langstrom linger by the window with their cigars. Ethel Stein makes her way to the bathroom. Rolands and Loretta sit down again and chat over cigarettes and whiskey. Miriam empties ashtrays. Sam goes to the kitchen.

Mel hustles me over to a corner of the room. With a Broadway smile and the smooth-voice treatment, he says, "What are you really doing here, Cantor? You're playing like you don't give a damn. But you're eyeing me so much that if I didn't know better I might think you want a date." If his grin gets any wider, its wattage could light up the whole neighborhood.

But the grin's tight around the edges, not the smile of a guy at ease with a little banter at a friendly card game. It seems my strategy of unsettling Mel is working as well as his strategy of winning at cards.

I say, "You've got a suspicious mind, Mel."

"With good reason," he says. "First you show up at the ad agency asking about Edie. Now you show up here. You stalking me?"

"Is that what it feels like?"

"Yeah, that's what it feels like. So what's your story, Cantor. If this is still about Edie, I don't have another damn thing to say. She and I were washed up a long time ago."

"Yeah, so she said. But listen, your name came up today at Goody's. You know Danny Bell?"

His shrug's as tight as his grin. "Met him a few times at the bar. We're not exactly old pals, so why would he ask about me? I hardly know the guy."

"You know he's Goody's son?"

"Really? No, I didn't know. Huh, how about that. But why would a guy I've said hello to maybe three times talk about me?"

"He didn't. Goody mentioned you. He said you know enough about stage makeup to disguise yourself if you want to."

"Sure, I'm an actor," he says. It comes across with a practiced nonchalance meant to telegraph two things: that he's not put off by my disconnected questions, and that he's as good as any Broadway idol or Hollywood star. He's failing at both. "So, yeah," he says, "I know all about stage makeup. But why would

149

Goody mention it? Never figured Goody would talk about me at all." The great actor can't seem to hide the trace of bitterness at being overlooked by the Broadway crowd.

The players at the other table take a break now, too. The dealer, Harry Fine, stops by to give me a hello, then goes off to get a drink. The other players mill around, smoking, drinking, stretching their arms and limbering up their fingers.

I see Sam Fine come back from the kitchen. He'll call our table back soon, so I can't play this slow game with Mel much longer, can't just inch my way toward getting him to show his hand. It's time to turn over a card. "Edie's dead," I say.

I can't tell whether Mel's staring at me or looking through me. His baby blues don't move, don't blink, until he says, "And you think it's got something to do with me?"

"Does it?"

"Why should it?"

"Don't you want to know how she died?"

"And I bet you're gonna tell me."

"Beaten bad, stuffed into a burlap sack, and dumped in a shed by the East River."

He says nothing, just gives me that stare again, that piercing stare that might be an expression of horror or might be a performance to hide his guilt.

I press again. "And oh yeah, there was some excitement at Goody's late this afternoon. Stage Door Johnny took a knife in the back. He's dead too. It'll probably show up on the eleven o'clock news."

This time there's a glint in Mel's eyes and a hint of a smile at the corner of his mouth that gives me the creeps. "The sonuvabitch never gave me a mention in his column," he says. "I don't give a damn that he's dead." He takes a pack of smokes and a book of matches from his shirt pocket, shakes out a cigarette and puts it between his lips. He strikes a match, says, "I bet a lot of people wanted him dead."

"Yeah, I guess a Broadway gossip columnist makes a lot of enemies," I say. "Any ideas about who might've done it? Or maybe you saw it."

The lit match stops halfway to the cigarette, the flame wavering under Mel's breath. He finally lights up, puffs the cigarette, exhales a line of smoke in my face. "You're fishing for something, Cantor. Why don't you just come right out and say it."

"All right: did you kill Johnny Delmore? That was his real name, by the way. And what about Edie and her father? Did you kill them too?"

Shock takes over his pretty face, but I can't tell whether he's shocked that I'd think he could be a killer or shocked that I found him out. But the shock drains away, and here comes the high-wattage smile again. He punctuates it with a buddy-buddy clap on my shoulder. "What the hell are you talking about, Cantor? C'mon, let's play cards."

I'm no longer in the mood.

Outside, Thirty-Second Street is pretty quiet, which is typical of this residential neighborhood at this hour. Lights are still on in a lot of the windows of the apartment houses and remaining brownstones that line the block, but other windows are dark, the apartments' occupants turned in for the night. Only a few cars drive by, some slowly, their drivers looking for parking spaces. One car, a flashy two-tone '52 Mercury coupe shimmers its black and yellow paint job as it passes under a street lamp. It rolls more slowly than the rest of the light traffic, which gives me that queasy feeling. But the driver rolls down his window, asks if I'm leaving my parking spot. I shake my head no, wave him away. My stomach unknots when he drives off. He's not my stalker.

I lean against my car, light a smoke, take some time to think.

The guy in the Mercury wasn't Mel, who couldn't have gotten down here before I did anyway. So Mel's still in the mix of possible murderers, possible stalkers who want me ground to dust.

I still can't figure why Mel might hate me enough to put me

through the wringer. Except for card games and the occasional hello in our neighborhood, we don't run in the same circles. I can't recall ever doing him dirty. Hell, I wouldn't even know what to do him dirty about. And I really can't figure how he'd know about my connection to Vivienne or which paintings of hers to steal.

But none of that wipes out the possibility that Mel has his own reasons to knock me down. He sure got real testy real fast under my questions. Maybe he's made it his business to know a lot about me and who I pal around with, who I do business with. One thing I know, though, one thing that was clear tonight: the way Mel handles the cards, the way they move under his touch, he's got the hands to slip Vivienne's front door lock without a sound.

But so does Handy Dave Handy. I saw it in the way he flips those shot glasses, never breaking even one, always pulling off perfect landings on his pyramid of glasses. If he can do that, he can pick a lock fast and on the quiet.

And though Dave's no art expert, his connection to Adele might lead him to my dealings, maybe even to my clients, even to Vivienne.

But what about Adele? Yeah, she'd probably be able to get a line on Vivienne's paintings, but does she have the hand skills to pick a lock and pull off a heist? Well, maybe. I know she can frame and unframe some pretty delicate artwork and never pull a thread of canvas or clip a chip of paint.

And now there's that late entry into the horse race, Danny Bell. I know he's got the hands to pull off some very neat heists, even if his last one was a bust. As far as I know, though, unlike Mel, Dave, and Adele, Danny has no connection to Edie Angeli. But a guy like Danny, a longtime player on my side of the Law, maybe he had a handshake with *Dominic* Angeli, maybe he was one of the few people who could get to him.

Edie would know. Edie might remember seeing Danny around the mansion. Maybe that's why Edie's dead.

None of this answers the big questions: who's after me and

why? It's like having someone jump onto my back and hold on tight but no matter how I twist and turn I can't see their face. I feel them, though, feel their weight like lead pressing down on me, feel their arms wrapped tight around me, crushing me, squeezing the air out of me.

"Cantor!"

The call of my name yanks me out of the suffocating bleakness of my thoughts.

It's Mel. He's walking out of the apartment building and coming toward me. He waves his arm, says, "Hey!" but a crushing wallop to the back of my head silences whatever else he says. It silences everything.

Something that sounds like shrieks slices into my head. The shrieks slice and slice until they cut into the core of my brain and force slits of light into my eyes. The light is red, and it doesn't stay still. It moves, it slides away and slides around again.

I hear, "Wake up, Gold, you're not dead," and feel shaken by the shoulders. My eyes open a little more. I see a thick, tough face, Sergeant Adair's face, smeared by the swirling red light. Adair looms over me, grabs my arm, helps me up from the pavement.

I trip over something. It's Mel. There's blood all over his shirt. A crumpled white paper sticks out of his mouth. I catch a few letters of what's written on the paper: *ntor*. The last four letters of my name.

I reach for it, but the world spins as I bend down. Adair steadies me. "Don't touch that note, Gold. You don't want your prints on it, not with another dead body at your feet and a bullet in the guy's chest."

Adair leans me against my car, then carefully pulls the note from Mel's mouth by the paper's edge, flicks it open and shows it to me:

I'M HAVING SUCH FUN, CANTOR. AND

WHAT LUCK THAT YOUR FRIEND
SHOWED UP!

Adair says, "That last bit, that second sentence, it's in the same crude style, but looks like it was written fast, on the spur of the moment. You see that?"

I don't know if it's because the knock to my head is making everything jumpy, but that exclamation point seems to be jumping up and down, laughing at me.

Chapter Seventeen

My head's starting to clear. I see more lights on in apartments. I see people leaning out of windows. I hear people chattering, hear TV shows through open windows, hear old standards competing with rock-'n'-roll on radios. A crowd of rubberneckers is held back by uniformed cops. Everything and everyone is smeared red from the twirling lights of cop cars and the coroner's meat wagon.

Mel would love it, a starring role in New York's longest running show: Murder on the Pavement.

Adair says, "Someone heard a shot and called it in."

"They see the shooter?"

"Sure. He was a tall guy in a short coat, or a hefty dame in a shapeless dress, or maybe it was a teenage kid in a black jacket, or maybe the kid wore a suit and tie. Y'know, the usual mishmash. So what's the coincidence of you and Burns lying on the same sidewalk?" Adair's slipped into grill patter, that no-nonsense way cops have of asking a simple question.

"Friendly game of cards. I already told you that's how I knew Mel."

Adair looks up at the apartment building, then back to me. Through a smile that has no humor but plenty of sneer, he says, "Anyone up there want the guy dead?"

The last thing I want is for Adair to raid the card room,

question everyone, bust them for gambling, and ruin Miriam and her brothers' racket.

Adair reads my face, says, "Look, I'm not gonna bust up the card room. That's not my beat."

I say, "Nobody up there's a killer, sergeant. Gamblers, sure, but not killers." I don't mention EeZee Zhang, the Mah-Jongg king of Chinatown. He's been known to plug a guy or two. But as far as I know, he had no beef with Mel, and he has no reason to have beef with me. "And I'd appreciate it if you didn't report the address to the vice squad either."

Adair gives me a look that says he'll remember the favor, puts it into his back pocket for another time. Then he nods, says, "I gotta check your gun, Gold. Hand it over."

"What for? I didn't shoot the guy."

"But you're the only one the killer is playing deadly games with. Someone's throwing bodies at you, Gold, and the deaths get weirder and weirder, like they're trying to drive you nuts."

There's nothing weird about a murder by gunshot, except for what Adair's hinting at about Mel's killing.

It gives me the willies to hand over my gun to a cop, but I don't want to give Adair an excuse to haul me in for resisting, so I pull my gun from my rig and give it to him.

Adair checks the chambers: a bullet's missing. He sniffs the gun. "Recently fired," he says. "The shooter's a real jokester."

And the joke's on me. Whoever killed Mel knocked me out first, pulled my gun from my rig, shot Mel, and put the gun back in the rig—fingerprints carefully wiped, of course. The only prints on the gun now are mine. If my head didn't hurt so bad, I'd laugh.

Adair says, "I gotta take your gun for a ballistics check, Gold." He pockets my .38.

"And you'll give it back."

"You're kidding me, right? Something tells me you don't have a license and the gun's not registered."

"Then how do you know it's mine, sergeant?"

"Very funny."

Adair offers me a lift, but riding in a cop car has never held any appeal, so I drive myself home. It's not easy. The blow to my head was one helluva wallop. The attacker must've used a lead sap. The pain's settled down to a dull ache, but the lights of the city and the traffic lights at street corners won't stay still. By the time I park the Buick at my place, my eyes feel like they've been stretched out of their sockets and flung in every direction.

When the elevator opens on my floor, all I want is a stiff drink followed by a hard fall into my cozy bed. What I get is Adele at my apartment door.

"Cantor! Oh, I'm glad I caught you. I was about to write you a note. Look, I know it's late, but I was out with friends at a jazz joint in the neighborhood, so I thought I'd drop by. I didn't want to leave things the way we did at the gallery this afternoon." There's enough drama in her voice and dark eyes for a Shakespearean tragedy.

"You could've just called me on the phone," I say. "Or maybe not. Maybe when we split, you tore up my telephone number."

"Maybe I should've tossed your number," she teases, "but I didn't. In fact, I almost called you tonight from a booth at the jazz club. But I figured, well, since I'm already in the neighborhood . . ." She finishes with a shrug and a sophisticated smile.

The jazz joint evening explains Adele's outfit: billowy black coat, black V-necked sweater, slim black slacks, black leather saddle-pouch bag hanging from her shoulder, and a long necklace of oddly shaped amber stones, another of her avant garde adornments. Adele can pull it off, though. She pulls the whole outfit off. She gives Beat style a dark glamour. The loose knot of hair at her neck with stray strands against her face, her thick black eyeliner, and blood-red lipstick add a Gothic touch. Adele couldn't look anymore lethal if she'd been wielding a knife.

Or a gun. My gun. Sure, Adele's outfit would fit right in at a jazz joint, but all that black could also hide her in the night. Maybe she wasn't at a jazz joint at all. Maybe she's been tailing me—or had me tailed—all day, and caught me at Thirty-Second Street. She could've sapped me and plugged Mel and still got a good head start to my place while I was out cold. For all I know, Adele Perkins came to my door tonight to slip another mocking note under it.

But I'm too tired and too wrung out to play deadly emotional games with Adele. "Look," I say, "okay, we're friends again. You're right, though, it's late, almost midnight, and I've had a tough day. So if it's okay by you, how about if we make up another time."

"Now, Cantor," she says, and runs her fingers along the lapel of my coat, "since when have you ever turned a lady down for a drink? Especially when she's sure you're planning to pour one for yourself anyway. You look like you need it." Her fingers slide up to my cheek.

"One drink," I say, immediately regretting it.

Inside my apartment, I hang up my coat in the hall closet, toss my cap on the closet shelf, but drape Adele's coat over the hall table in a not-so-subtle hint that her stay will be brief. I turn on a lamp in the living room and go to the credenza to pour our drinks. "What's your pleasure?" I say.

Adele says, "Whatever you're having is fine."

I pour two tumblers of Chivas, give one to Adele, who's made herself comfortable on the couch, her saddle-pouch bag beside her. She's kicked her shoes off, drawn her legs up under her. "You've redecorated since I've been here," she says. "I like the red couch and club chairs. Very bold. Very you. The art on the walls is first-rate too. How much of it did you steal?"

"That's a rude question, Adele." I give Adele her drink, then sit across from her in one of the club chairs. "That's like asking you how many people did you kill." No sense beating about the bush.

If Adele's annoyed by my question, she hides it behind a sideways smile that seems to enjoy the idea of being a killer. "If you're going to ask me horrid questions," she says, "you could at least show a little courage and not retreat to the safety of that great big chair. You're not the type to hide, Cantor."

I'm tired, too tired to play verbal hide-and-seek with Adele, but I don't dare let her get the upper hand. So okay, I'll play for a while, because she's right, I'm not the type to hide. And it's time to stop my stalker from hiding too. It's time to drag whoever it is into the light, even if it's only the light of one lamp in my living room.

I sit down on the couch, take a pull on my scotch, keep my eyes on Adele, who's eyeing me over the rim of her glass.

The whiskey gives me a needed kick, enough to start my little game with the possibly deadly woman facing me at the other end of my couch.

I say, "So, here's another horrid question, Adele. Why did you throw the aryballos I gave you at Dave Handy?"

It's Adele who's doing the hiding now, or at least she tries to by turning her face away. "Did Dave tell you about that?" she says.

"No, a dead man told me."

Adele keeps her face turned away while she fumbles with the chunky amber stone clasp of her leather bag. She can't do it one-handed. Frustrated, she finally puts down her drink on the side table and uses two hands to open the clasp. She reaches inside the bag.

I sit up straighter, ready to slam her hand if it comes out of that bag with a knife or a gun.

Adele pulls out a pack of cigarettes and a book of matches. She lights a smoke, takes a deep draw, then a long exhale before she looks at me again, her dark eyes pinning me like a butterfly to a wall. "Is this the second time today you're accusing me of murder, Cantor?"

"Am I? And don't you want to know who's the dead man who told me about your athletics with the aryballos? Anyway, it's already tomorrow."

"So just who am I supposed to have killed this time?"

"Take your pick," I say. "The guy who told me about the aryballos? Or the guy I mistakenly thought might've been the killer."

Adele picks up her drink again, takes a long sip, then puts the glass down, holds it in her lap. The gesture's meant to be a casual one, but Adele's knuckles are white. She's clutching the glass hard. "You might not believe this, Cantor, but I loved that little jar. I hated myself for smashing it."

"Then why did you?"

"Heat of the moment," she says with a shrug. "You know how passionate I can be. Remember, Cantor?" She's uncurls one leg, rubs her toes against my thigh.

"Sure, I remember," I say, not thrilled that my voice has gone shaky. I slide her foot away. "And the memory is swell. Maybe it will rock me to sleep tonight. But right now I'm more interested in the chilly here and now than our hot nights of yesterday."

"They were hot, weren't they," she says, giving it the sultry treatment. "You know, there were lots of times I was tempted to call you up just to get some of those hot nights back." She finishes her drink, kills her cigarette in the glass, then slides herself to my side of the couch. "Maybe I should have called, because you're right, Cantor, the here and now is chilly. My day's been chilly ever since you left the gallery this afternoon."

"I didn't leave, Adele. You threw me out."

"Because you accused me of being a murderer."

"Well, are you?"

Her hand slides up my thigh. She whispers in my ear, "If that's what you want me to be."

I've heard some pretty inviting lines in my life, but never a more titillating one. Not because I want Adele to be a murderer, but because of the shiver passing through her body at the idea of being one.

I start to wonder whether the way to get to the truth is through Adele's body, not her mind. A mind as brilliant as hers could tangle the truth into a thousand knots, but her body might be more honest. It always was.

Or maybe it's my own body that's talking. My mouth certainly isn't; it's busy tasting Adele.

I don't love this woman. I'm not even sure if I like her. But right now, how I feel about Adele isn't as high on my list as how she feels about me. The way she's writhing beneath me on the couch, kissing me ferociously one minute, stroking me gently the next, it's as if she can't make up her mind if she likes me, loves me, or hates me. Hates me seems to be winning; at least, it has more heat, more lust. More danger.

She pulls my suit jacket back off my shoulders, then smiles a gorgeously wicked smile when she sees my empty gun rig. "Too bad your toy's gone," she says.

"I've got others," I say.

"Do you want to shoot me?"

"Do you think I have a reason to?"

She answers with a long, deep kiss, then pulls away, licks her lips. "Let's not kill each other, Cantor," she says.

"At least not yet," I say.

"No, at least not yet."

I wake up on the floor. Adele's beside me. She's asleep. We're both naked. Light from the living room lamp slides across her breasts, brushes her belly, glides along my hand as I move to let my fingers take some more pleasure of her body. But I stop just as my hand gets close to her flesh. I have a more strategic use for my hand right now, while Adele is asleep.

I get up from the floor carefully, quietly, and take Adele's bag from the couch. I open it, search the bag for a mocking note she might've planned to slip under my door before I unexpectedly showed up and ruined her joke.

There's no note, but among the usual female supply of lipstick, a gold compact, a comb, tissues, a wallet, and loose change is a large pad of paper and a pen.

I flip through the pad. The paper is pretty standard, plain white sheets, just like the notes from my stalker. But of the nearly

161

two million people in the borough of Manhattan, probably one million have the same or similar pads of plain white paper.

I scan pages of Adele's notes about various artists, dates of events, scribbled telephone numbers, grocery lists—the sort of business and personal notes one makes at the spur of the moment when something comes up, an idea comes to mind, or someone mentions something you want to remember. None of the notes are in block letters. But they wouldn't be. Adele had no reason to disguise her own scribblings.

When we met earlier in the hallway outside my door, she said she was going to leave me a note. Maybe she really did mean a note telling me she'd dropped by. Maybe it's the truth. Or maybe I interrupted her before she wrote in those clumsy letters the latest threat to my health and welfare.

Right now, there's only one truth in front of me: Adele's naked body asleep on my Persian carpet.

I lower myself beside her again, let my fingers resume what they'd planned.

Adele wakes a little, says my name.

"Do you hate me, Adele?" I say.

"Deeply," she says.

The front door buzzer drills into my head, ruining a perfectly good sleep. My eyes squint open, sliced by the light through the living room window.

Adele stirs too. We're still on the floor. We're still naked.

The insistent buzzing finally rousts us. Adele grabs her clothes from the floor and makes a dash for my bedroom. I slip into my trousers, throw on my shirt, toss my skivvies under a couch cushion, and go barefoot to the door.

When I open it, Danny Bell greets me with a smile wide and garish as a Times Square billboard. His eyes, though, are narrow and penetrating, like the eyes of a rat who hasn't eaten in days. The rest of him is no comforting sight either. The combination of his black-and-white herringbone tweed coat open to reveal a dark blue suit and a peach-color shirt could cross your eyes. His black snap brim trilby gives him the cocky dignity of a brat expelled from reform school. "Sleeping late, Cantor?" he says.

"What time is it? And what are you doing here, Danny?"

"It's a little after ten," he says with a big show of pushing up the sleeve of his coat and checking his flashy watch. "Listen, after I saw you yesterday at my Pop's place, I got an idea I think you'll go for."

"Is that so. What kind of idea? Your last idea didn't work out too well."

"Aren't you gonna ask me in? The hallway's not really the place to discuss business."

I'd rather choke to death than talk business with Danny Bell this morning, but the sooner I let him in, the sooner I can get him out.

I cock my head for him to come inside. "Let's talk in the kitchen," I say. "I'll make some coffee." And hide Danny from Adele. Frankly, I'm not in the mood for that particular conversation.

In the kitchen, I measure out coffee in the basket, fill the percolator with water, and put it on the stove. Danny takes off his coat, drapes it over a chair, but keeps his hat on when he sits himself down at my kitchen table. He lights a cigarette, exhales, and gives me the big grin again. I wish he'd stop. Looking at it is exhausting. "I think you're gonna like what I have in mind, Cantor," he says.

"I already don't like it. I don't like anything before I've had my morning coffee."

"But I know you like money. I mean, look at the way you live. Nice apartment, a new car all the time, custom-made silk suits. You don't live life on the cheap, Cantor. And neither do I. That's why we're a sweet combination for a little something I've worked out."

"Does Goody know you're here, Danny?"

"Nah. Listen, I love the guy, I really do. Couldn't ask for a better Pop. And it was fun growing up around all those show biz

163

people. Slick crowd. But my Pop and I don't see eye to eye on how I should live my life. I gotta do things my way, y'know? I bet you know what I'm talking about, Cantor. You go your own way, too, no matter what, no matter who you've got to elbow out of the way."

If the guy's trying to get on my good side, he's botching the job. "Let's get something straight, Danny: the only people I elbow out of the way are people who try to elbow me into jail or oblivion."

"Okay, sure, whatever you say." His shrug is stiff, tense. His shoulders snap up so high they nearly slap his ears. But he hasn't taken those rat's eyes off me. "The fact is, Cantor, you can't live your swell life without cash, lots of it, and I'm here to bring you a deal that could net us both armfuls of the stuff."

"And just why do you need me? You're a damn good lifter, Danny, despite burning your fingers on that jewelry heist, which, if you remember, I told you was a lousy mark. Some jobs are better left alone, and that was one of them. After you got nabbed, I couldn't help you out."

"But y'see?" he says through a fast, hard pull on his smoke. "That's just it. I've got the talent, but you've got the brains. *And* you've got the contacts and know-how we need for this job."

I need coffee so bad by now my hand shakes when I pour a mug for myself and one for Danny. The first sip, though, of the strong black stuff kicks me into gear. The second sip sharpens my morning brain enough to sense booby traps in the story Danny's peddling. "Listen, Danny, maybe I'm the perfect partner, or maybe I'm the perfect patsy. So maybe you'd just better lay it out. What do you want my brains and know-how for?"

He takes a gulp of coffee, gives me that smile again. Its wattage threatens to give me a headache. "It's gonna be a delicate lift," he says, "but I can handle it. What I need is someone who can work out, y'know, the logistics of the heist and where to peddle the potato. That person is you, Cantor."

"And just what is this delicate lift and where is it supposed to happen?"

Danny takes another pull on his smoke, exhales through his teeth. He pushes his trilby back on his head, leaving blond tufts to stick out like a street-corner teenager's. "You're gonna love this, Cantor," he says. "The whole job's right up your alley. It's a painting, a small one of Baccho or Bacchi or something like that I think they call it. It's coming in—"

"Hold it right there," I say. "You're talking about the fifteenth-century painting of Bacchus some workmen found last year in an attic in Rome and that the Italian government is loaning for a show at the most important museum in the city." Vivienne's museum. Vivienne's department. Vivienne's show. The show she wore a classy blue sheath for to coax cash from Mister Moneybags over drinks.

"Yeah, that's the one," Danny says. "It's coming in next week to Idlewild Airport. An armored truck is gonna pick it up and drive it from the airport to the museum."

"And you know this how, Danny?" Every inch of my skin prickles. It's a feeling I get when I sense something's not kosher. Danny Bell reaching way out of his patch ain't kosher.

His smile's changed from Times Square slick to back-alley sly. "I, uh . . . let's just say I've been keeping my ears open a little wider since I got out of the joint. Look, Cantor, I can lift the potato; you can unload it. You have the contacts. You deal with people who come across with the big money, right? So whaddya say? We can—wait a minute—" Danny's enthusiasm drops fast as a stripper's last veil. He's not smiling anymore. He's frowning. "Unless you're already planning to do the job yourself," he says. "Oh boy, listen Cantor, you're a good lightfinger, everyone knows that. But I'm better. Everyone knows that too. Or at least they used to know it. That jewelry bust that sent me up the river? It killed my name on the street. I can't get a fence to talk to me. Even Mom Sheinbaum's been giving me the cold shoulder, and she was always happy to move my stuff because she could count on me for quality goods. So y'see, pulling off this job could set me up again, but I need your help to do it. C'mon, Cantor, help a pal out."

There's begging in Danny's eyes, but there's pushy challenge too. The first is pitiful, the second smug. Neither of them endears him to me. "That stretch upstate didn't teach you a thing, did it, Danny," I say. "And what I said about that loused-up jewelry job still hasn't sunk in: there are some jobs you walk away from. That was one of them, and so's this one." But I don't tell him why I'll walk from the tempting fruit of the Bacchus. I don't tell him it's because I won't stab Vivienne in the back. I'll steal for her, but I won't steal from her.

He says, "What's the matter with you, Cantor? It's a peaches-and-cream setup, sweet and smooth. The Baccho, Bacchi, whatever you call it, it's coming in on—"

"I know when, where, and how it's coming in, Danny. Which is why I'm leaving it alone. It's not as peaches-and-cream as you think. That truck will be spiked. There'll be enough armed guards in it to end the Cold War and start a hot one."

Danny fidgets in his chair like the seat's suddenly crawling with ants. He stubs out his smoke, pushes his hat forward to a rakish angle, and gets up, snarling, "Thanks for nothin', Cantor. This is the second time you've turned me down for a sweet job, in case you've forgotten. You think you're too classy for me, huh?" He grabs his coat, the flashy herringbone tweed scraping across my vision as Danny scrams out of the kitchen. A minute later I hear the apartment door slam.

I'm glad to be rid of the guy, but his idea of heisting the Bacchus gnaws at me.

I take a last gulp of coffee, head back to the living room. The room's empty. Adele must still be hiding in the bedroom. I'll rescue her after I make a phone call, one she doesn't need to hear.

I dial the number. After two rings, I hear the velvety voice say, "European paintings department, Vivienne Parkhurst Trent here."

"Good morning, Vivienne," I say. "Listen, put me on the security detail collecting the Bacchus from Idlewild."

"How the—how in the world do you know about that?"

She can't see my smile through the phone, but maybe she

can hear it. "How long have you known me, Vivienne?"

"Touché," she says. I'm sure she's smiling, too, when she says it. "But because I do know you, Cantor, I'd be a fool to let you anywhere near that painting."

"Listen, I don't want to steal the Bacchus. I want to protect it. The security guys at the airport and on the truck won't know the things I know about protecting a stash. I need to be on the tarmac the minute that plane lands."

There's a brief silence at her end, then, "Let me see what I can do."

We hang up. I head to the bedroom, happy to tell Adele she can come out now.

Or maybe we'll both stay there, play around again, this time on my big, comfortable bed. She can keep trying to convince me that she hates me. She tried last night with every ferocious kiss. I enjoyed every bite.

I give a light rap on the door, say, "Adele, honey," not bothering to hide the craving in my voice. I open the door and walk in.

The bedroom's empty. Adele must've left on the quiet while I was jabbering with Danny in the kitchen.

I need another cup of coffee, maybe spike it with a dash of scotch to quiet my frustrated libido. On my way back through the living room to the kitchen, I spot something that flattens my fleshly cravings but twists my gut: a patch of white near the front door.

Chapter Eighteen

I pick up the note. I can't worry about leaving fingerprints. Even Adair would figure, hell, the note's in my apartment, it would have my prints.

Before I even open the note, wild ideas wrestle with each other in my head. The easiest one to deal with thinks maybe Dave Handy came by this morning before he went to work at the bar, slid the note under my door. The other two ideas are scarier: Danny had it in his pocket all the time and left it on his way out of my apartment after I didn't play ball with his harebrained plans, or Adele wrote it while I was in the kitchen with Danny, dropped it on her way out the door. This last idea is the toughest to take.

I unfold the paper. Those grotesque letters hit me like knuckles to the throat:

> TOO BAD ABOUT YOUR
> PAL ON 32ND STREET.
> DID YOU SLEEP WELL,
> CANTOR? I HOPE SO.
> YOU'LL NEED YOUR ENERGY
> BECAUSE THE GAME'S NOT
> OVER. NOT UNTIL YOU'RE
> ON YOUR KNEES. NOT

UNTIL YOU'RE NOTHING.
GET THE PICTURE?

My throat's so dry it feels like I've swallowed the Sahara. My insides are having a hard time staying inside. But it's my mind and soul that are fighting a savage war: terror at being stalked, terror of the unseen threat that clings to me, eats at me. But all of that slams up against my anger at the coward who wants to toss me off the world.

Yeah, my stalker's that crummiest of crumbs, a coward. Only a coward hides behind teases and taunts. If someone thinks I did them dirty, then say so to my face, have it out with me. They might even be right. Maybe I owe them an apology, or cash, or a favor, or a kiss. What I don't owe them, what I won't give up to anyone, is my life or how I live it.

My phone's ringing when I get out of the shower. It's Adair.

He says, "Lab report came back. Just as we figured, no usable prints on any of the notes. The paper was wiped, left nothing but smudges. And except for the bar napkin, the paper is all standard stuff that anybody could have. The ink, too. So no help there. And no prints on your gun except yours. Ballistics confirm that it's the weapon used to kill Birnbaum, or Burns, or whatever he called himself. Can't these show business people be truthful about anything?"

"Glad you're still calling it my gun, sergeant. But it's okay if you don't give it back."

He laughs at that, a quiet wiseacre laugh because he gets my drift: with the ballistics report on that gun, a gun that's now in police custody and labeled as mine, I can't use it again. I can't use the gun to put a bullet in some guy's knee even if he's coming at me with a shotgun and two thugs to help, not unless I want to take a hard-time vacation courtesy of the City or State of New York.

I move the conversation along. "By the way, Adair, another

note showed up this morning at my door. Same weird lettering, same threats. The writer even admits—well, sort of sideways—that they did the Burns killing."

"Hold onto that note until I see you. It'll go into the evidence file. Listen, Gold, I get it that it's gotta be pretty hairy, having some character play hide-and-seek with you and killing people along the way. How are you holding up?"

"Sergeant Adair, I didn't know you cared."

"Who said anything about caring? I just need you not to buckle until we catch this character. So I need you alive." He hangs up.

First time I've smiled all morning.

The crowd at Pete's is having lunch when I arrive about a quarter to noon. The place has the deliciously mingled aromas of burgers, pastrami, mustard, fries, and always coffee.

Doris pours me a mug as I take a seat at the counter. "Nice suit, Cantor. Dark green looks good on you. You're lookin' a little tired, though. Rough night?"

"Depends on what you mean by rough," I say with a wink.

She gives that a chirpy laugh, then puts down the coffee pot and leans across the counter. "Listen, I saw on the news last night about what happened to Stage Door Johnny. I gotta tell you, Cantor, I feel lousy about me sending you and that cop over to Goody's and all. I've stayed clear of the doings of your life all these years, but I'm not some naïve ninny. I know there's a shady side to you, and I don't judge how you live your life or make your cash. But I don't need cops askin' me questions."

"Doris, I'd never put you in danger, not from cops or anyone else. That's a promise. If I ever thought I did, I'll buy my coffee somewhere else."

"Over my dead body," she says. "You're my best tipper." Then she pinches my cheek. "So what'll you have?"

"Couple of eggs over easy on a bialy. And keep the coffee coming."

Doris disappears into the kitchen. While I wait for my food, I drink my coffee and take a careful look around the luncheonette, see if anyone's paying more attention to me than I'd like. Neither Dave, nor Adele, nor Danny are here, but I haven't ruled out a dark horse. I can't rule out anything. I can't rule out anyone in the City of New York.

So I look around, catch a guy reading a newspaper, a couple of young fellas yakking about auditions, a guy with his horn case on his lap while he eats his eggs, and a neighbor who touches the brim of his fedora in greeting then stuffs his chubby cheeks with a burger on a bun. It's the usual sort of Theater District and jazz club crowd. My crowd.

I let myself relax a little, but only a little when my food comes.

Sig's dining room is the sort of place where meals are an obligation, not a joy. Unlike Vivienne's dining room, which advertises taste as well as power, Sig's dining room, a long gray-walled room with a sleek but massive sharp-cornered walnut table and great big walnut chairs that look as welcoming guillotines, is a heavy-fisted statement of pure power. Even the sunlight in the widows seems to ask permission to come in.

Sig's having lunch when I arrive. As usual, he's impeccably dressed, this time in a double-breasted black suit, his white shirt crisp, the knot of his black-and-gray striped tie centered precisely below his Adam's apple. But I'm not here to talk to Sig, I'm here to talk to his guest, Mom Sheinbaum, who's making the most of her guest status by filling her plate with samples of all the fare on the table.

Mom's in one of her sensible cotton dresses, this one a pale green that makes her look like a large wave rolling in on the ocean on a sunny day.

Sig invites me to sit down and have lunch.

"No thanks," I say, "I just had a bite." I sit down anyway.

"Are you here to discuss the murder that took place with

your gun last night on East Thirty-Second Street?" The words roll out through Sig's fleshy lips in his slow, terrifying rhythm that sets my teeth on edge. "I understand Sergeant Adair is handling that."

Sig's not my stalker, but he's just as creepy. My stalker's been making it his or her business to know what I do. Sig Loreale makes it his business to know what everybody does. If you're a shoemaker, a plumber, a thief, or a cop, he'll know your every move, just like he knows that I was on East Thirty-Second Street when Mel Burns took a bullet with my gun, and that Adair's the cop on the case.

"Adair's looking into it, yeah," I say.

"Then what brings you here, Cantor," he says. "It is in your interest that you and Sergeant Adair make progress."

"Depends what you call progress, Sig. Look, I'm here to talk to Mom, ask her a few questions."

Mom stops slathering mustard on her sandwich of roast beef on rye. She looks at me across the table like she's getting ready to spank me. "Dragging me into your mess again, Cantor? I had to leave my house and stay here just to avoid the trouble you bring me."

I'm in no mood for her scolding. "Listen, Mom, the sooner I find whoever's causing the trouble," I say, "the sooner you can go home to Second Avenue and the sooner you can be rid of me. Do we have a deal?"

She shrugs, says, "So ask your questions already," and finishes slathering the mustard. Then she takes a hefty bite.

"What do you know about Danny Bell?" I say.

Mom takes her time chewing the roast beef sandwich, all the time keeping her eyes on me while she tosses my question around in her head. After she finally swallows the mouthful, she says, "Danny Bell?"—her Lower East Side dialect renders his name as *Dennih*—"That *nudnik*? He's dead to me. He's been dead to me since he loused up that jewelry job. A real shame, too, 'cause he always brought me better goods. But that jewelry heist was a stinker, a real prison job. That's when I knew that, sure, the guy's got great hands, but a *narishe kop*, a stupid head. Can't do business with a stupid head."

I start, "How about—?"

Sig cuts me off. "Just a moment, Cantor. I believe Mr. Bell is the son of that Broadway bartender, a Mr. Goodman. Am I correct?"

"Yeah, that's the guy."

"And there was an incident at Mr. Goodman's bar yesterday. That gossip peddler, Stage Door Johnny, was killed." Sig pronounces Johnny's moniker as if it's barely worth the use of his lips and tongue. "Knifed, I understand," he says. "So, Cantor, are you telling us this may have something to do with the situation I've instructed you and Sergeant Adair to take care of?"

"Not may have," I say. "It definitely has something to do with it. Whether Danny Bell was involved in killing Johnny, or was just an innocent latecomer to the scene, well, that's the question, isn't it. And maybe that makes him the subject of those other questions: like did he kill Dominic and Edie Angeli, and did he do last night's murder of Mel Burns on Thirty-Second Street. And is it Danny who's orchestrating this elaborate murder spree and leaving taunting notes behind just to get to me?"

Sig's been finishing the last of his salad while I've been making my spiel. He takes up his napkin slowly, dabs his mouth just as slowly, then says, "Does Mr. Bell have a reason to want to get to you?"

"Could be," I say, "but I don't have enough to pin it down. But Mom might have something for me."

She shrugs while she chews.

"Listen, Mom," I say, "I know Danny's approached you since he's been out of the joint."

"And I told him he can just take his business elsewhere."

"Did he mention a new heist he's planning?"

She waves the idea away, says, "I never even gave him a chance. I don't want to hear anything the *shmegege* has to say."

"That must've made Danny mad."

"Yeah, good and mad," she says with a laugh. "He thought

173

he could get away with callin' me all sortsa names. But then I tell him to know his place when he talks to me. He got the picture. What's so funny?"

My own little chortle has all the humor of a bad joke, but still a joke. "It was a picture he was planning to heist. Listen, did he mention me at all when he tried to bring the idea to you?"

"Mention you? No. Wait—yeah, he did mention you, but not about any job. He said to tell you hello if I see you."

"That's it? Just to tell me hello?"

"Yop, that's it. He said it over his shoulder on his way outta my place."

As parting shots go, that one makes me edgy, the way those taunting notes make me edgy. "One more question, Mom. That phone call threatening you, the call with the disguised voice. Could it have been Danny on the phone?"

Another big bite of the sandwich, another long chew, and then a shrug. "Coulda been," she says. "I dunno. Maybe, maybe not. Like I been tellin' you, the voice was fake."

"Or maybe a woman's voice?"

Another shrug. "Coulda been, I guess. Got a particular woman in mind?"

"You know anyone named Adele Perkins?"

"Never heard of her."

Sig says, "You appear to be just fishing, Cantor."

"I am, Sig. I'm fishing for the shark that's out to devour me."

Outside Sig's building, I linger on the sidewalk while I mull over Danny telling Mom to give me a hello. Something about it is all wrong, the kind of wrong that makes my nerve ends stand up and complain.

I light a smoke, try to settle down from that edgy feeling. The nicotine soothes a bit, but it doesn't help answer the question about why Danny gave Mom a message that was about as sincere as a gigolo's smile.

I'm tangled up thinking about it when I get jostled by a

passersby. Yeah, yeah, I know, it's not kosher in New York to just stand around on the sidewalk and clog up the pedestrian flow.

And then I realize that the jostler left a little something behind, a slip of paper in my hand.

Reading those contorted letters brings that edgy feeling back, but this time with a murderous bite:

SIG LOREALE CAN'T HELP YOU, CANTOR. NO ONE CAN HELP YOU. THE KILLING'S NOT OVER. THE NEXT ONE WILL CRUSH YOUR HEART. AND THEN I'LL CRUSH YOU.

I search the street, fast, think I see a familiar form in a billowy black coat among the crowd heading toward the subway at the corner. I push my way through the throng.

I wish I was surprised, but I'm not surprised. I should've known because of all she showed me yesterday at her gallery and last night at my place. The heat of Adele's passion and the heat of her anger are the same heat: both fueled by hatred of me.

I'm almost at her. I push past angry citizens giving me the stink-eye or the middle finger or a "Hey! Watch where you're goin'!" All I think about is what I'll do when I get her, when I grab Adele and spin her around to face me. I wonder what I'll see on her face, in her eyes. I wonder what my rage will let me do.

I'm steps away and getting closer, straining my legs, stretching out my arms until they hurt in their sockets. My fingers finally grab a handful of her billowy coat. She screams, I spin her around. Her terrified face glares at me.

It's not Adele.

I let her go. She scrams, fast. So do a bunch of other people who want no part of whatever nasty business they think I'm up to.

I search more faces on the street, study the faces of men in fedoras and homburgs, look at women in hats: flowery hats, flat little hats, or elegant hats with veils. I don't recognize anyone, but I can't shake the feeling that among all these strangers on Fortieth Street is a shark who's laughing while they sharpen their teeth.

Chapter Nineteen

The next one will crush your heart. The killer's words pound like a hammer in my head as I push into the phone booth at the corner of Fortieth Street and Sixth Avenue. Inside the booth my hand shakes when I drop a dime into the coin slot. I force the shaking to stop. I'll be damned if I'll let my stalker get the better of me. I won't let the SOB break me. I don't dare.

I dial Vivienne's office at the museum. Her phone rings, keeps ringing. She can't still be at lunch; it's almost a quarter to three in the afternoon. Maybe she's in one of the galleries. Maybe she's in a meeting. Maybe—

I'm gone from the booth so fast I'm not even sure I've hung up the phone.

Traffic in the uptown lanes on Fifth Avenue is hell. The city keeps talking about doing something about it, like closing the street to everything except cabs and busses, or making Fifth Avenue one-way downtown and Madison Avenue one-way uptown. But talking about is all the pols at City Hall ever do.

Meantime, I lean on my horn and scuttle around traffic as if the Buick is a spider with eight legs. It's the sort of driving that might draw the attention of cops, an outcome I usually try to avoid. Right now, though, if a cop car stops me I'll tell them to leave their siren on and make it snappy uptown to prevent a murder. But there's never a cop around when you need one.

By the time I park across the street from the museum my nerves are standing up and complaining again. My legs aren't any happier with me either when I run up the broad front stairway like I'm on fire.

Inside, I barrel through the enormous Great Hall, nearly knock the eyeglasses off a stuffy guy in tweeds reading a museum guide, and scare a crowd of Ladies' Club types who've been standing around tut-tutting over a classical Greek statue of a near naked Amazon.

My legs want to divorce me again as I bound up the long Grand Staircase to the second floor. I move so fast my breeze blows through the curly hair of a little girl who's holding her mother's hand as she pretends she's a princess descending the stately marble stairs of her imaginary palace. I'm so fast through the European paintings galleries that the Medieval and Renaissance paintings are just blurs of color.

I finally arrive at the discreet door to the curatorial offices. As always, it's locked. Only museum personnel have keys.

There's just a sparse crowd in the gallery: a few black-clad art students seriously examining every brushstroke of Rembrandt's *Aristotle with the Bust of Homer*, and another clutch of Ladies' Club gals breezing by a group of Franz Hals's Dutch barroom scenes. The art school hipsters pay no attention to me. The club ladies look at me with everything from shock to disgust to wondering whether to call the authorities or just get away from me fast.

I don't give them the chance to bother with any of it. I slide my case of lockpicks from the inside pocket of my suit jacket, and after quick, silent work, my body blocking the action from the ladies' view, I slip the lock and disappear through the door. No doubt the ladies are relieved that I'm out of their sight, though they may withdraw their memberships to the museum.

The hallway's quiet as I make my way to Vivienne's office at the far end. All I hear through the doors of the other offices are normal sounds of the museum's business: someone's talking on a phone about acquiring a Medieval icon from a hesitant owner; someone's typing; a few people are having a meeting about staff schedules. None of the voices in the meeting are Vivienne's. When I arrive at Vivienne's door, there's no sound at all, which scares me.

I forget about doing the polite thing and just open the door and walk in. There's no one at Vivienne's elegant eighteenth-century mahogany desk. I see no one in the spacious office, its gray-green walls bathed in sunlight from the Fifth Avenue windows and covered in masterpieces big and small by European masters. Some of the pictures trigger memories of my adventures in heisting them.

But my jaw's tight, my gut's twisting, as I look for signs of struggle or spots of blood. I can't get rid of the sickening feeling that my stalker got here ahead of me to make good on the threat to crush my heart by doing murder.

"Did you forget how to knock?"

It takes a minute for my insides to settle back into place when I hear Vivienne's voice come at me from behind the open door. I turn around, see her closing a drawer of a file cabinet. In her slender navy-blue skirt, creamy silk blouse, and pearls at her neck, she's as elegant as royalty and as sensual as a pinup. It's that irresistible combination of her twin bloodlines again: the high-born Parkhurst sophistication and the gutter-born Trent spice.

"No, I didn't forget how to knock," I say. "I just didn't want to waste the time. Listen, Vivienne. You can't stay here. You can't go home either."

Her eyes narrow, her hands go to her hips, and her attitude turns stiff as steel. "I've already told you, Cantor, I won't be chased from my own home, and that goes for my office here at the museum, too. I've worked too hard to earn it."

"That won't work this time, Vivienne. The threat to you isn't abstract anymore. It's real and it's coming for you. It may already be on its way. In fact, I was afraid it got here ahead of me."

She goes to her desk, opens a drawer, takes out her handbag, opens it and takes out the nickel-plated .22 she'd carried with her the night of our aborted dinner and her date for drinks with Mr. Moneybags. "If I'd been sitting at my desk when you burst in without knocking, well, you might've had a hard time walking for a while."

Her adventuress act is seductive. I'd love it at any other time, in any other place, especially a bedroom. But that's a daydream for another day. "Vivienne, I know you're a great shot, but you'd make a lousy assassin. Before you could even open the drawer, you'd be dead. You'd never get to take out your handbag. Your little .22 would still be asleep inside. Listen to me; get your coat and hat, take your gun with you, and let's get out of here."

Her steely attitude melts. Her face pales. Her special beauty of elegance and gutter-blood is tainted by fear. "Just where am I supposed to go?"

"Let me worry about that." I use the phone on Vivienne's desk to call Judson.

When I get him on the line, he says, "I wondered where you'd gotten to. Haven't been able to reach you for a couple of days. By the way, Red Drogan called, said he asked around the docks if anyone saw activity at Pier 32 the night Edie Angeli was killed."

"And?"

"And mostly nothing, though one tug boater thought he saw someone pushing a wheelbarrow with something in it. He didn't think much about it since the city sometimes uses that empty pier shed to store maintenance supplies. Crews show up at all hours hauling all kinds of stuff."

"Interesting. Listen, here's what I need you to do, Judson, and do it fast."

Ten minutes later, Vivienne and I are inside the museum's service dock, a tucked-away spot at the side of the building where trucks and vans deliver or pick up works of art. Two big guys, art handlers in gray overalls whose hands can handle a porcelain teacup with the delicacy of tatting lace, look us over. One of them says, "We didn't get a work order for anything comin' in or goin' out, Miss Parkhurst Trent."

"Oh, quite right," she says. "This is just a test run for a possible acquisition. No need to trouble you with it, Bobby, unless it really happens."

Bobby shrugs and goes back to jabbering with his pal.

I give Vivienne a nod and a sideways smile of appreciation for her quick thinking. Her position at the museum has its privileges, and she just used one of them. As far as Bobby is concerned, he never saw Vivienne today, and I simply don't exist.

After another few minutes, Judson arrives driving a green delivery truck. He pulls up close to the loading door, giving me and Vivienne cover when we get into the back of the truck, unseen by anyone from the street.

I don't ask Judson how he secured the truck so fast or who he got it from. Judson has a set of connections I'm smart enough to take advantage of but not stupid enough to question.

He drives like an upright citizen, staying with the flow of traffic, making clean stops at every red light and stop sign. Unlike my drive uptown, this trip is better off without attracting the eyeballs of prowling cops.

We finally pull into the basement garage of an old apartment building on West Fifty-Seventh Street. Judson says, "A buddy of mine has a place here. He's out of town until next week."

Vivienne says, "Nice of him to leave you his key."

Judson and I say nothing about that.

We take the service elevator from the basement garage to the ninth floor, then walk through the service hall into the main corridor, a respectable if dusty hallway with a worn rose-colored carpet and walls that try hard to be beige in a respectable if dusty building.

At the door to apartment 903, Judson nods and I take out my lockpicks.

Vivienne rolls her eyes, says, "I should've known you wouldn't need a key. I guess there's no point in getting my locks changed at home anytime soon."

"Keeping me out isn't the problem, Vivienne," I say, more or less under my breath.

I open the door to apartment 903.

It's a studio apartment with blue floral wallpaper that's still holding its own but tired enough to look forward to the day it's allowed to peel.

The nubby brown sofa in the middle of the room is no spring chicken either.

"It's a sofa bed," Judson says, and opens it, revealing crumpled sheets, which probably haven't been changed in weeks. "Uh, I think clean sheets are in the closet."

The rest of the room isn't any more inviting. Crumbs crunch in the gray shag carpet. There's a television set in a scratched mahogany cabinet, a bulbous dark green chair with a textured leaf pattern popular before the war, and a torchiere with a chipped glass shade standing in the corner opposite the two windows, their Venetian blinds partially closed.

Vivienne sits down on the sofa, says, "Well, I've seen worse." The woman is full of surprises. Someday I'll have to ask her about it.

Judson points to an arched hall. "The bathroom's through there," he says, then points across the room, "and the kitchen's over there."

Vivienne says, "Just what does your friend do for a living, Judson, that he can reside in such splendid surroundings?"

"This and that," Judson says, shutting down that particular conversation.

I wander into the kitchen. It's clean enough, well-stocked with cooking utensils in the rust-stained white cabinets and drawers. There's nothing much in the refrigerator: a bottle of soured milk, a block of stale cheese, and a package of moldy white bread.

Back in the living room, I note the number on the phone on

the side table next to the sofa, then use the phone to call Doris at Pete's Luncheonette, ask her to put some sandwiches together, a couple of dinners that can be eaten cold or just heated up. "And a container of your good coffee." I tell her Judson will pick it up later. Doris takes the order, doesn't ask questions.

Vivienne says, "I can't hide here forever, Cantor. I have work to do."

"And I've got to keep you alive to do that work. I'm trying to find whoever it is that's making our lives miserable. Frankly, I've had just about enough of the bastard."

"Are you getting close?"

"Maybe. Anyway, I seem to be making him—"

"Or her."

"Yeah, or her." Thoughts of Adele and her anger fly around in my mind. "But yeah, I seem to be making whoever it is antsy. Their threats are coming faster, getting closer, getting nervier. When people get nervy is when they make mistakes. I plan to do all I can to force more of those mistakes. Meantime, you're safe here, Vivienne. Judson will be back later with grub."

"What about clothes? I'll need clean clothes. Maybe I'll call George—"

"Sure, go ahead and call him, let him know you won't be home tonight, but don't tell him where you are. And don't have him come here with clothes. Someone may be watching your house. They could follow George here. So for the time being, Vivienne, just take off your coat and hat and make yourself comfortable. I'll figure something to keep you in clean linens." I say it with a smile.

Judson chuckles.

Vivienne gives us both a schoolmarm's *tsk*, but she takes off her coat and hat.

Judson drives clean again on our way back to the museum. No fancy maneuvers, no sudden stops. He's just a guy driving a delivery truck, like so many in New York, while I'm out of sight in the back.

"Drop me at the museum's service door," I say through the sliding panel to the driver's cab.

"Don't you want me to drop you at your car?"

"Uh-uh. It's better if I come out of the building through the main entrance on Fifth Avenue. If someone tailed me up here, then they saw me go in. I want them to see me coming out."

Judson, keeping his eyes on his lane in Fifth Avenue traffic, nods that he gets the picture.

When we arrive at the museum, I get out of the truck and ring the service door bell. Judson doesn't drive away until art handler Bobby opens the door and I'm inside.

"Miss Parkhurst Trent not with you?" he says with more curiosity than I'd like.

"She's checking a location," I say with a straight face, and make a quick exit up the stairs into the museum.

I find my way through staff hallways and through a door that opens into the Arms and Armor gallery, a big hall decked out to look like Camelot. Medieval armor is mounted on painted steeds as if the knights are still riding them, jousting spears thrust forward, heraldic banners waving. A bunch of schoolkids are dazzled by the spectacle, throwing their imaginations into overdrive: the boys pretend to be knights; the girls either giggle or pretend to be princesses pining for their knights in shining armor. Two little girls, though, take their make-believe in a different direction, striking the poses of the knights. The two girls spark memories of my own childhood and my first trip to this august institution, when Mom Sheinbaum brought me here in my first cab ride, my first trip above Fourteenth Street, my first exposure to the bigger, prettier world I knew right away I'd do anything to live in.

I don't have time for nostalgia, and I make it quick through the Medieval galleries and back through the Great Hall to the Fifth Avenue entrance.

It's almost five o'clock. I'm just one of the crowd spilling out of the museum before it closes for the night. But I linger down the stairs, giving whoever's stalking me a chance to spot me. It's time to get ahead of the chase. It's time to lead it.

Chapter Twenty

I take my time at my car before getting in. I adjust my cap, look at my watch, give whoever's tailing me all the time they need to get a bead on me. I also give myself the time to glance around, see if I can spot the creep. I can't be sure they've even followed me here, but I've survived on the dark side of New York long enough to put my trust in those instincts that keep me alive: like the way my skin prickles when someone's disturbing the air. My skin prickles now.

I get into the Buick's driver's seat, kill time there too. I adjust my rear- and side-view mirrors, use them as eyes in back of my head to have another look around the street. I look at the neighborhood's high society dames stepping out of Fifth Avenue's high-hat apartment buildings, watch them tell their doormen to hail them cabs. I examine the faces of the avenue's well-tailored gentlemen, almost all of them in gray or brown fedoras or homburgs and conservatively cut suits as they get in and out of cabs and limousines. I take a good look at passing pedestrians, delivery guys, governesses pushing fancy baby strollers or holding toddlers' hands. I look at parked cars, see if anyone's inside. I look at traffic, whose slow crawl lets me see who's driving, who's a passenger, and who might be looking at me. I look at all these faces, see a lot of strangers, but I don't see Adele Perkins, or Danny Bell, or

Dave Handy. And yet my skin still prickles.

I drive to Louie's Garage, drive in from Twelfth Avenue, pull into my rented space, and close the garage door. Whoever's interested in my comings and goings will see me go in but they won't see me come out, because they won't see me leave by the back door and disappear into the alleys behind the garage. I'll be damned if I'll lead them to my office. And if my stalker does go into the garage and out the back door, the down-and-outs who populate the alleys will do what they always do to strangers and others who don't belong. It's not pretty.

My walk through the alleys is the usual mixture of greetings here and there from the alley's secretive denizens, accompanied by the soothing whoosh of traffic from Twelfth Avenue, and the waterfront's symphony of ships' horns, buoy bells, and the shouts of dockworkers loading and unloading cargo. It's the first peaceful moment I've had all day.

Inside my office, I'm alone. Judson's out returning the truck and picking up the food order from Doris.

I head into my private office, pull out the bottle of Chivas and a glass from my desk drawer, and pour a hefty dollop. I down it in one swallow.

It's not doing as much as I'd like to soothe my mood, help me get control of my emotions. I need to get out from under the choking grip of feeling watched, waiting for the next murder, waiting for the next taunting note by a stalker who's determined to crush my life.

Why the hell are they after me? If I can figure that, maybe I can figure who's behind it.

I pour another slug of scotch, down this one in one swallow, too, then lean back in my chair and close my eyes. In the darkness behind my eyelids, I take a deep look into my life, visit people I've known or made love to or worked with or did dirty. I'm in a rough racket in a life-and-death world of tough guys and dangerous dames, killers, crooks and cheats of every kind, men and women who gave up trying to fit into the straight-back world or never even bothered. The smart ones know the game, play it as honorably as they can, and accept the occasional slip of the underworld's code. Some, though, are stupid enough to hold grudges. They're the underworld's festering sores, wallowing in the pus of their grievance until the pus finally spews in a violent eruption, forcing a big shot with power, like Sig Loreale, to clean up the mess.

So who's the festering sore coming after me? Whose scab did I rip open?

My mind wanders to Handy Dave, Adele, and Danny. All three have me on their mud list, or at least Adele did, but after last night, maybe she's changed her mind. Hell, after the way we explored each other last night, the way we knew each other's needs, maybe I've changed *my* mind about *her*. Maybe someone who's caressed your body can't kill your body.

Who am I kidding? A long history of spouse- or jealous-lover murders tosses that theory out the window.

I do get a laugh, though, thinking about the sophisticated Adele pushing a wheelbarrow in the dead of night. I wonder where she'd even get one, then figure she might have one stored in the basement or back courtyard of the gallery's building, use it to move sculpture or framing equipment.

Dave and Danny could easily get hold of a wheelbarrow too. Saloons often keep them in their basements to move deliveries of booze.

The Chivas isn't doing a damned thing to help me sort out the who's who of any of that, or settle on a reason why someone wants to destroy me, maybe even kill me. But I know something that stands a better chance of restoring my balance. Something that always settles me down and cleanses my troubled mind.

I fill my glass again and take my drink downstairs to the basement, open the vault, step into my world of beauty and dazzle.

Business has been good lately, lots of deliveries made to clients who've come through with the cash for treasures they hire me to get and don't ask questions of how I get them. So the shelves in the vault aren't as full as they might be, but there's still enough here to satisfy my hungry soul, restore my confidence in what I do and who I am.

The first thing my hand touches is a small, ornate early nineteenth-century round gold box decorated with Egyptian designs in multicolored enamel and a big ruby on top of the lid. I smuggled it out of Rome for a banker here in New York who says he fell in love with it when he saw it in a small museum in Italy and he wants it as a gift for his wife. I think he's lying. I'd lay odds it's for his mistress. In any event, the little lady will have to wait until the guy pays up.

Nearby is a seventeenth-century Russian necklace of tiny pearls and silver beads woven into a delicate silver filigree. According to the daughter of the exiled Russian aristocrat who ran for his life during the revolution of 1917—and who swears the last Tsar's youngest daughter, Anastasia, escaped the murder of her parents and siblings and is still alive—the necklace was immortalized in a now lost painting of the royal family. Well, maybe it was, but the exiled aristocrat and his daughter aren't immortal, so you might say their window of opportunity to pay me is limited.

I drift over to one of the most colorful items still in my possession, though it won't be here in my vault for long. It's a watercolor and ink on paper of the gods Shiva and Parvati by an unknown master in late fifteenth-century India. The image sparkles with color and glows with highlights of silver and gold. The collector in Boston who purchased it, a longtime client who's always been good for the cash, wants me to hold it until she returns next week from a trip to somewhere she didn't mention and I didn't ask.

I could linger here in my vault all day, wallow in the beauty that surrounds me, take delight and have a few laughs remembering some of my more hair-raising escapades to heist them, but I've got a life to live, a life I insist on living, a life these objects bring the kind of cash to that allows me to live my way.

I take a last gulp of my scotch, close the vault, and head back upstairs.

I pour myself another drink, take a swallow, and notice my watch says it's a few minutes after six o'clock. I dial Rosie's number, counting on her habit of going home for dinner between a day in the cab and pulling a night shift if she has nothing else planned.

I luck out. She picks up the phone on the third ring.

After our hellos, I ask her to stop by my office. "If you haven't eaten yet, I'll spot you to dinner."

With a soft but sly laugh, she says, "You're too late, Cantor. I've got a dinner date." There's a subtle trace of satisfaction in her voice, a vestige of her triumph over her hurt that I could return only her lust but not her love.

"My loss," I say. "But can you make a quick delivery? It's too dangerous for me to be seen at the location."

"Dangerous for who?"

"For the woman getting the delivery. Listen, Rosie, I'll make it worth your while. How does a C-note sound?"

She doesn't answer right away, letting me dangle and feel like a heel for throwing money at her. "Sounds about right," she finally says, her delivery flat and dry as pavement. "See you in about twenty minutes."

I spend the time pulling a few things from my stash of clothes in my closet: a couple of white shirts, a pair of black trousers and a pair of brown, a gray overcoat, a few pairs of socks, a handful of underwear—which makes me grin—and a pair of pale blue silk pajamas.

By the time I have it all folded into a paper bag, Rosie's at the alley door.

She steps inside. I have to catch my breath. Rosie's dressed for her dinner date. Her brown coat is open to reveal a pink sheath that accents the best parts of her. Her silvery blond hair peeks out from a brown pillbox hat with a net veil that dips just below her eyes.

Whoever's Rosie's date tonight is a damned lucky woman.

She notices me admiring her but doesn't mention it. She just smiles a satisfied smile, says, "What's the package and where's it going?"

I give her the paper bag of clothes, tell her the address on Fifty-Seventh Street and the apartment number. "And here's your hundred," I say, folding the cash into her hand.

She puts the money into her handbag, but she's not smiling anymore. "Y'know, Cantor, I appreciate the cash you pay me as my cut when I'm part of one of your jobs, and I'm always ready to pull you out of a scrape, like when I picked you up on Seventeenth Street the other night. But this is the last time I take your cash just to be your errand girl. And I'm taking it just to make you feel lousy."

She sashays out the door, and, yeah, I feel pretty lousy.

But not as lousy as someone else thinks I should feel. Someone who thinks I should be ground to dust.

I make another phone call.

Adair says, "You just caught me, Gold. One more minute and you'd have to call me at home, but you can't because you don't have my home number and I wouldn't give it to you in a million years. But I've got *your* home number, and I've been trying to call you for over an hour."

"Then I guess you have something to tell me."

"More like something to show you. Look, I'm hungry. Let's go get a bite to eat."

"Meet me at Pete's. The same place we—"

"Yeah, I remember. The place with the good coffee and the smarty-pants waitress."

Adair's already at a table slurping a bowl of pea soup, a ham sandwich on the side, when I walk in a little after seven. The place is buzzing with a neighborhood crowd grabbing a light bite before their eight o'clock curtain at one of the nearby theaters, or before the first show in one of the clubs. The cigarette and cigar smoke in the air makes everyone look like they've just stepped out of an Impressionist painting, softening even the painted faces of the two has-been showgirls at a table next to the wall.

I stop at the counter, and after I give Doris my order of a pastrami with mustard on rye and a cup of coffee, she leans over the counter, speaks softly. "Your guy picked up your phone order about a half hour ago."

I nod. Doris leans back from the counter and goes to the kitchen with my sandwich order.

I join Adair at the table, say, "So what've you got to show me, sergeant?"

He pulls an envelope from his pocket. It's got his name on it in those weird letters. The envelope's also marked PERSONAL. Adair says, "That *personal* bit is why the desk sergeant didn't open it when some flashy dame walked into the precinct and told him to give this to me. Someone's either getting sloppy, starting to lose their marbles, or they're the slickest player in the city. Takes a lotta nerve to deliver something like this to a cop in his own house."

What the desk sergeant calls flashy someone else might call fashionable, even unconventional. Like Adele. My skin prickles again. "Besides calling her flashy, did the desk sergeant describe the woman who brought the envelope?"

Adair's tough face doesn't wear a snicker well. It makes me want to rub it off his face with a cheese grater. "He called her a boozy floozie wearing bourbon for perfume and in an out-of-style flashy green dress."

That lets out Adele. Still, she could've given some down-and-out dame a few bucks to carry the note, like maybe she gave the kid on West Eighth Street some pocket change to deliver a note when I left her gallery yesterday. Or maybe Adele had nothing to do with either of them. "Let's see it, sergeant."

Adair opens the envelope, pulls out a folded sheet of paper, opens it, and hands it to me.

What's written in those creepy letters makes my skin not only prickle; it burns with a fire that heats deep into my flesh, like being scorched by the air of hell.

WHY WOULD YOU WANT TO HELP
A NO-GOOD LIKE CANTOR GOLD,
SERGEANT ADAIR? LEAVE HER TO
ME. EVEN JAIL'S TOO GOOD FOR
HER.

I say, "I guess I made them mad when they couldn't find me today. So the SOB went after you."

Adair swallows a slurp of his pea soup, then says, "Yeah, you're good at disappearing, Gold. The department's been trying to nail you for years, but somehow you're never where we think you'll be or doing what we're sure you're doing."

I'm not sure if he's complimenting or cutting me.

Doris brings my pastrami on rye and my cup of coffee, then walks away, smart enough to not even pick up so much as a word between me and a cop. On her way back to the counter, she answers a ringing phone in a booth in the back.

I take a bite of my pastrami sandwich, savor its tang when I see Doris come back to our table. "Phone call for you, sergeant. It's your precinct," she says, not happy about it. "How'd they get this number?"

"We're the New York City Police Department," he says, getting up from the table. "We can get any number we want, and a cop always lets his precinct know where he is."

He goes off to the phone booth.

Doris says, "Look, Cantor, you know I always stay out of your business. You're a good customer and you're an okay person in my book. But this is the second time you've been in here with a cop, and that means trouble. I need this job, I can't have—" She stops talking and I stop eating when we see Adair walk back from the phone booth.

His rough face is hard and pale as stone. "They just found the body of the woman who brought the note to the precinct. She was slashed to ribbons. Nothing left of her but sliced flesh and a shredded dress."

Chapter Twenty-One

I used to think of murder as a darkness, a devouring black shadow that sucks up all light. It isn't. Murder is red. Murder is the twirling red light atop cop cars and coroners' wagons, smearing everything with swashes of blood red: the night, the street, the rubberneckers straining past the police line to gawk at the bloody corpse, Adair's face under the brim of his fedora, me. All red.

Dominic Angeli. Edie Angeli. Mel Burns. Stage Door Johnny Delmore. And now this woman lying in a puddle of blood in an alley off Eighth Avenue, down the block from Adair's police precinct. All of them murdered and smeared in red.

Up to now, I figured there was at least a rationality to my stalker's murders. Each victim had a connection to me, even if that connection was thin and sideways, like my connection to Dominic Angeli through Sig Loreale and a shared underworld. But I don't know this woman, at least I don't think so. Her face is so cut up her own mother wouldn't know her. And the killer didn't stop there. Her body's shredded, the skin on her hands cut to the bone.

Whoever did tonight's killing, whoever sliced this woman into a bloody pulp, isn't rational. They've graduated to crazy. Or maybe they always were.

A uniformed cop says to Adair, "The photographer is on his way, sergeant. The coroner's guys had a look at her, though."

Adair says, "Any identification?"

"Nope. Just a five-spot and sixty cents in change in her purse and the usual female stuff, y'know, a lipstick, a compact, those sorta things. No wallet, no driver's license, no nothin'. Someone really wanted to erase this dame. And one of the coroner's boys said it looks like the killer worked fast. He could tell by the slashes."

Adair says to me, "You have any idea who she is, Gold?"

I shake my head no.

The police photographer arrives. Adair and I step out of the way to let him do his grim work. With each flash of his camera as he moves around the body, sections of the woman flicker into view: tangled blond hair matted with blood; chest and stomach and hips mangled in her torn green dress; shredded hosiery on her bloodied legs; one foot shoeless, the other in a cracked patent leather shoe with a broken heel; all of it adding up to . . . no one.

The brutality of her murder makes me sick. Her anonymous death breaks my heart. The craziness of it scares the hell out of me.

Until it doesn't. Until I sense something in this woman's death, brutal and wild as it is, that isn't crazy at all, but a well-thought-out plan to bring me back into the killer's sights. They couldn't find me today, couldn't follow me, so they decided to do something about it. They set up Adair with that note to him, which naturally brought him to me, and brought the two of us to this alley off Eighth Avenue.

My skin prickles again.

I scan the crowd of rubberneckers, look for anyone who's more interested in me than the dead woman. I pick out individual faces: a frightened woman in a feathery hat, the man beside her trying to lead her away; a couple of snickering potato-faced teenagers in leather gang jackets; a tired guy who looks like he just finished a double shift in one of the factories near the river; other men and women exhibiting varying degrees of interest in the murdered woman and the police activity around her. No one's paying particular attention to me, other than a passing glance followed by the disgusted looks I'm used to.

The police photographer finishes taking his pictures. The coroner's crew moves in, loads the woman's body onto a stretcher and carries her to their wagon parked at the Eighth Avenue end of the alley.

Adair says, "I'll make sure the coroner's office does everything they can to get an identification. The killer didn't leave us much, even got rid of her fingerprints, but maybe she had local dental work. Now, that's what I'm going to do, Gold. What are you going to do?"

"I'm going to make your dreams come true, sergeant. At least for a little while."

"Yeah? I don't waste my time dreaming about you, Gold, but if I did, you wouldn't like the ending. So what the hell are you talking about?"

"I'm going to let you arrest me."

The crowd of rubberneckers has thinned now that the grisliest part of the show's over. The remaining bunch gets a kick out of seeing me led in handcuffs to Adair's car, its red light still twirling.

The red light's punctured here and there with the white flash of news cameras. I try to give them my good side.

Adair presses me into the back seat of his car. He gets into the driver's seat and pulls away from the crowd. "Someday this is gonna be real, Gold," he says. "Consider this a rehearsal."

It's a short drive down the block to the precinct. A few newshounds run alongside the car. Adair might think this a rehearsal, but as far as I'm concerned this is the whole show and Adair's just a supporting player.

I give the news crowd a wink and a smile because, hell, I'm the star.

The wink and the smile disappear fast when we walk into the precinct. Instead, I give Adair a sharp stare to get me out of the cuffs.

Now it's Adair who's smiling, taking his time to uncuff me while he enjoys his bit of power over me.

"Show's over, sergeant," I say.

"Yeah, yeah," he says, finally taking the bracelets off. "Listen, I hope you know what you're doing. You think you can actually outsmart whoever's got it in for you? So far they're killing everyone but you, but you know you're the endgame target."

"I'm just trying to stay ahead of the game," I say, "sometimes by being the animal in the shadows, sometimes by being the bait. Tonight it's the shadows."

"Sure, that's your favorite playground, isn't it."

"It has to be," I say. "It's the only way I can make my way through your rotten world without letting too much of the rot find me. Now get me out of here."

He leads me along a hallway to a side door of the precinct. It opens to a courtyard off-limits to the public, where cops park their cars.

Adair says, "Enjoy your freedom, Gold, if you can stay alive to keep it."

A night's worth of freedom is what I bought with my little theatrical in handcuffs. With any luck, my performance convinced my stalker that I'm cooling my heels in a jail cell, not getting out of a cab and walking into the Green Door Club. And even if my stalker didn't actually see me led away in the steel bracelets, the eleven o'clock news and tomorrow morning's papers will take care of it.

Meantime, all I want is to drink in peace in the place where I'm always welcome, where the sweet side of my life ignores the dark side.

The Friday night crowd is warming up when I walk in around nine o'clock. The start-of-the-weekend mood in the place is a tonic, all of us sharing relief from the snares of life: theirs probably from jobs they don't like and where they have to hide their true selves; mine, from being stalked. The Green Door Club provides freedom from whatever haunts or hunts us.

Peg pours me a Chivas as I slide onto a barstool. "You look like you could use a friend," she says.

"You volunteering?" I joke.

"As long as I don't have to stick you in the shower to sober you up," she jokes back. She gives me a wave and a smile as she takes care of a drink order for a couple at the far end of the bar.

I sip my scotch, have a look around the room, see if maybe I can spot that friend Peg and I joked about. A friend just for tonight, a soft friend with a soft heart and a soft body. I see a few lovelies who could fit the bill: a brunette who glitters in purple taffeta, a blonde who knows how to wear a black cocktail dress, a redhead who knows how to carry off a pastel green sheath and whose attitude seems to know about a lot of other things I'd be interested in. But I'm out of luck: all three lovelies are on the dance floor or sharing drinks with some other lucky so-and-so.

The three-piece combo on the bandstand shifts from the mellow ballad "Only You" to a slow and sexy Dinah Washington tune, "Teach Me Tonight." More couples drift onto the dance floor, teaching each other things I wouldn't mind learning.

A woman with a voice smooth and warm as fine brandy says, "I've been watching you from the other end of the bar. Are you alone?"

The voice belongs to a charming brunette with a pixie haircut, blue eyes that beckon, and a sculpted face that cameras probably love. She's wearing a black knit skirt that hugs her like it wants to make love to her, and a pale lavender knit top with a scooped neckline that dares my imagination. If I had to guess, I'd say she's probably a little young for me, but she had to prove she's at least twenty-one to get into the club, and I figure she's maybe a year or two past that, so I just drop my guessing game and enjoy the fresh glow of her youth.

I say, "Who do you have in mind for companionship?"

"Will I do?"

"Nicely," I say. "How about a dance?"

She nods her assent and we take our places among the couples swaying in and out of the shadows on the dance floor. I slip my arm around her, draw her close. "What's your name?" I say.

"Lydia," she says. "Lydia McKenzie. And yours?"

"Cantor Gold."

She pulls back from me a little, gives me a curious smile. "Cantor. That's an odd name."

"I live an odd life."

"Maybe you'll tell me about that life someday."

"Maybe. But not tonight."

She says, "No, not tonight," and puts her head against my shoulder, lets her body move with mine.

It's as if she's whispering to me with her body, telling me what she needs and what she wants to give. There's tenderness in her closeness and desire in her sway. I answer her tenderness with a caress of her back, answer her desire with my lips along her neck. With each movement of our dance, our conversation warms, grows more honest. The way she presses against me talks of her pain, and I'm surprised and saddened by the amount of it in one so young. She draws out *my* pain, accepts it, answers it by stroking the scars on my face and running her fingertips along my shoulders and down my jacket.

And then she stops, leans away from me. Even in the flickering light and shadow of the dance floor, I can see her face go pale. Her hand's found the bulge of my gun under my jacket. "Is this what I think it is?" she says.

"I told you, I lead an odd life."

"A dangerous one?"

"It's not dangerous right now," I say, and kiss her neck again.

"Are you a dangerous person?" The way she says it has no fear in it but plenty of curiosity.

"Not when I don't have to be," I say.

"But sometimes you have to be."

"This isn't one of those times," I say, my lips still caressing her neck, my hand gently stroking her back.

"Then why does it feel dangerous?"

It takes me a minute to work through my regret at having to take my lips from her neck so I can look at her, search her face, search those beckoning eyes to see what she's talking about. I came here tonight to leave my deadly business outside the door, and yet this youngster, whose experience of the world would barely fill a shot glass, got right into the soul of me, figured me as carrying the darkness around like a bulging suitcase.

"Well, Cantor Gold," she says, smiling, but ending our dance though the music's not over, "I came here tonight after a tough day at a crummy job. I came here looking for a good time, a few laughs to wipe my own troubles away. I didn't come looking for a risky night. But if I'm ever in the mood for a different kind of play, I'll come looking for you."

She lets go of my hand, drifts back from me with an apologetic smile, leaving me standing alone in the crowd on the dance floor like a weed in a flower garden.

The music changes. The band's taking a break, the slow and seductive "Teach Me Tonight" replaced by a rock-'n'-roll number from the jukebox, a bunch of guys shouting "Shake, Rattle and Roll." Several couples leave the dance floor. Younger couples remain, joined by more of the younger crowd.

My arm's tugged on my way off the dance floor. It's Lydia McKenzie.

"C'mon, Cantor Gold," she says with a buoyant laugh that's as irresistible as a double scoop of my favorite ice cream. "Maybe we can shake some of that risky stuff out of you."

The next thing I know, she's corralled me into dancing something resembling a Lindy Hop, a newer, wilder version that asks my bones to fling themselves around under my flesh.

It feels good. It feels ridiculous, the kind of ridiculous that forces you to smile, then laugh as you rock and roll your body and swing your partner around you. Lydia's laughing. I'm laughing. The music's surging. The beat vibrates through the room. People are singing the repeating lyrics, shouting the nonsense syllables. It's pure energy, rebellion. It's freedom.

The end of the song brings a loud, "Whoop!" from the young dancers as they drift back to tables and the bar. The music on the juke changes again, back to a slow tune, Nat "King" Cole's velvet-voiced rendition of "Tenderly."

Lydia's in my arms again. I didn't invite her, she didn't ask, we just did it, and now we're moving slow and slinky on the dance floor.

I don't know where this is going. I don't know if this is even a good idea. Lydia's movement against me says she's not sure it's a good idea either. But we keep dancing. Maybe she needs to experience a different side of life a little bit. Maybe I need her freshness and warmth, even if we share ourselves with each other for just one night.

When the dance is over, we walk hand in hand to the bar, slide onto a couple of barstools. Peg pours us our drinks: my scotch neat, Lydia's seven-and-seven, a favorite of the younger set. Peg also gives me a side-eye. I guess even Peg doesn't think my dalliance with the young Lydia is a good idea.

I don't care anymore whether we're a good idea or not. I bought myself a night of freedom and I'm going to rock-'n'-roll it till the sun comes up.

Lydia and I linger over our drinks, sliding our way toward the your-place-or-mine part of the conversation, when I hear, "Hey, hi there, Cantor. Glad I caught you."

I turn around to see Ike Martindale. I know it's Ike and not Ivy because the haircut's slicked, the gray double-breasted's tailored, the white shirt's unbuttoned at the collar, and the green tie's open at the neck.

"Well, well. Hello, Ike." I keep my voice and my smile as pleasant as I can, do my best to hide my frustration at being interrupted at the critical moment of my chat with Lydia. "And just why are you glad you caught me here?"

"So I could thank you. I tried phoning you, even dropped by your place before coming over here, but you're never home, you son-of-a-gun." That rides on a wink at Lydia.

"I'm surprised you still have my number. It's been a while, Ike."

"You never forget phone numbers of people who matter to you, right?"

"Nice to know I matter. But what's all this about thanking me? Thanking me for what?"

"For shaking me out of the shadows." Ike gives a wave to Peg, who's pouring drinks at the other end of the bar. "Listen, Cantor," Ike says after Peg nods that she'll be right over, "when you showed up at the ad agency the other day, it really shook me. I mean, you have more guts than I'll ever have, but seeing you shook me out of the lie I was living. I've been brooding about it ever since, making myself nuts. I had to face it, face the lie, otherwise I'd keep on strangling myself, know what I mean? You saved my life, Cantor. You really did. So thanks to you, I'm back. I'm me. Ike Martindale, alive and well, spiffed up and decked out."

"You saying you quit your job? Pretty gutsy, Ike."

Ike's shoulders slump a bit, the bravado a little less flashy. "Uh, no, I didn't quit. Look, I'm not making excuses, but I really love my job. Worked plenty hard to get it and keep it. So, sure, the McClure & Fineman advertising agency can have Ivy Martindale, or at least that's who they see. But after hours? On my own time? Ivy gets hung away in the closet with the other skirts and blouses, and Ike Martindale steps out, free as a bird."

I'm happy for Ike, I really am, but that life sounds pretty schizo to me: living a lie for half your life, living true for the other half. The idea makes my eyes cross. But maybe Ike's got the bravery angle inside out. Maybe Ike's the brave one, surviving the lie to protect the truth.

Peg pours Ike a bourbon and water, says, "Good to see you again, Ike."

"You can thank Cantor."

Peg says, "Is that so?" and gives me another side-eye before going off to fill more drink orders.

Ike sips the bourbon, says, "Aren't you going to introduce me to your friend?" with a smile that's just this side of lecherous. A night of sudden freedom must be busting the bounds of Ike's previously courtly behavior.

I say, "Lydia McKenzie, Ike Martindale. Actually, Lydia and I were just leaving, Ike. See you around sometime."

"Sure. Listen, will I see you at Mel Burns' funeral tomorrow? A few of us who worked with him figure we'll pay our respects. The guy could be a braggart and a pain in the ass, but he had a golden voice. And murder is a helluva way to die."

The mention of Mel Burns puts a sudden spike in my good mood. I didn't want to think about Mel, or Edie, or Edie's gangster father, or Stage Door Johnny, or that nameless woman slashed to ribbons in the alley. I didn't want to think about murder and all the madness and hate behind it. I didn't want to think about whoever the hell it is who hates me.

But here it all is, dropped in my lap by Ike Martindale, the old pal whose life I supposedly saved just by showing up as myself.

Lydia says, "Cantor?" as if she's caught scent of the sudden change in me. Her blue eyes aren't beckoning now; they're full of curiosity of the saddest kind, the kind that wonders what went wrong but knows there's nothing she can do to fix it.

"I have to go," I say.

Chapter Twenty-Two

It's almost ten-thirty by the time I walk into my apartment and find another note slipped under the door. Picking it up, I wait for my usual reaction to these invasions of my life: pounding heart, twitching nerves. But none of that happens. I'm steady as a dull day.

I'm steady and calm because I've had it with being scared. I'm sick and tired of looking over my shoulder all the time. This guy—or dame—wants to find me? Fine. Let them. Let them look me in the eye instead of hiding behind wacky scribbles.

I open the note. It's longer than the others. I guess the writer had time on their hands when they couldn't find me. I almost laugh, but can't because what's written in the note is no joke:

> TOO BAD ABOUT THE BOOZER IN
> THE ALLEY. DID THE SIGHT OF HER
> SHOCK YOU, CANTOR? NICE PLAY
> BY THE WAY, GETTING YOURSELF
> CUFFED AND STASHED IN THE POLICE
> COOLER. I ALMOST BOUGHT THE
> ACT. BUT I KNOW YOU, CANTOR.
> I KNOW YOUR GAMES. AND I KNEW
> YOU HAD TO COME HOME SOONER
> OR LATER. YOU CAN HIDE FROM ME

ALL YOU LIKE. IT WON'T MATTER.
YOU'RE DONE FOR IN THE END.
MEANTIME, CONGRATULATIONS
ON STASHING MOM SHEINBAUM
OUT OF MY REACH. I GUESS YOU
STASHED YOUR MUSUEM DOLLIE
SOMEWHERE, TOO. WELL, GOOD
FOR YOU. I CAN'T GET TO THEM.
NOT YET, ANYWAY. BUT I CAN GET
TO YOU.

I toss the note onto a side table in the living room on my way to the credenza where I pour myself a scotch. After a swallow, I take the drink with me to my favorite club chair, pick up the phone on the side table, and start to dial Adair, figuring I should fill him in about the newest note.

But I stop dialing, pump the cradle to get a new dial tone, and call a different number instead.

Vivienne's ambivalent "Hello?" is more question than greeting, as if she's not sure if she should've answered the phone at all. When I tell her it's me on the line, her, "Oh, hello, Cantor," is more relaxed, relieved.

I say, "All settled in?"

"As much as anyone can settle into a shabby apartment as a hideout. I think even John Dillinger might've turned up his nose. Thank you for the food, by the way. And the coffee's delicious. You must let me compliment the chef when all this is over. So if you don't mind me asking, when *will* all this be over?"

"I'm working on it, Vivienne. Just sit tight for a while. Meantime, you need anything else? Books, magazines? I can have them sent over."

"How about my own clothes?" she says. "Your underwear's not exactly a great fit."

"Is that what you're wearing?" My imagination is having a swell time.

"Wouldn't you like to know. Too bad you can't come over

and have a look," she teases, "but I guess that's too risky if you're still being followed. Any new developments, by the way?"

"Yeah. Another note was slipped under my door. Same crazy letters, same smug threats."

Vivienne gives that a delicate grunt, then says, "Whoever's behind all this sure likes to be theatrical, don't you think? I mean, those melodramatic notes written in those crazy-shaped letters. Very theatrical, even childish, if you ask me."

"But grown up enough to murder," I say. "And the threat to you is real, Vivienne."

"So you've said. Listen, Cantor, I appreciate that you're trying to protect me, but I have the same repugnance about hiding as you do. I'll give this place one night, but in the morning I think I'll grab a cab and just go home. This place is too dreary to spend a weekend."

"Dreary is better than dead, Vivienne," I say, without an ounce of anything soothing in my delivery. "Look, I know you've got your great-grandad Trent's fierce streak. It's one of your more alluring qualities. But don't let that gutsy Trent spirit suffocate your intelligence. If you show up at your place, you'll put a target on your back. Maybe George's back too."

Vivienne doesn't argue. She doesn't say anything. Her quick breath after I mention George says it all. She'd never forgive herself if any harm came to the old guy.

I change gears into something calmer, even light. "Just relax, watch some television. It'll take your mind off things."

"It doesn't help," she says with a mildly annoyed sigh. "I was watching *Person to Person*—you know, that show where Ed Murrow wastes his newsman's talents interviewing movie stars. He was interviewing Kim Novak when you called. Made me think of you."

"Ed Murrow makes you think of me?"

"No. Kim Novak. I'm sure she's your type: gorgeous, blonde, busty."

"I've been known to cast my eye at brunettes too, Vivienne."

Vivienne's silence isn't fearful this time, just thoughtful. She finally says, "Good night, Cantor," with a small laugh.

"Good night, Vivienne. I'll give you a call tomorrow."

We hang up, but I can't help lingering over an image of Vivienne in my underwear. I'm even smiling about it when I dial Adair's precinct.

"He's gone for the night," the desk sergeant says.

"I suppose you won't give me his home number," I joke.

"What're you, a comedian?"

"I've got that reputation. Look, just get in touch with Adair and tell him to call Cantor Gold. He's got my number."

"Cantor Gold? Hey, aren't you supposed to be downstairs in the cells?"

"And here I thought all cops know by now that I'm never where I'm supposed to be. Just have Adair call me. It's important. He'll want to talk to me."

I hang up and finish my drink, pour myself another, and dawdle in the nighttime view out my window while I wait for Adair's call. My view of the city always soothes me. The neon lights of my neighborhood advertise good times, zesty nightlife, the kick-up-your-heels life of jazz clubs and Broadway shows. So why do I feel like there's grit in my eye?

Thoughts of Dave Handy, Adele Perkins, and Danny Bell circle around in my brain. But nothing about who they are, what they do, how they feel about me—none of it seems to connect. It's like trying to put a plug into a wall socket that keeps moving.

My phone rings. I pick it up. After my "Hello," I hear Adair's "Whaddya want?"

"Another note was slipped under my door. Another doozy. Longer this time. Figured you oughta know. Anything new on your end?"

"It's almost eleven at night, Gold. I'm done for the day, relaxing with a beer and the TV. I was having a good time ogling Kim Novak when the precinct called. So, no, nothing new at my end. Now, if you don't mind, I'll get back to ogling—"

"Wait a minute, Adair." I think that grit might've just fallen out of my eye. Maybe it was the mention of the luscious Miss

Novak, maybe it reminded me of Vivienne and something she said, which reminded me of something Ike Martindale said, but something definitely kicked over in my head. Pieces of this and that suddenly run behind my eyes like the headline news zipper on Times Square, telling me what's what.

"What is it, Gold?"

"Uh, nothing," I say. "Listen, I'll be in touch if something new develops." I hang up without even saying goodbye, because for what I'm about to do the last thing I need is a cop tagging along to scare the prey away.

I wear my neighborhood's Friday night after-theater crowd like a cloak of protection, staying safe inside the throng when I need to, separating from them and standing in the light of a neon sign or under a streetlight when I want to be bait.

The killer knew I'd come home, so I'm betting that the killer knows I've come out again. I don't care if I'm being followed. *I'll lead you into the jaws of hell. And if you're not following me, I'll find you, because I know who you are.*

But I am being followed. I know it. I feel it in the breeze of the cool night air along the scars on my face. It's in the tingle along my spine, the scrape along the back of my neck, sensations I pay attention to, sensations that have kept me alive all these years. This isn't the first time a threat's come for me, but it's the first time I know from who but I don't know why.

It doesn't matter why anymore, if it really ever did. Someone hates me. Well, so what. Someone hates me and the way I live my life, so they're out to crush me and erase my existence. Well, so what to that too. Bigger, more powerful forces than the killer who's on my tail have tried. The Law's tried. The Law's bully boys have tried. All the tentacles of the straight-back world have tried. I'm still here.

The killer's not snapping at the bait yet, so I move on, move through the crowd of men and women all spiffed up for a night on the town. Men in fedoras or snap-brim trilbys or porkpies, with overcoats open to sharp suits. Women in swirling coats open to colorful dresses, the ensembles topped off by extravagant or elegant hats. New Yorkers who stride the street with purpose. Tourists looking at the lights, at the marquees, the tall buildings, looking everywhere but where they're going. Everyone moving. No one knowing there's a cunning cat setting a trap for the murderous rat among the crowd, both of them on the prowl.

I'm not far from the street corner now, where I can turn onto the main stem: Broadway. Broadway's crowds are thicker. They'll give me even better cover when I want it. The lights there are brighter, making me handier bait. Maybe Broadway's where the killer will either make a move or get caught in the glare. I'll be ready.

I slide my hand inside my suit jacket, wrap my fingers around my .38.

"Gold!" A hand's suddenly on my shoulder.

I spin around, pull my gun from my rig, aim it straight into the face of Sergeant Liam Adair.

In the neon light of a jazz joint's sign, Adair's fedora looks like a party hat and his usually tough face looks like a pink marshmallow about to melt.

I put my gun away. We both reclaim our breath. Adair's finally able to speak. "What're you so jumpy about?"

"Let's just say I thought you were someone else. How long you been tailing me, sergeant?"

"Just a few minutes." The neon pink is still washing over Adair's face, but at least his cheeks are solid again. "I pulled up to your place," he says, "saw you walk out but lost you in the crowd. What's the matter, Gold? You look disappointed, like you're sorry I'm not the person you were looking to kill."

I've never found it beneficial to tell a cop my intentions, especially if he gets them only half right. He'll only make a mess of the other half. Better to just change the subject. "What're you doing here, Adair?"

"I didn't like the way you cut off our phone call," he says. "Gave me the twitches, like you were up to something. Looks like I was right."

"This is my neighborhood, sergeant. Can't a citizen take a nighttime stroll through their own neighborhood anymore?"

"Depends on why they're strolling, or maybe where they're strolling to. Look, Gold, I've played on the up-and-up with you on this case, at least as much as my badge will allow. And whether you believe it or not, it's my job to keep people alive, even the likes of you, and even without Sig Loreale's say-so. So whatever mischief you've got planned, you might want to think twice about going it alone. My badge can help."

"Your badge might get in the way."

"But my gun won't."

We stand there staring at each other, get bumped now and then by the crunch of passersby.

A smile spreads slowly across Adair's face. It's a happy smile but a worried one, the kind that says he knows what's coming, and likes it, but doesn't trust the situation either.

When the smile's completed its trip across his lips, Adair says, "You know who the killer is, don't you, Gold. You know who's out to get you. How'd you figure it?"

If I don't give Adair something, he'll just keep pestering me. "Because there are some phone numbers you never forget. Listen, Adair, in the general run of cops, your badge is probably one of the cleaner ones. If you want to keep it clean and shiny, your best bet is to go home, have another beer, and pretend you never saw me. Good night, sergeant." I start to walk away.

He grabs my arm. "If you're planning to kill someone, Gold, that's not a good idea."

"I never plan on killing."

"But you won't back off from it either," he says. "Listen, you're a thief, an outlaw, a criminal who hates everything the Law stands for, but you're not stupid. Get a grip and play it smart, Gold. Bring me along on this so I can bring the sonuvabitch in and make sure they get a reservation for the electric chair. Do this the right way, because if you don't, I'll come after you with the full force of my clean and shiny badge and bring the whole police department with me. Even Sig Loreale won't be able to save you."

Not that Sig would bother.

I guess Adair means well, but he doesn't get the world I live in, doesn't get how it works, how I live in it, survive in it. And he doesn't understand how far I'll go to keep him from entering it. He's about to find out.

I slide my gun from its rig, pull my gun hand back into the sleeve of my overcoat so only a tiny tip of the barrel sticks out. It's soon enveloped by the bulky rolls of Adair's belly.

The shock on his face is as electric as the neon sign washing it pink. "You wouldn't dare, Gold."

I don't answer. I just drift back into the moving mass of people on the street, my .38 pointed at Adair but hidden from the crowd.

I forget about turning onto Broadway. The bright lights that might've set me up as bait would make it too easy for Adair to spot me. Five'll get you ten he's already trying to follow me. But like I told him, this is my neighborhood. I know where the lights are and I know where they aren't. I know the alleys at the back ends of theaters and nightspots.

I slide into one of them now.

Chapter Twenty-Three

I've exchanged the cool night breeze of the street for the clammy chill of the alley, giving a harsher feel to the new tingling along my spine, the scrape at the back of my neck. I'm being followed. But it's not Adair. It could only be someone who knows the back ends of Broadway as well as I do.

I pull my gun out slowly and quietly, turn around, but in the darkness of the alley see only a shadow. We're two shadows hidden behind the brightest boulevard in the world.

"It could only be you," I say to the shadow. "Of all the people I might've figured for this twisted exercise in murder, you're the only one who ticks all the boxes." The narrow alley amplifies the sound of my voice, the sound of everything. The crinkle of a cigarette pack sounds like electric sparks. The scratch of a lighted match sounds like a crack of lightning. The match's flame illuminates the shadow's face: Danny Bell is grinning at me under the slim brim of his hat, his narrow rat's eyes catching the light.

The match goes out. He's a shadow again. He says, "And just what boxes would those be, Cantor? C'mon, you're supposed to be the smart one. Show me how smart you are before I ruin your life forever."

"Too bad I wasn't smart enough," I say. "Too bad I didn't wise up fast enough, or five people wouldn't be dead. And that last one, Danny, that poor boozer of a woman. She had nothing to do with me. You just didn't want her to finger you as the guy who gave her that note to take to the cops. Killing her the way you did, slicing her up like that, you crossed the line, Danny. You crossed the line from being an everyday brutal killer to a sick bastard."

"Shut up about that, Cantor," he says, sounding more like a bratty kid than someone who's done time with the big guys in Sing Sing. "You have no right to lecture me. You're no saint yourself, y'know. And, anyway, it looks to me like maybe you're not so smart after all if it took you this long to figure me."

That stabs me, but the wound has less to do with my lack of smarts and more to do with heart. "Maybe it took me this long because I didn't want to look too hard into my own backyard," I say. "I could handle all the hate in those notes if it came from the usual sources who hate me: cops, upright citizens, the morality mob who want my kind to burn in hell. But you and I share a world, Danny, a hard world, sure, even a dangerous one. But it's a world where the straight-backs and their cop enforcers can't push us around, and they can't tell me how to live my life or who to take to dinner or to bed. I like that world, Danny. So I didn't look too deeply there because I was foolish enough to think that no one in our world had a good enough reason to toss me out of it."

"So sorry I disappoint you, Cantor." I can't see his face but I can hear his sneer.

"You didn't just disappoint me, Danny. You broke my heart."

His snicker bangs against the walls of the alley. "You have no heart to break, Cantor. You're just a swaggering dagger who thinks she's too classy to work with the likes of me. So you poked around in boxes to find me, huh?" There's so much ice in Danny's voice I swear I feel the temperature in the air drop. "I'm curious," he says. "I'm curious about what you found in all those boxes that led you to me."

The Danny Bell I've known for years isn't the guy who's facing me in the alley. This isn't the flashy but friendly lightfinger.

This guy is a stranger, a shadow. He's nothing but darkness, a killing darkness. He's killed five people. He probably figures to kill me. I'm tempted to pull the trigger of my .38 and get rid of him before he does the same to me.

But cold-blooded murder's not my style. And besides, in the darkness of the alley, I can't be sure I'm the only one with a gun. So far, all I've seen of Danny is by a lighted match and the glow of a cigarette that's still burning. Otherwise, he's a shadow, maybe a shadow who's pulled a gun in the dark. Or maybe he's pulled a knife. The guy's nasty with a blade, too. The way he quietly shivved Stage Door Johnny in the middle of a crowd, and sliced the lady boozer to shreds, was the work of talented hands. So unless I want to wind up on the alley's cobblestones with a bloody hole in my gut, I'd better stay sharp, give Danny something better to do than kill me if that's what he has in mind.

So I go into my song and dance. "Okay, sure, Danny, you want to know what I found in the boxes? All right, here's the first box, an easy one I should've picked up on sooner, but murder got in the way: you know my racket, you know how I work, maybe even who I've worked with, so you were able to trace my connection to Miss Parkhurst Trent and the artworks I supplied her."

The tip of Danny's cigarette shines bright as he takes a deep drag. Through an exhale of smoke that glows pink in the cigarette's burn, he says, "The dame might as well have left her front door open. Easy job."

"Which brings me to box number two," I say. "Yeah, an easy job because you've got good hands, Danny, a thief's hands, the kind of hands that can pick a lock and get into Miss Parkhurst Trent's house without a sound. You're a pro, Danny, a lightfinger with the skill to get in and out with the goods without knocking over the furniture."

"Well, thanks a lot for finally giving me a little credit."

"You're welcome. Okay, now box number three: you've been in the game long enough to be familiar with killing, even if you'd never done it yourself. Maybe prison educated you to be a killer, or maybe it was there all along. And even before prison, you'd know who's who on our outlaw side of the street. You'd know or could find out who might have a connection to me, even a sideways one. Dominic Angeli was pretty sideways to me, but I guess you knew he had dealings with Sig Loreale, and everyone knows I've done business with Sig. But there's something I can't figure, Danny. Something you were able to pull off that some people thought was almost impossible."

"Yeah? What's that?" He sounds proud as a strutting schoolyard tough.

"How the hell did you get close enough to Dominic Angeli to kill him? The guy was practically a recluse, with plenty of thugs with guns to shield him."

"Oh that," he says. "It wasn't so hard." I think his shadow just puffed out his chest. "The old boss was cheap. Paid his boys peanuts compared to what they were used to when Angeli had real power. I heard all about it from one of the guys in Sing Sing."

Mom Sheinbaum had the same idea about the lack of loyalty among Angeli's troops. I guess word gets around.

Danny keeps talking. "My prison pal told me his cousin was a guard up at Angeli's country place, and this cousin was always looking for any action to make a few bucks. So I gave him a nice few bucks; a hundred nice bucks to let me into the compound. And like you said, Cantor, I'm good at getting in and out without knocking over the furniture. The only thing I knocked over was Dominic Angeli." Danny's laugh is as childish as anything Vivienne might've imagined.

"Yeah, the prison grapevine is famous for useful gossip, or so I hear," I say. "And let me guess: Miss Parkhurst Trent's paintings were already in your car when you drove up to the compound, and the guy you bribed helped you stash Angeli in the trunk, maybe even helped you get him into the warehouse, right, Danny?"

"Hell no," he says, going from merely childish to petulant

and insulted. "I handled that all by myself. I got real strong in Sing Sing. You have to be strong in prison if you want to survive. But you wouldn't know about that, would you, Cantor. You're too smart to get caught and sent up. The smart, classy Cantor Gold. Too smart for the Law. Or maybe the Law's just too stupid."

"I count on it," I say with a grin Danny can't see, but which I enjoy nonetheless.

"I bet you do. But keep on humoring me, Cantor, about all those boxes."

They guy's too happy to hear about his string of murderous triumphs. It makes me queasy, but it gives me time to get a bead on what he might be up to, what he has planned for me, figure if he intends to kill me, and how. I still don't know if he's got a knife or if a gun's pointed at my gut. So I keep talking to keep him from killing. "Okay, Danny. Here it is: after knocking off Dominic Angeli, setting up Edie's killing must've been easy. She didn't hide away like her father, so a clever fellow like you would have no trouble getting to her. The wheelbarrow bit was especially clever. What did you do? Haul one up from the basement of your father's saloon? And his place isn't too far from Pier 32. Not a big trip to push a wheelbarrow carting a body hidden in a burlap sack through empty streets in the middle of the night. How am I doing so far, Danny?"

The tip of his cigarette glows red again as he takes a pull. His exhale is hard and fast. "Sounds like your grapevine is as good as mine, Cantor," he says. "But is that all you've got?"

"Oh, I've saved the best for last, Danny, the two boxes you should've been smart enough to avoid. They're the ones that nailed you. Tell you the truth, I could kick myself for not figuring them sooner, but you know how it is; sometimes things stare you in the face but they're too close to your eyes to see the whole picture. And then one night in a bar, an old pal says something. And later you're chitchatting with a lady friend on the phone, and she says something. And soon you remember what the old pal said and it bumps up against what the lady friend said, and all of a sudden everything's clear as clean glass."

The more I talk, the more drama I throw into it, makes Danny take deeper drags on his smoke, the burning tip lingering longer and brighter in the shadowy alley. My spiel becomes a play to rattle him, give me a chance to get whatever weapon he's carrying away from him.

So I go on talking, keep the patter up to keep the pressure on. "That's what happened, Danny. That's how these last two boxes got ticked: the pal at the bar mentioned that there are some phone numbers you never forget, and later the lady friend—Miss Parkhurst Trent as a matter of fact—was of the opinion that those notes you wrote were overly theatrical. Uh-huh, this caper was theatrical, all right, right from the get-go, when you phoned Mom Sheinbaum and disguised your voice. Mom's phone number is one of those numbers you'd never forget, Danny, especially after you got out of prison and tried to do business with her again. And the disguised voice? It was good, real good, so good that Mom didn't recognize you, someone she's had conversations with for years. She couldn't even say for sure if the caller was a man or a woman."

"Y'mean like this?" he says in a voice that coils through the alley and up my spine. He sounds like a wraith, a little girl, a little boy, an old witch, and an angry ogre all in one terrifying sound.

I have to let my nerve ends settle before I say, "You must've picked up that trick at your dad's bar, hanging around all those show biz types since you were a kid. You must've picked up plenty of makeup tricks too. Y'know, your dad said he wouldn't know his own mother if some makeup maven did her up with greasepaint and fake hair. But it wasn't Goody's mother he didn't recognize. It was his own son. It was you, Danny. That's why when I saw you, you looked like you'd just gotten out of the shower because that's exactly what you did. You'd washed off the fake hair and greasepaint and then walked back into the bar, sweet and innocent as an ice cream sundae. So you see, Danny, the person behind all the notes and all the killings could only be you. All those boxes got ticked, and when I opened them, you're inside all the boxes."

The red tip of Danny's cigarette corkscrews in the darkness when he tosses it. His foot makes a scraping sound against the cobblestones when he stubs it out. "Yeah, I learned a lot at my pop's bar," he says in his own voice, which is a relief. "One of the things I learned was that I didn't want to end up like him, working a million hours a day just to keep a bunch of Broadway phonies liquored up and happy. Sure, his saloon is a hot spot, even written up in the papers. But you should see him after closing, Cantor, when he comes upstairs to the apartment over the bar. The guy's dead on his feet. You never saw a guy so tired. Well, I knew real fast that kind of life wasn't for me. I never want to be that tired. Know what I mean, Cantor?"

"You're preaching to the choir, Danny. The straight-and-narrow life can grind you down."

"You said it. As a matter of fact, y'know what?" The question rides on a snicker that crackles through the alley. "I think we're not so different, you and I, Cantor. You wanted a bigger life than just the Coney Island honky-tonks, and I wanted more than just a saloon."

"We're not anything alike, Danny. You're a good lifter, but—"

"But nothing. I'm the best. You said it yourself. I've got good hands and the skills to move in and out like a shadow. So why'd you have to do me dirty?"

Well, it's about time. If the guy's out to crush me, I'd like to know why. "What the hell are you talking about, Danny? When did I do you dirty?"

"You ask me that? You have the nerve to ask me that? Because of you, Cantor, I got sent up the river. It was no picnic in the joint, believe me. A bunch of guys would beat you bloody for a cigarette or a stick of gum."

"Then you shouldn't have done the job that sent you there. I warned you not—"

"Shut up. I'm not done. It's because of you, Cantor, that Mom Sheinbaum won't give me the time of day. Because of you, my name's mud all over the street."

I hear a footstep, a scrape on the cobblestones. Danny's taken a step toward me. I keep my finger on the trigger of my .38 and put a little kindness into my voice, maybe slow up the action enough for me to figure what kind of weapon he's coming at me with. "I'm sorry for you, Danny. You got a lousy deal, no doubt about it. But I didn't deal you that hand. When you told me your plans for that jewelry heist, I told you it was no good. I told you not to do it. I was looking out for you, Danny."

"Don't make me laugh, Cantor. Sure, okay, you told me not to do it. So, yeah, it was a stupid job. And yeah, okay, I shouldn't've done it. But it's what happened afterward. That's when you did me in."

"Is that so? How you figure that?"

"When I got pinched," he says, almost whining, "you could've sprung me."

"Danny, I don't have keys to the jailhouse."

"Cut the jokes," he says. "Sure you do. That fancy lawyer of yours is like a great big jailhouse key. I asked him to take me. He's famous for getting people off. He's sprung you from the lockup more times than I can count. But he said no. He said it was a losing case."

"Because it was. You were caught red-handed, Danny."

I hear another snicker, the kind that presses bile through his teeth. "You could've put in a good word for me with the guy, Cantor. But you didn't. You didn't lift a finger to help me out. And when I was cooling my heels in Sing Sing, when all I had was time, I used that time to think. Oh boy, did I think. I thought about the day I told you what I had in mind for another job, a different job than the jewelry heist, a sweet job even you said was a good play. I thought about how I told you I was willing to go in on it with you. Together, we could've hauled in a fortune."

"And I told you I'd think about it, and I wasn't kidding, Danny. I did think about it."

"I bet you did." I hear more scrapes of footsteps on the cobblestones, see Danny's shadow grow a little bigger as he moves toward me again. His angry whine drifts closer, rolls along the walls of the alley. "I bet you thought about it all the way to the grand finale," he says, "when you and Mom Sheinbaum walked off with buckets of cash after she fenced the goods for you. Yeah, you thought about it. You thought about how leaving me to stew in the joint would get me out of the way so you could take that job for yourself. You had no right, Cantor. You had no right to take my place!"

"Listen to me, Danny. You know the game. If I didn't do that job, someone else would have because you were right about that one. It was ripe for the pickings."

"It was *my* job, Cantor! You should've split the cash with me!"

"Then why didn't you come see me when you got out? We could've worked out a deal. But I didn't even know you were back in town until I saw you at Goody's. Sounds like another of your bad decisions, Danny. And I didn't try to get you out of the way. You got yourself out of the way by pulling that bad jewelry job. And now you're telling me you killed five people just to get back at me?"

"It worked, didn't it, Cantor?" His laugh could scrape the skin from my bones. "It drove you crazy. It made you look over your shoulder and wonder who's after you. It made you scared. I made you scared."

"So now you're planning to kill me, right, Danny? Is this the big finish?"

The sound of his *tsk* is very close to me now. "You have no imagination, Cantor. I won't kill you. That's too easy. I'll just make your life as miserable as you've made mine. I'll hurt you where it hurts most."

"You figure you'll turn me in to the cops for the job I did without you, is that it? Send me behind bars? I'll survive it, Danny."

"Nah, that's not your soft spot, Cantor. Your soft spot is a lot, uh, curvier. It's all those women. I'll take your women away from you."

I let a small laugh escape. Can't help it. "We don't fish in the same pond, Danny."

"Oh, I don't have to fish in your pond to take the ladies away," he says. "I just have to make sure they don't want to come near you. You're nothing without your women, Cantor, but when I get through with you, no woman will want to touch you, not even that snooty Parkhurst Trent dame."

That's when I know Danny has a knife and not a gun. What he wants to do is straight out of a horror movie. He wants to do to me what he did to that poor boozer woman, only without killing me. She was just a rehearsal.

I swear I'm moving fast, lifting my gun arm fast, but the air in front of my face suddenly feels like it's moving faster than my arm. So why does time seem to slow to a crawl?

And then there's a slashing, burning pain next to my left eye! A gagged grunt bursts from my mouth. Instinct sends my gun arm up fast again. A gunshot cracks the air.

I hear, "Gold!" I see lights, a car's headlights and a red swirling light at the entrance to the alley. The red light smears Sergeant Adair, a .38 Police Special in his hand.

Danny Bell is at my feet, howling like a wounded dog. Red light washes over him. Blood oozes from his shoulder.

I kick his knife from his hand.

Chapter Twenty-Four

It twists me up to think I'd owe even a small favor to a cop. Owing my life or limb to a cop is a damn big favor. The very idea itches my brain, like a buzzing fly that can't find a place to settle.

A uniformed cop leads Danny away. I'm surprised I feel sorry for the guy. He's looking at five counts of murder he'll go to the chair for, blaming me every step of the way to the death house. I feel even sorrier for his dad. I can't help wondering if the miserable fate of Goody's son might kill the father, and if the Broadway colony would do Goody the honor they bestow on their fallen: dim the street's marquees and lights.

Adair says, "Don't bother to thank me, Gold. You wouldn't mean it anyway."

I hold my pocket handkerchief against the bloody wound next to my eye and answer Adair with just a shrug and a smile. The idea of Adair saving my life or even just my flesh is tough enough to handle. The idea that he saved me from committing murder is as hard to take as the idea that this cop knows me better than I'd figured any cop ever could.

My smile hurts my face, so I lose it. "I guess you tailed me after all," I say.

"More or less. You really know how to get lost when you want to, Gold, or I might've found you sooner. I might've saved you from adding another scar to that pretty face."

The last person who ever called me pretty was my mother when I was five years old. She changed her description of me by the time I was six.

Adair says, "You should have that looked at, Gold. That's a nasty gash."

"Nothing a splash of alcohol, a bandage, and a fifth of scotch can't handle," I say and start to walk away. "Good night, sergeant."

"See you around, Gold." The way he says it, flat, toneless, scares me more than Danny Bell ever did.

A thorough wash and a dab of alcohol stings my wound. A gulp of scotch from the glass perched on the bathroom sink kills some of the pain.

The Cantor Gold looking back at me in the mirror looks like someone who's been through too many wars. And Adair's right, that new slash next to my left eye will add to the assortment of battle wounds already claiming real estate on my face. But they tell my story, each scar a pictograph of what it takes for me to live my life and stake my claim to a place in the world.

I make a bandage from the first aid supplies in my medicine cabinet, tape it to the wound, then carry my drink to my favorite chair in the living room. I don't bother to turn on any lamps.

Outside, the city's lights are still blazing. They'll stay that way until dawn, especially the lights of the theaters and jazz joints in my neighborhood. Their neon colors float into my darkened living room and all over me.

The Chivas and a cigarette do their job, take the edge off my rough night. My mind starts to amble around. I think about calling Vivienne, tell her the good news that the threat to her is finished. She can go home.

I ditch that idea. It's well past midnight. Maybe she's already in bed, asleep—I enjoy a tangy daydream of Vivienne in my skivvies under the covers—so I figure the good news will keep till tomorrow. Besides, I have a sweeter idea: I'll go see her in the morning, help Vivienne clear out from Judson's pal's apartment, and take her to breakfast to celebrate her freedom.

Now, though, maybe I should give Sig a call, tell him what's what, tell him that there'll be no more killings to gum up the gears of his rackets or threaten his hold on the town's cops, and that Mom Sheinbaum can go back to Second Avenue. But at this hour chances are good that Sig and Mom are all tucked up and asleep too.

Okay then, I'll call Sig tomorrow, before I trot over to rescue Vivienne from her shabby hideout. And, anyway, the cops on Sig's payroll might call him up any minute with the news. Fine. Let them be the ones to disturb his sleep.

The knife slash still stings, but it could've been worse. I guess I have the darkness of the alley to thank for Danny's knife missing my eye. I don't doubt he was out to blind me, then keep on knifing my face to disfigure me, make me look like the ogre he's convinced I am.

This wound, though, like the others that made all the scars on my face, will heal. Danny's knife attacked the wrong part of me. But his taunting notes didn't. Those notes attacked my soul, or at least tried to. But the guy missed the mark there too. There's already a wound to my soul, and it takes up all the space. It's the wound that won't heal, the wound I try to smother in booze and new cars and new women. But that wound will never heal, because the only woman who can take the pain away is lost to me.

So I'll go on salving my poor damaged soul and my too-often-pummeled body with good scotch and the sweet strokes of all the women who'll have me.

I have to wonder, though, if those women would have me if Danny had succeeded in giving me an ogre's face.

But he didn't.

Acknowledgements

Ah life, just one disaster after another. These last few years have been tough on us all. Covid really gummed up the works, trapping us in our homes, limiting our social lives. There were a few breaks in the misery, some periods of hope when the plague seemed to be receding (and I got to go back to Paris! Whoopee!), but then the Omicron variant arrived and loused everything up again. To paraphrase the famous joke: You make plans, Covid laughs. Maybe by the time you read this, Covid will have stopped laughing, or at least the laugh will be reduced to an annoying snicker.

Unfortunately, for me, the one-disaster-after-another scenario became all too real. To be frank, my survival and the ability to keep a roof over my head has been sorely tested. But one soldiers on, right? And one writes, meets deadlines, keeps going as the professional author I've always aspired to be.

I could not do it alone, could not survive alone. It may not have taken a village, but it certainly took friends. Thus, I must acknowledge these friends, people who have big, exquisite hearts. I love you all: Claude Pollack, Claudine Dumoulin, Kate Fitzgerald, Jacalyn Burke, Barry Katz, Mitchell Karp, Cora Jane Glasser, Ramekon O'Arwisters, Carlo Abruzzese, Dana DeKalb, Peter Goldstein, Lynn Ames, and Cheryl Pletcher. And as always, my fine pal and hometown New York anchor Allan Neuwirth, a special nod to magicienne extraordinaire Belinda Sinclair for tips on card playing for a scene in the book, and the magnificent team at Bywater Books. Without all of you this book could not have been completed.

About the Author

Native New Yorker Ann Aptaker's Cantor Gold crime/mystery series has won Lambda Literary and Goldie Awards. Her short stories have appeared in two editions of the *Fedora* crime anthology, *Switchblade Magazine's Stiletto Heeled* issue, the *Mickey Finn: Twenty-First Century Noir* anthology Volume 1 and the upcoming Volume 3, and in *Black Cat Mystery Magazine*. Her novella, *A Taco, A T-Bird, A Barretta and One Furious Night*, was published by Down & Out Books for their *Guns And Tacos* crime series. Her flash fiction, *A Night In Town*, appeared in the online zine *Punk Soul Poet*, and another flash fiction, *Rock 'N Dyke Roll*, is featured in the Goldie Award winning anthology *Happy Hours: Our Lives in Gay Bars*. Ann has been an art curator, exhibition design specialist, art writer, and was a professor of Art History at the New York Institute of Technology. She now writes full time.

Bywater
BOOKS

At Bywater Books, we love good books just like you do, and we're committed to bringing the best of contemporary writing to our growing community of avid readers. Our editorial team is dedicated to finding and developing outstanding writers who create books you won't want to put down.

For more information about Bywater Books, our authors and our titles, please visit our website.

www.bywaterbooks.com

CPSIA information can be obtained
at www.ICGtesting.com
Printed in the USA
JSHW022238040522
25607JS00003B/10

9 781612 942377